W9-CDW-583

the OBSESSION

JESSE Q. SUTANTO

sourcebooks
fire

Copyright © 2021 by Jesse Q. Sutanto
Cover and internal design © 2021 by Sourcebooks
Cover design by Nicole Hower/Sourcebooks
Cover images © Marcus Garrett/Arcangel; Stephen Rees/Shutterstock
Internal design by Danielle McNaughton/Sourcebooks

Sourcebooks and the colophon are registered trademarks of Sourcebooks.

All rights reserved. No part of this book may be reproduced in any form or by
any electronic or mechanical means including information storage and retrieval
systems—except in the case of brief quotations embodied in critical articles or
reviews—without permission in writing from its publisher, Sourcebooks.

The characters and events portrayed in this book are fictitious or
are used fictitiously. Any similarity to real persons, living or dead,
is purely coincidental and not intended by the author.

All brand names and product names used in this book are trademarks,
registered trademarks, or trade names of their respective holders.
Sourcebooks is not associated with any product or vendor in this book.

Published by Sourcebooks Fire, an imprint of Sourcebooks
P.O. Box 4410, Naperville, Illinois 60567-4410
(630) 961-3900
sourcebooks.com

Library of Congress Cataloging-in-Publication Data

Names: Sutanto, Jesse Q., author.
Title: The obsession / Jesse Q. Sutanto.
Description: Naperville, Illinois : Sourcebooks Fire, [2021] | Audience:
    Ages 14. | Audience: Grades 10-12. | Summary: After freeing her mother
    from an abusive relationship, Delilah Wong refuses to play a part in
    Logan's delusional romance -- but how can she convince him to let her
    go?
Identifiers: LCCN 2020035331 (print) | LCCN 2020035332 (ebook)
Subjects: CYAC: Dating (Social customs)--Fiction. | Stalking--Fiction. |
    Drugs--Fiction. | Racially mixed people--Fiction. | Singaporean
    Americans--Fiction. | Suspense fiction.
Classification: LCC PZ7.1.S8823 Ob 2021 (print) | LCC PZ7.1.S8823 (ebook)
    | DDC [Fic]--dc23
LC record available at https://lccn.loc.gov/2020035331
LC ebook record available at https://lccn.loc.gov/2020035332

Printed and bound in the United States of America.
VP 16

To my husband, Mike, who has always been there for me—but like, in a non-stalkery way.

PART ONE
boy meets girl

logan

Ms. Taylor gave me a smile, the kind I'd secretly dubbed the Soothing Guidance Counselor Smile. She wore it the way she wore her soft cardigan, a conscious choice made to put "problem students" like myself at ease.

"How was your summer, Logan?"

"Fine." My summer had been spent in a haze of Netflix and scrolling through pictures of Sophie until inky night gave way to watery sunlight and my brain felt like it was about to dribble out of my ears. "It was great, actually. I got lots of rest." My voice came out thick and slow. Maybe because I hadn't been sleeping well and always felt like I was groping my way through a fog. Maybe because I had a permanent lump in my throat.

"That's wonderful to hear, Logan."

Why did she always have to say my name at the end of every sentence?

"Are you feeling prepared for the new semester, Logan?"

"Yeah," I said. "I'm ready to join the team again."

Ms. Taylor's smile lost some wattage. "Let's come back to lacrosse later, after our chat."

I tried to find the familiar anger, the old gunpowder barrel of energy that would wrench me out of this murk and make me feel something. It was there, I knew it was. I could feel it lurking at the edges, reaching out for me. But I was so tired.

Honestly, I wasn't even sure if I cared about getting back on the team. But Dad said what I really needed was to get back to sports. Get a good sweat going, thrash it out on the field, like if I could only run hard enough, I'd be able to outrun Sophie's ghost.

"When we talked last spring, you were going through a really challenging time."

I winced at the memory of my last session with Ms. Taylor. I'd been consumed by rage then. I'd called her a bitch and then something worse, and she'd sat there silently, looking very disappointed.

"I'm sorry," I mumbled.

Ms. Taylor smiled. "Thank you, Logan. I appreciate that. How are you feeling about being back at Draycott?"

Like I was thrust into a graveyard. Ghosts everywhere. But

I had to move on. Sophie would've wanted me to move on. "I'm fine, really. I was just kind of derailed by my classmate's death. Made me question my own mortality or whatever." How ridiculous to refer to the love of my life as my *classmate*, like we were strangers who passed each other in the hall.

Ms. Taylor gave me a sympathetic grimace. "I understand."

No, you fucking don't. No one knew Sophie like I did. No one had any idea how her death had completely devastated my life. We never dated, not officially, but our love was the real deal. Nobody understood, though. "She's leading you on," they told me, but they didn't know what Sophie was like when it was just us.

I tuned out the next few minutes as Ms. Taylor rambled on about how she expected great and wonderful things from me and how she'd have a chat with Coach about letting me back on the team and how I totally would be allowed back as long as I pulled my grades up and didn't mouth off to teachers again and behaved like a good little boy.

"You'll be fine, Logan. I believe in you. You're a good kid," she said, getting up. "You're going to do great things this semester, I know it."

Her words stayed with me as I walked back to my dorm room. *Do great things.* It felt more like a threat than anything. Do great things, or get suspended again, maybe even expelled. Do great things, or get rejected by every college and be a loser for the rest of your life.

I checked my phone. I had close to an hour before the assembly. The early-morning sun was painting everything a golden hue. The lush, rolling fields, the ivy wrapped around Draycott Academy's sandstone buildings—everything shone with warmth. Another slow wave of resentment. Before Sophie died, I would've stood still and taken it all in. I would've asked her to walk with me to the rose garden to admire the dewy flowers before telling her she was more beautiful than any rose. Now, beauty was wasted on me.

I trudged back to my room and got ready for class. But by the time I put on my navy-blue blazer, gathered all my books, and messed up my hair in just the right way, I was exhausted. I walked to the common room, where Josh was finishing up his coffee. He waved at me and smiled. Was his smile just the slightest bit strained? I tried my best to smile back like I meant it.

"Hey, man! How was your summer?" he asked, giving me a one-armed hug.

"It was okay. How was yours?"

Josh started yapping about how his folks had taken him and his sister to Bordeaux for the summer. Somehow, I managed to follow him out of the dorm.

Summer was still clinging to the air with sticky stubbornness, never mind the fact that it was already September and Draycott Academy was surrounded by lush, green Northern Californian hills. All around us were excited cries like,

"Omigod, did you guys hook up over the break?" and "Did you see Jenna's new boobs?" Groups of too-cool-to-care seniors and terrified freshmen chattered and shriek-giggled, and I was so done with my schoolmates. It wasn't even nine o'clock yet, but my shirt was already sticking to my back with sweat.

I struggled to pay attention to Josh's incessant chatter. I wasn't imagining it; there was definitely a strained quality to his cheerfulness, like he was determined to talk to me the way he used to be able to.

What was he even going on about? Something about hooking up with a French girl over the summer. *Try harder!* I'd lost so many friends over the past year. I couldn't afford to lose Josh, too.

"Sounds hot," I said. That was the most I could come up with.

Josh laughed like I'd just said something exceptional. "Yeah, man! It was totally hot!" He gave me his usual not-a-care-in-the-world grin, but I didn't miss the flash of concern in his eyes. I wasn't sure if he was worried about me or about his own social status.

Someone shouted as we made our way across the quad, catching my attention. A handful of sophomores were playing with a Frisbee in the commons. They leapt and ran like gleeful Labradors. I watched them and wondered what it was like to be so invested in a game. I used to be into this stuff too, but for the life of me, now I couldn't remember what that felt like. Distracted, I started when I bumped into someone.

No, not someone. Her.

My phone slipped out of my hand, and the screen lit up when it bounced on the ground.

9:01 a.m.

I'd remember those exact numbers for the rest of my life—the exact time, down to the minute, when the universe lifted its slow, giant hand, reached straight through my skull and into the center of my brain, and said, "You've gone through enough, Logan. Here she is. I am delivering her to you personally. She is all yours."

I wanted to grab her, feel her warm flesh beneath my fingers, and check if she was real. Her face was eerily similar to Sophie's, and they swam in my mind and overlapped.

"I'm so sorry!" she exclaimed, and her eyes met mine for a split second. She crouched down and picked up my phone. "I hope I didn't break it." Her voice was sincere and shy, and she was biting her lower lip slightly, her eyebrows furrowed like she was genuinely worried, and god, I wanted tell her it was okay. Everything was okay because she was here, and I bet she tasted like strawberries at the height of summer.

I searched my mind for something memorable to say, something to put a smile on those lips of hers.

"You did."

Oh god, why did I say that? It was true that there was a giant crack on my phone, but really, *who gives a shit?*

Panic crossed her face. "I'm so sorry! I'll, um, I'll pay you back—um, but it might have to be in installments—"

Were those tears in her eyes? Holy crap. "It's fine," I said. I meant it to come out reassuring, but it came out gruff. I might as well be hobbling, waving my cane, and yelling at kids to get off my lawn.

Josh must have sensed the disaster (finally!), because he laughed and said, "Don't worry about it. Logan here can afford, like, a million of these things."

I wanted to throttle him. I at least had the excuse of the Sophie fog. Josh was just a massive idiot. He probably thought he was making the situation better, like telling girls my family was loaded would help me get laid.

The girl's forehead turned red, and her entire face shut down.

FuckingJoshfuckingguidancecounselorfucking—

"I'm so, so sorry, I—" Her voice cracked a little.

I couldn't bear to see her perfect face so tortured. I mumbled something about it being okay and walked away. I didn't look back, even though her presence, her aura, everything about her, burned a hole in my back. And I was left alone with Josh. Josh, who couldn't possibly grasp what had just happened, how the skies had parted so the universe could bring down this gift to me. And how I'd royally messed it all up.

I fed Josh some bullshit about how I wasn't feeling well, though in fact I was feeling like I'd come back to life. Mortified, yes, but mortification was better than being a zombie. I bounded after her. Hungry, famished really, to catch more of her. She disappeared into Wheeler Hall, where the science classes were located, and when I pushed through the double doors, I was greeted by a sea of students, all tanned skin and newly dyed hair.

I'd lost her.

I spent the next period hiding in one of the restrooms at Wheeler so no one would notice I was cutting class. It wasn't like I could explain why I had to do this. No one would understand. They'd judge me again. Just like Mom did, when she found all those pictures and videos of Sophie. Not that it mattered; this was all in the past. It was as though everything that had happened with Sophie was to prepare me for this girl. I closed my eyes and thought of her.

Though guys like Josh wouldn't find her hot, I noticed her subtle beauty. She looked half-Asian, half-white. Sophie was of Japanese descent. At first glance, the girl could have been Sophie's sister. There were differences, though. Sophie was all about the makeup—her lips always colored and glossed, her skin smooth and airbrushed, her eyes lined so her gaze was piercing and impossible to ignore. I never once saw Sophie without makeup, even toward the end, when everyone said she was losing it. Even then, she still caked the stuff on.

This girl looked like Sophie unmasked. Fresh, naked. Maybe just a touch of balm on those heart-shaped lips. What would it be like to kiss her? To taste her?

I willed myself from thoughts of the mystery girl's lips to the rest of her. The way she moved, the way she hunched her shoulders ever so slightly, the way she turned her head and cast her eyes downward, not quite at her feet. The flash of alarm that had sparked through her eyes when I dropped my phone. She was shy. That much was obvious. I couldn't mess this up. I'd lost so much already.

I came out of my hiding place and stationed myself on the landing between the first and second floor. A short while later, the bell clanged and kids flooded the hallway, blocking my view. I wanted to scream at them to stop chattering, stop fucking moving—

And there she was, walking next to Aisha Johnson. So, a senior then, like me. I couldn't not move toward her. She was so magnetic, how could all these idiots not notice her? I had to remind myself to keep some distance between us.

"—not so hard once you get used to—" Aisha was saying.

Someone jostled me, and I missed the next few words. I wanted to strangle everybody around us. Luckily, once we were outside, I could make out more of what they were saying.

"—volleyball tryouts later—" the girl said, and her voice was like a finger flicking a light switch in my head, making everything suddenly, stunningly bright.

"Ah, I'm so excited!" Aisha said. "I'm so glad you're here, Dee!"

I expected "Dee" to smile and tell Aisha how glad she was to be here too, but instead, an awkward silence followed.

"Um, sorry. I didn't mean like—um. Obviously I'm not glad about what brought you here..." Aisha's voice trailed off, and she fidgeted with her hands.

"No, it's fine. I know what you mean. I missed you so much when you started boarding here. And yes, I know we kept in touch, but it's just not the same."

"Definitely not the same." Aisha grinned at her. "Do you need a tour of the place?"

"No, I pretty much know where everything is."

"Oh yeah, I forgot you started working here over the summer instead of hanging out with me."

Dee laughed.

"Oh man, I can't believe we're going to the same school again. After all this time. Delilah and Aisha, united again!"

Delilah.

I said it silently, letting my tongue caress each syllable, tasting it.

Delilah.

The name of my destiny.

I followed her until she disappeared into the next class, and then I stood there for a while, smiling my first real smile in a long time.

Do great things.

Ms. Taylor had no fucking clue how great this semester was going to be.

CHAPTER TWO

logan

When classes ended, I hurried back to my room. With each step, my mind outran my feet by a thousand paces. I couldn't wait to see Delilah again. She had brought me back to life.

I locked the door, because the last thing I wanted was Josh popping his head in. I was a romantic, and romance was hard for some people to understand. I will never forget the way Mom reacted when she found my Sophie folder. And when she finally did speak to me, days later, she'd spat the words out like they left a foul taste in her mouth. "Don't ever let me find anything like that on your computer again." And that was that.

I put on my headphones to shut out the noise of people in the hallway. Then I opened a web browser and started my search.

Unlike last year, when the Sophie fog had made even the simple act of typing an ordeal, my fingers flew across the keyboard.

And boy, did I learn a lot about my girl.

I found her Instagram easily enough, but Facebook told me her full name: Delilah Laura Wong. She had a Chinese name: Shu Ping. It meant *peaceful book*, which suited her. She was an old soul, like me.

Goodreads told me her favorite books—upmarket suspense novels by someone named Tan Jing Xu. I bought all of the author's books, picturing Delilah's fingers, long and slim, caressing the pages, her index fingernail caught ever so lightly between her teeth (she was a nail-biter, I was sure) as her deep, brown eyes took in the words. I imagined her resting her head on my chest as she read. What would her hair smell of? Roses? Jasmine? Maybe frangipani. Definitely some sort of flower.

I wasn't expecting Google to have much on Delilah, but a quick search rewarded me with a whole bunch of news articles. Her father was an oil rig engineer who'd died in an offshore explosion large enough to be caught on satellite, leaving her with a trust fund from his life insurance. Mom worked at some giant tech company in Silicon Valley, which meant she was out of the house more often than in. They lived ten miles away from school. Delilah did not board; the life insurance money was only enough to enroll her at Draycott as a day student.

My heart hurt at the thought of what Delilah had been through. I knew the sort of loss she'd had, the hole it gouged in your entire being, so big and gaping you didn't think you could possibly continue, while everybody else kept on living and expecting you to limp along like you didn't just have a part of you ripped out. But I got it. I was the only one who really got Delilah.

So, on to Instagram and Snapchat. Back in her old school, Delilah was an outgoing girl. There were hundreds of pictures of her laughing with friends, their skinny, tween-girl arms twined around one another's necks. Aisha was in quite a few of them. Delilah looked so different from the pale, silent girl who turned up at Draycott that I sat there, staring at my computer for a long time, mourning the death of Happy Delilah.

I understood transformations all too well. The version of me right now was nothing like the version I was during freshman year. Sometimes my idiot friends would repost some old photos and tag me in them, and it always hurt to see what I looked like at the time—lanky, all elbows and knees. It had all changed when I met Sophie. She was a sophomore then and was the most beautiful thing I had ever come across. She'd bewitched me. I knew I had to change myself to be worthy of her, and I did. I hit the gym hard. I choked down protein shakes. I tried out for various sports teams and made friends with the right people. It took about a year to leave that skinny, awkward kid behind. And it was all worth it.

Delilah's transformation was a different one. A heartbreaking one, but maybe Happy Delilah wasn't really gone.

Maybe she was just hiding under all the layers of grief. My purpose was clear as day. I was meant to restore the old Delilah.

Too bad she'd largely stopped posting on social media weeks ago. On one hand, I liked that she wasn't like every other kid our age, faking everything on social media, desperately gobbling up every Like they could get their hands on. On the other hand, it made my job so much harder than it needed to be.

As I paced about my room, scratching the side of my neck with increasing ferocity, Sophie's voice floated through my head.

I could see her plain as day, her lips curled into a nice-but-mostly-naughty smile. *Nothing worthwhile ever comes easy, Lolo. You must know that by now.*

She was right, as usual. Shame on me, getting frustrated so easily. Since when did love come easy? I had to figure shit out. Delilah may not be the type to publicly check in at every location she visited, but others sure were. Others like Aisha.

Aisha's Instagram was a cacophony of selfies, smiling faces, kissy faces, long legs being showcased at a million different angles. Aisha had nice legs. Aisha also liked to announce her whereabouts to the world at all possible moments.

@Aishazzam checked in at Freddy's.
Come hungry, leave happy! #FreddysBurgers #PiggingOut

@Aishazzam checked in at AMC Draycott.

Movie night with the girls! #PopcornTime

I scrolled through nearly a year's worth of banality—if only Delilah knew the lengths I was going to for her sake— before striking gold:

@Aishazzam checked in at 1876 Woolworth Dr.

Sleepover with the BFF! #JustLikeWhenWeWereKids

And there was a picture of her and Delilah in matching pajamas.

I stole out of the dorms that same night, climbing out my window and keeping in the shadows until I was off school grounds, then I ran. And it felt. So. Good. I was Lazarus. I was alive again. Everything was amazing. I wanted to fly through the sky, shouting, but I managed to keep my excitement inside.

It took a bit of effort, but I managed to make myself sit down when I caught the bus to Woolworth Drive instead of pacing around and freaking the other passengers out. Delilah's neighborhood was nice; modest but respectable. Trimmed lawns and lush trees lined the sidewalk. I stopped across the street from number 1876, my throat sandpapery and dry, a fist squeezing my heart, because there she was: my Delilah, sitting in her room on the second floor braiding her hair, her curtains wide open, putting her on display for all the world to see. Really, she should be more careful. She was so luminescent, she could easily attract some creep's attention.

My heart squeezed tighter at the thought of some asshole taking advantage of Delilah's naivety. *It's okay*, I told myself. *It's fine. It's why I'm here, to protect her. I will never let anything bad happen to her.*

Never.

CHAPTER THREE
delilah

I was sorting through the latest inventory sheet for Lisa, the school librarian, when I heard the door open downstairs, startling me. Work always made me jumpy, especially when I had to take it home, like I did today, because Brandon—my mom's asshole boyfriend—didn't understand the meaning of privacy. All he knew was that I worked at the school library, and I didn't want him to learn any details about it. A glance at my phone told me it was five o'clock, too early for Mom to be back. Which meant it could only be Brandon, which meant—well, it meant nothing good. I hopped up, grabbed a textbook, and opened it at random. I hunched over the book at my desk because Brandon found it less threatening to see me curled over a book.

I held my breath, listening for his heavy footsteps, but all I heard were soft steps and cupboards being opened and closed. Then a feminine sigh. My breath came out in a whoosh. It was Mom. Weird. The only other time Mom had been home this early was when we received the news about Pa. Maybe something similarly awful had happened to Brandon. One could hope. That's a horrible thing to think, right? Still, I couldn't deny the coil of twisted satisfaction at the thought of Brandon pushing up daisies. Sick, sick, sick.

I crept out of my room—even though Brandon wasn't around, the habit was hard to break. I was used to creeping everywhere now, making my footsteps as diminutive as possible—and stopped on the third step to watch Mom as she emptied the dishwasher. She looked tired. She always did, I guess that's how most Silicon Valley employees look, but I liked to think she also looked happy when Pa was still around. Now she just looked haggard.

"Why are you home so early?" I said from the steps.

She jumped. "Sweetheart, I didn't think you'd be home!"

"Yeah, they called off volleyball practice today cause Coach had to take her dog to the vet."

"Awww. Is it okay?" Mom went back to stacking the dishes.

"Probably not."

"Oh, Dee. Don't start."

I swallowed my retort. Forced myself to take a deep breath.

"What were you up to?" Mom asked.

I shrugged. "Just doing some work for Lisa." I'd started working there over the summer, just so I didn't have to stay here in this house and watch my mother scurry about like a frightened rat, trying to appease Brandon's endless demands. I'd never thought anything involving the library could be interesting, but my second month there, I walked in on Lisa dealing with inventory, and she trusted me enough by then to let me help. And, as it turned out, I was a natural. Lisa often told me I was the best assistant she could ever hope for, and I was pathetic enough to lap up any compliment thrown my way.

The corners of Mom's mouth lifted, though I wouldn't call what she was doing *smiling*.

"You know, I wish you wouldn't work, Dee," she said. "We can afford Draycott. I'd much rather you spend your time studying or going out with your friends like a normal teen."

Once again, I had to bite back my caustic reply. These days, there were thousands of unsaid retorts burning a hole in my throat. *I'm doing this because of you,* I wanted to yell until my voice stripped the flesh off her bones. Also, it was rich of her to say we could afford Draycott when we'd had to defer my enrollment for almost a year, until Pa's insurance money finally came in.

Instead, I said, "Why're you home early?"

"Oh, you know. Thought I'd take some time off work. I haven't had a vacation in five years, so why not?" Mom's eyes flicked toward me, pale, nervous. I could smell the lie on her, coming in waves so thick, it was almost visible.

I narrowed my eyes. "You're taking a vacation from work," I said flatly. "You, the woman who returned to work one week after giving birth, are taking a vacation."

"It's been known to happen," Mom chirped.

I sighed. "What's really going on, Mom?"

"Well, I've been thinking about how nice it would be if I had more time at home, you know? I could do all the things I've always wanted to do but never had the chance to…"

"Like what?"

Now that she was finished putting the dishes away, Mom had no choice but to look at me. She didn't do it for very long before she picked up a dishrag and started wiping at the kitchen counter absentmindedly. "Like baking."

"Baking," I parroted back.

"Yes, baking. I loved baking when I was younger."

"Mom, you don't take time off work because you want to bake. What the hell is this all about?"

"I just needed a break, okay?" Mom cried. "Is that all right with you, Dee? Do I have your permission to take time off work? Do you know how hard it is for a woman working in tech, Dee? You know the amount of shit I take every single day from men who think I don't deserve to be there just because I happen to have a vagina?"

"This is because of Brandon, isn't it?" I growled. I knew

I was being a jerk, but it wasn't the fact that she'd taken time off. It was the fact that this was *my mom* taking time off, and my mom never took time off work. She'd always been a tech designer first, wife second, mother third, and I loved her for it. And now, all of a sudden, here she was, an aspiring baker? It was all wrong. It smelled like Brandon's doing.

"Well, he and I have been talking, yes, about how nice it would be if I—if we started a family, and—"

"A family?" I squawked. "You're thinking of procreating with that man? Jesus Christ, Mom! You've lost it. Look at what he's done to you, to us! You still can't rotate your wrist without it clicking!" My entire world was spiraling out of control. "Mom, you're smarter than this. Why do you keep him around? You can do so much better."

"Sweetie, it's not as simple as that. I'm in my forties; it'll be a miracle if I can conceive at my age, and there aren't many men out there who would be willing to take me, you know, what with all my baggage and my craziness." Mom laughed her new laugh, the one she'd developed about a month after Brandon moved in.

"Mom, listen to me. Brandon's been brainwashing you. All that stuff about nobody wanting you isn't true. You're a catch! I bet half the guys at your company are lusting over you." But even as I said it, I knew I'd lost her. This was my fault, all of it. Pa had been the engineer in charge of making sure the rig ran smoothly, and he'd missed something, or he'd miscalculated—whatever it was, his mistake led to the explosion and left us with nothing but twisted metal and a thick layer of oil that spread poison across the ocean beneath a cloud of greasy, black smoke, an ecological disaster that the world mourned.

And in the months following his death, I'd taken all the fury boiling inside me and flung it at Mom's face, and she'd had no one to turn to but Brandon. I had ripped her apart piece by piece, and Brandon had been there to catch the bits that remained. He'd pretended to put her back together, but his glue had turned out to be poison, too. By the time we were done with Mom, she was nothing but a shadow of what she used to be. I'd realized this too late. I could rage as hard as I wanted to, and Mom would still believe that she needed Brandon to get by. This was my doing.

"Look, Dee, I just need you to be supportive, okay? Can you do that for us? I'll be home a lot more from now on, and I would really like us to get along."

"What do you mean you'll be home a lot more? I thought you were just taking a vacation. It's temporary, right?" I asked.

"Well, it's temporary, but if it goes well, maybe it can become something more permanent."

"And what would we live on?"

Mom smiled. "Oh, sweetie, Brandon's assured me he'll look after us, I mean, look how well he's looked after our finances—"

I blew up then. "How well he's looked after our finances? You mean him taking your paychecks and—"

The door banged open. Brandon expected us to tiptoe around him, but he loved making explosive entrances. "Boy, am I glad to be home," he grunted, stripping off his gear and flinging it to the floor.

Mom shot me a warning glance. Like I needed a reminder that her live-in boyfriend was a monster. I rounded my shoulders and bowed my head (eye contact was a dangerous thing around here) and started walking toward the stairs, but Brandon stopped me.

"What's going on with my two favorite ladies?" He dropped onto the couch, making the entire thing sag, and manspread his legs, taking up more space than he should. "Babe, can I have a drink, please?"

"Coming right up, sweetheart," Mom cooed. The effect was somewhat spoiled by the shrill note of fear lacing her voice, but Brandon did not seem to notice. Or, if he did, he relished it.

"What have you two been up to?" he said, beaming at me.

"Um, not much. I was just finishing up my homework—"

"Yeah? You need any help with schoolwork?" Brandon said. His expression was earnest—eager. Even after everything, he liked to think of himself as a Nice Guy.

I was too well trained by this time to laugh in his face. Instead, I wrangled my expression into a simpering, grateful one and said, "Thank you, Brandon, but I think I've got it."

"Aw, come on. Let me help. I'm practically your dad by now. Didn't he like to help with your homework?" He gave me a big smile, one that said, *Aren't I sweet?*

You're not my fucking dad, I wanted to say. Pa was the exact opposite of Brandon in every way. He was soft-spoken, his fingers as elegant as any pianist's. He'd moved here from Singapore for grad school. That was when he met Mom, and what was supposed to be a two-year stay in California turned into twenty. Even though he'd lived in California for so long, he never quite lost the Singlish accent. He tried hard to hide the accent in public so it wouldn't mark him as a foreigner, but at home, he'd relax and I'd tease him for punctuating all of his sentences with *lah*.

He taught me many of the hallmarks of Singlish—saying *aiya* instead of *oh my god*, one of the delightful Hokkien curse words that sounded so much fiercer than your usual English ones. He liked to cook us Singaporean dishes—chili crab, Hokkien mee, roti prata.

We visited Singapore twice when I was little, and though the heat slowed me down to a sweaty crawl, I fell in love with the country immediately. I loved everything about it, the breakneck speed at which everybody spoke, the way people so casually included you in everything, the cleanliness and efficiency of the place. And Pa's family was there—loud and welcoming, always shoving food in my face. It was the reason I was working my ass off on my studies and at work. I was going to apply to Pa's alma mater: the National University of Singapore.

Brandon thinking he could replace Pa made me want to plunge a knife in his eyeball and twist. I scrambled my brains for something to say. Something that wouldn't get me in trouble. I'd made the mistake of asking him to help with my math homework once, when he insisted, and he'd stared at my textbook forever before—well, never mind. So math wasn't in the cards. Same with Shakespeare. In fact, anything that made him feel stupid was off-limits.

I'd taken too long to think. Brandon's face had lost its generous smile, and his jaw was now clenched. His jaw was always the first to tighten up. Then it would be his fist, and that would be that.

"Somebody thinks they're too smart for good ol' Brandon," he said in a joking tone, but beneath the singsong voice was a small vibration of anger.

"No, no! I don't want to waste your time with my stuff," I said hurriedly. "You have more important things to deal with." I forced a halfway sincere-looking smile onto my face, my insides shriveling up with hatred. It was, ironically, mostly hatred toward myself. I still hadn't forgiven myself for not being the badass I'd always thought I would be. The past year or so, he had broken me down, softened me until

I was nothing more than this useless, simpering lump with a quavering smile. Keeping my head down and my shoulders hunched had stopped being a survival trait and started becoming an actual habit that I did everywhere, even when Brandon wasn't anywhere in the vicinity. I was becoming less me, less present, less alive. And I deserved it for being so pathetic, for not fighting back.

Brandon frowned. "Nothing's more important than the two leading ladies of my life."

I forced my smile to remain. "That's so sweet of you, Brandon. But I'll be fine, really."

"Well, offer's on the table if you need my help."

"Uh-huh," I said. Time for a quick change of subject. "Hey, how was your day?"

Brandon leaned back, but his gaze remained on me. "Funny you should ask. I was just at your school."

My heart dropped a beat. "Oh?"

"Yeah, you know, Dee, I gotta say, I'm not a fan of that place. Don't know why your dad wanted to put you in there so badly. It's kinda... Well, it's pretty much filled with spoiled rich brats. And all the shit that's happened there, man..." Brandon shook his head.

I nodded along.

"Aren't you gonna ask me why I was there?"

"Why were you there?" I replied obediently.

He side-eyed me in what he probably thought was a

mysterious detective way. "Two years ago, someone was operating a drug ring there."

Ice prickled down my back. This was a dangerous topic, one I really needed to stay far away from.

"It was all a huge clusterfuck. You know what Mendez is like. She couldn't leave well enough alone. Had to dig deeper and deeper."

He didn't know. He had no idea. I wanted to tell him I knew all this already. People at school still talked about the infamous drug-fueled case from time to time. Hell, it shook even the school staff. Lisa herself told me about it one quiet afternoon, her voice hushed and her eyes wide, always checking to make sure we were alone. Lisa never gossiped, so that afternoon was a one-time event. I bet I knew more details than Brandon did about the drug ring. But of course I couldn't interrupt Brandon, Mr. Important Policeman.

Mom came by with his drink before going back to the kitchen.

Brandon swilled his glass for a while, his thumb scraping the rim. He was wearing this faraway look. "Of course, in the end, nothing happened. The place is untouchable. The trail had gone dry, anyway. Whoever was running the drug business closed up shop."

I made an *aww, that really sucks* face.

"But now we got word someone's started selling again."

He pointed a large, stubby finger and glared at me. "Have you and your friends been buying, Dee?"

He might as well have picked up our solid oak coffee table and smashed me in the head with it. "I don't—I really—"

Brandon threw his head back and guffawed. "I'm messing around, Dee. That look on your face! You are the biggest fuckin' nerd I've come across. 'Ooh, I'm Asian, I can't do anything fun! Must study hard!'" He raised his hands and leaned back a little. "Uh-oh, call the PC police! I made a race joke!"

Somehow, I managed to force a smile onto my face. "Ha ha," I bit out.

He winked at me. "I'm messing with you. I don't really believe that. You're a great kid, Dee."

"Thanks, Brandon." Sometimes, I imagined Brandon dead. *Maybe he slips while going down the stairs and breaks his neck. Maybe he gets caught in a gunfight and a bullet rips through his skull. Maybe—*

Brandon grinned and took a sip of his whiskey sour. He made a face and called out to Mom. "Hey, babe, can you bring me some ice cubes?"

"Okay, sweet stuff," Mom chirped.

That was my cue to leave. I was halfway to the bottom of the staircase when I heard Mom whisper, "Shit."

I paused. Pre-Brandon, my reaction to my mom swearing would have been laughter, followed by me giving her a hard time. But there was actual terror in Mom's voice, and it was contagious. I crept back to the kitchen and raised my eyebrows at her.

She tipped the ice box toward me and gestured at it. Empty.

"I'll go to the store and buy some," I whispered.

Mom blinked rapidly, her eyes shining with tears. "I—I'd have to ask him for money," she said.

My chest tightened. How wrong, how fucking awful it was that my mom was reduced to this. How could she have let him bully her into letting him take over the finances? And now here we were, panicking because we'd have to ask Brandon to give us a few of Mom's hard-earned dollars so we could get him ice for his goddamn whiskey.

"Don't worry, Mom, I'll pay for it. It's why I got the library job." And why I was working so hard at it, squirreling money away.

Mom smiled gratefully, then her smile froze when Brandon called out, "Any luck on that ice?" Already there was a dangerous tone to his voice.

Mom took a deep breath and plastered a smile on her face, even though Brandon wasn't in the kitchen to see it in its full terrified glory. "We're out of ice cubes, sweetie. Dee's just about to go to the store and grab a bag." She ushered me out of the kitchen.

"Out of ice?" Brandon's voice had gone silky soft. He hefted himself off the couch, and suddenly, there he was, a mountain of muscle and sudden, swift punishment.

My bones turned to water. The urge to curl up in a tight corner with my head in my hands almost overcame me.

"Who was the last to use the ice?" he said, still in that velvety voice.

Mom was opening and shutting her mouth, but no words came out. And then I recalled she'd poured a whole bunch of ice cubes into a water bottle last night and then pressed it to her back, where he'd—

"It was me."

It took a moment to realize I'd spoken. They were both staring at me. *Shit, shit, shit.*

"No, Brandon—" Mom started.

"Shh," Brandon whispered, putting a finger to his lips. He turned toward me, and when Brandon turned to face you, he did so with his entire body, and it felt like seeing a large bull that had been happily munching grass but now realized you were there and you were wearing red.

Time held its breath. The only sound in the room was the roar of my blood rushing through my ears. I should run right now. I shouldn't even take the time to grab anything on the way out, just run until there was no more air in my lungs. But I was a useless, watery thing, and so I stood there, trembling, as he advanced upon me.

"Brandon—" Mom pleaded, but like me, she was broken too. She wouldn't actually do anything.

"Funny story, Dee," Brandon said, in a conversational

tone, his voice still soft, soft as snowfall. "You know what they call it when an officer kills someone by accident?"

"Please let me get the ice now, I'll be quick," I squeaked.

"Don't worry about the ice. Answer my question."

I scrambled through the mess that was my mind. "Um...I don't know...um, a misdemeanor?"

"Paid vacation." Brandon broke into a face-splitting grin. "Hey, why do you look so scared, Dee? I'm just playing around." He smacked my shoulder and roared his laughter at Mom. "Look at her! Shaking like a leaf!"

"Why don't you go get the ice now, darling?" Mom said to me, her cheeks trembling with the effort of keeping the manic smile on her face.

I slunk away quickly, Brandon's laughter echoing through my head.

CHAPTER FOUR

logan

*Things that had irked me for the last two years—like listen-*ing to the guys sing dirty versions of our school anthem, or wrestling in the corridors on the way to class, or pranking each other in the showers—things I'd given up for so long, became enjoyable once again.

Even Josh noticed the difference. One evening, as we walked back to the dorms from the dining hall, he punched me on the shoulder and said, "It's really great to have you back, man." I could've sworn there were actual tears in his eyes. Jesus, the guy was so hopelessly loyal. I couldn't even give him a hard time about it, because *I* had tears in *my* goddamn eyes. I punched him back, and it felt so good to horse around again.

Three weeks after I laid eyes on the love of my life, I finally got the chance to talk to her.

After dinnertime, before lights-out, the boarders had free roam of the grounds. Draycott was known for its rolling grounds—endless carpets of lush green connecting the buildings with paths curling along the borders like graceful calligraphy. Most kids took full advantage of their surroundings and sprawled across the grass to hang out. The more adventurous, or those looking for quiet nooks to hook up, go farther from the main grounds and sneak under the dark trees, past the tangle of branches and thorny blackberry bushes and down to the river. The less outgoing went back to their rooms, the ambitious curled up at the library, and I, well, I checked out of Draycott and drove down to the animal shelter.

Volunteering at the local shelter was Ms. Taylor's idea. She'd given me a lengthy talk about the amazing healing powers of animals, yada yada, and I'd agreed just so she'd stop. And it wasn't bad at all. I'd expected to be put to work scrubbing out kennels, but as it turned out, I was given the task of taking the bigger dogs out on walks. They didn't usually let anyone under eighteen take the animals for walks, but Ms. Taylor gave them a call, telling them how much it would help me, and since there were only a couple months left before my eighteenth birthday, the local shelter relented. I liked dogs, especially big ones. I liked how they were always panting, like they couldn't have enough of life and they had to gulp down every moment of it.

One of the dogs I was often assigned to walk was a monstrously huge and hopelessly friendly Lab mix called Daddy. Daddy was a really sweet, hyper dog who thought he was the size of a Chihuahua, so when I asked if I could take him out on extra-long walks, the shelter employ-ees went, "God, *yes*, please tire him out." It took me and Daddy less than fifteen minutes to run the two miles from the shelter to Delilah's street. I could go faster, but Daddy was a bit overweight, and by the time we were done with the two miles, he was panting hard. Once we made the turn to her street, I tugged on Daddy's leash and slowed our pace to a brisk walk.

I headed for number 1876. It was dark enough now for the streetlights to come on and the windows of the houses to glow soft orange. I bit my lip, savoring the way my heart rate increased slightly once I turned onto Delilah's street. I loved the anticipation, knowing she was there at the end of my journey. My prize, my perfect goddess, displayed through her window for me.

Delilah's house was on the corner. Lucky me. It meant I could observe her from two different angles, and I didn't squander that piece of good luck. Over the past couple of weeks, I'd walked up and down the two streets, looking for the perfect position, one that would give me the best view. And my luck had held; no one had found the little camera I'd installed in a tree across the street from her house.

I can't be here for you 24/7, Delilah, but I need you to know that I'm always with you. Always.

I checked to make sure no one was around before reaching up to the second branch of the tree, where the camera was tucked nice and tight. Daddy chose that moment to give a particularly ruthless yank on the leash. The momentum launched me forward and I pitched face-first onto the sidewalk. The breath was knocked out of my lungs, sort of like when I first saw Delilah, except a lot less pleasant. Somehow, I still had the presence of mind to keep a firm hold on the leash so Daddy's plans of a great escape were immediately dashed. *The things I go through for Del—*

"Are you okay?" a voice said. A voice I'd recognize even in my dreams.

Shit. Panic stabbed through my rib cage. *Shit, shit, shit.* Delilah. Had she seen me stretching my arm up into the branches? Was she wondering what the hell I was doing here? She was going to freak the fuck out—nobody understands romance—and Ms. Taylor would hear about this, and I'd be suspended again, except this time it would be worse, it would be so much worse—

Calm. Down.

She wasn't looking at me the way people sometimes did, like they thought I was going to do something totally off-the-wall. But I still had my fail-safe—Daddy. He automatically cleansed me of all suspicion.

I hoped.

I stood up and brushed myself off, taking a few moments to make sure my breathing was settled and my voice wasn't going to come out high with nervousness. But when I did look up, I realized I was hopeless. God, she was beautiful. I caught myself and forced out a casual, "Hey." Then, before my brain could catch up, I said, "Oh, hey, Delilah, right?"

She glanced up at me, recognition dawning on her features now that she could see my face.

"You're in my chemistry class," I mumbled.

"Yeah, I know who you are." She didn't quite meet my eye as she said it, which was typical Delilah. Instead, her eyes hovered somewhere around my chin.

I'd dreamed of so many ways for us to meet. Me falling on my face was not one of them. And now her eyes were focusing somewhere over my shoulder like she couldn't wait to go. I struggled to say something that would put her at ease. I knew so much about her, but none of that information was usable. I couldn't possibly say, "That Hainanese chicken rice dish you posted on Instagram two years ago and tagged as your all-time favorite food? I tried making it because I wanted to know how it felt eating something you loved. And it's really good. You've got great taste. I can't wait to try all those other Singaporean dishes you posted about." Yeah, not so much

"So, um, do you live around here?" Argh.

Delilah nodded, still not meeting my eye. "Yeah, that's my house right there. Do you live around here too?"

"No, I'm actually from out of state. I board at Draycott."

Delilah's eyebrows rose. "I didn't know they let you have pets at the dorms."

Thank god for Daddy. Look at him, sniffing his own balls, not realizing he'd just provided me with the perfect conversation starter. I gave Delilah a small smile. *Don't wanna creep her out with a full-on grin.* "They don't. He's from the shelter. I volunteer there once in a while, and they let me take him out on walks." I was careful not to sound like I was boasting; people did that so often—they talked about their time volunteering like they were Mother Teresa or some shit. Delilah wasn't the kind of girl who'd fall for that, so I made sure to keep it short—*no biggie, just something I do.*

"That's really cool of you," she said. The ghost of a smile reached her lips—*cherry lips, maybe raspberry, I love berries, Dee*—and she was finally seeing me, really seeing me. She liked what she saw, I could tell. But before I could capitalize on the moment, she glanced back at her house and her mouth tightened into a thin line. "I gotta go to the store."

"I'll walk you there," I said.

"No, I—I'll be fine."

I cocked my head to the side. "Come on, I gotta walk Daddy anyway."

"Daddy?" Delilah grinned, and I caught a glimpse of the

old Delilah, the one I'd seen in her pictures. It made my heart glow. "That's such a cute name."

Daddy perked up at the sound of his name, and I had to haul him back before he could pounce on Delilah and lick her to death. "Where are my manners?" I said. "Daddy, this is Delilah. Delilah, this is Daddy." I leaned closer to her and lowered my voice. "Careful, he's a bit of a perv."

Delilah laughed and crouched down to scratch Daddy behind his ears. I got a whiff of her scent—something that reminded me of pure, white petals. I had to stop myself from scooping her into my arms and inhaling all of her.

"Hey, big guy," she murmured.

Daddy sagged against her, panting happily. "See, he likes you," I said. "Come on, Daddy, let's walk Delilah to the store." I turned and started walking in the direction of the supermarket before Delilah could answer. She was a natural follower. I knew this much, at least. But part of me still crossed my fingers tight and prayed she'd follow my lead.

I smiled when I heard her footsteps walking toward mine. Phew. I searched for something to say. Again, I was faced with a mountain of information I'd so patiently gathered about her, none of it usable. I couldn't ask her about volleyball, nor could I ask her about Tan Jing Xu, nor could I ask her about Singapore—

Or maybe I could. I mean, it was no secret she was half-Singaporean. Most people would know stuff like that about their classmates, right? *Quick, before the silence overwhelms everything.*

"Singapore," I blurted.

Sweet Jesus, if I could only punch myself in the face.

"Sorry?" she said. The walls had clapped up around her, and she was looking at me warily.

"I just remembered—I think I overheard someone mention you're half-Singaporean," I said. I was babbling. I was a train veering off the rails and I had to save it, steer myself back, or I was going to end in a massive crash.

"Yeah...?" she said. Still with so much caution.

"My mom—" Great, I've brought up my mom. This could not get any worse. "She's one of the deans at Duke. Have you heard about the Duke-NUS program?"

It was a desperate last grasp at straws. Her dad was a graduate of NUS. Maybe it was dirty to bring up this connection, but love and war and all that...

Her face lit up, and it was worth it. "Yeah, I know about the Duke-NUS program."

"Cool," I said, joy rising through my chest. Her smile, I swear. "My mom's in charge of that program. Well, not in charge, but like, she's on the team, and she travels back and forth to Singapore quite a bit. She loves it there." Now I sounded like I was boasting, and I had to reel it back in, because I didn't want to boast, I just wanted to make a connection.

"Wow," she breathed, her eyes wide. "No way. That's amazing, Logan. Wow," she said again, and her gaze was fully on me, her attention all mine, and I was flying, flying into the stratosphere. "I love it there," she said. "My dad's Singaporean, and he took me a few times."

I didn't wait for her to realize she'd said "my dad's Singaporean" instead of "my dad was Singaporean." "Did you have roti prata? My mom's always raving about it."

Now she was beaming hard and I could die happy, I really could.

"Yes!" she said. "Oh, man, I love roti prata so, so much. I've been trying to find it here, but none of the Indian restaurants I've been to make it. The closest thing they have is paratha, and it's just not the same."

"That's cause it's more of a Peranakan dish than an Indian one, right?" Shit, now I was mansplaining and whitesplaining, and back the fuck up, Logan. "I mean, I don't know, I think I remember reading somewhere about it—" *When I looked it up because I saw so many pictures of it on your Instagram.* "I'm probably wrong."

"No, that makes sense," she said, appraising me. "I'm impressed you know so much about Singaporean food. Most people here don't know anything about Singapore. You know what people usually say when I tell them I'm half-Singaporean?"

"What?"

She pitched her voice high and squeaked, "'Ooh, which part of China is that in?'"

I laughed. "No way. People here aren't that ignorant. I mean, really? Singapore's obviously in Vietnam."

She narrowed her eyes at me.

"I'm kidding! It's right below Malaysia and next to Indonesia." I was a good boy, I'd done my homework. I could talk about Singapore for hours.

She laughed again—*I could listen to you laugh for days*—and lightly slapped me on my arm. My skin tingled where her fingers touched me, and if I were twelve years old, I'd swear not to wash my arm forever. *She wants me.* She wouldn't slap just anyone's arm.

"So what are you getting at the store?" I asked.

As it turned out, I'd asked the wrong question. The walls were back up. Delilah frowned and stared straight ahead. "Ice."

There was a pause, then I said, "What do you need it for?"

"It's just—for my mom's boyfriend."

Ah, yes. The ignoble Detective Brandon Jackson. I knew about Detective Jackson, and not just from my research on Delilah. A year ago, right around the time Sophie died, Detective Jackson and his partner had been put on a case at Draycott. They'd hung around the school for weeks, like a persistent and embarrassing rash. Detective Jackson was loud, obnoxious, and assumed everybody admired him, which of course turned the entire student body against him. I'd thought of him as a big, stupid, but well-meaning dog, not unlike Daddy, but Delilah did something when she mentioned him—she dropped her voice and gave a small, grim smile, as though she were afraid that mentioning him might summon him to our side.

"What does he need the ice for?" I asked.

"Um—you know. Just...stuff."

Something was off. Something that felt big, lurking underneath us the way a giant sea creature did, writhing right below the calm surface before bursting out of the water with its jaws open. I knew fear when I saw it. Even Daddy could sense it; he lifted his head and licked her hand, whining.

"Everything okay?" I frowned in concern.

Delilah turned away, but not before I caught her cheeks turning red. "Yeah, of course."

"That's not what Daddy says."

That coaxed a smile out of her, but she still looked tired, defeated. All the joy she'd shown moments ago had evaporated.

"Well, Daddy's wrong," she said.

I frowned at Daddy. "Are you losing your touch with the ladies, Daddy?"

The corners of Delilah's mouth lifted. "I don't think Daddy's as good with the ladies as he wants you to think," she said.

"Ouch."

Delilah laughed—a quick, nervous sound that was strangled almost as soon as it left her mouth. My grip on Daddy's leash tightened. I'd assumed, when I went through Delilah's pictures, that she'd curled into a tight, hard shell because the oil rig incident might have turned her and her mom into easy targets for the press. I never spared a thought for the possibility that her shyness was caused by something completely different. I imagined my fists crunching into Detective Jackson's meaty face and found the thought a pleasant one.

I had to take her mind off Detective Jackson. "So, how're you liking Draycott?" Pretty weak question to ask, given she'd been there for weeks, but I was running out of things to say.

"It's okay. I never thought I'd go someplace like Draycott." She hugged herself as she walked, her hands gripping her elbows. It made her look even thinner than she already was. "Sorry, I just—I kinda suck at conversations."

"You're better at it than you think you are."

She snorted.

"Of course," I added, "I'm only comparing you to Daddy, so the standards aren't exactly high."

Another quick laugh that was strangled as soon as it left her mouth. Another flash of my fists slamming into Detective Jackson's face. *What's he done to her?* Delilah was reminding me of Sophie in the worst possible way. Those final weeks before they found the drugs in Sophie's room, she'd behaved the same way—furtive glances, conversations weighed down with fear. I wasn't able to save Sophie. Hell if I was going to let the same thing happen to Delilah.

I stopped walking and touched her arm lightly, ignoring the zap, the spark, the whatever it was that told me our bodies were made for each other. I didn't let my hand stay on her arm. "Hey—um—I know this is out of the blue and we barely know each other, but if you need help, if you need anything at all, please tell me, okay?"

Delilah met my eyes then, and my breath caught in my throat. She wore Sophie's face—the expression of someone who was being hunted, that primal fear dancing frantically in her eyes.

"I don't know what you're talking about," she laughed, and the sound came out too high and too brittle. *Delilah, I know when you're lying.*

"I—uh—I hope you don't think it's weird, but I've seen you a couple of times at the Secret board…" I said, taking a giant leap into the world of risk.

At the lobby of the library at school was something called Post Ur Secret—a giant bulletin board where students were encouraged to pin up their secrets anonymously. We used to have an electronic version, an app called Draycott Dirt, but it got out of hand and devolved into a massive online bullying and trolling forum, and Mrs. Henderson banned any future such apps from being made. Then Lisa, the school librarian, suggested using one of the boards at the library as a more sensible outlet for students to let off some steam without it going out of control, and the thing became a huge hit. It was filled with all sorts of secrets. We weren't allowed to put any identifying information, so the board was also a great source of entertainment, an ongoing game of Guess Who?

Delilah's eyes were practically perfect circles and I wanted to reach out to hug her and tell her it was okay.

"I don't really post anything—I just like to look at the secrets there," she said.

"Hey, it's okay. I post on the board." Mostly stuff about Sophie, vague musings that couldn't be identified. "It's a good outlet for our feelings. But if someone's hurting you, the board won't help. Let me help you, Delilah."

Her eyes watered, and she blinked furiously, taking in a shaky breath, and I wondered how anyone could hurt someone like her. But it was going to be okay. I'd make it okay.

"That's really sweet, Logan. But I don't know what you can do. There's nothing anyone can do."

Sophie's words stabbed through my head. *"There's nothing anyone can do. I'm alone, Lolo. No one can help me."*

"We can report it. You don't have to go through this alone."

Delilah shook her head. "You don't understand. He's a cop. And my mom and I are so hated after what my dad did... Brandon can do whatever he wants to us and nobody would give a shit." She took a shaky breath. "There's nothing anyone can do."

"The school has counselors. They can help you." Hollow words, especially since I knew on a personal level how useless the counselors were. But I didn't want to leave her hopeless, and I couldn't tell her I would fix things. I would, but I'd have to be an anonymous benefactor.

"No, it's fine, really. If this gets out, if Brandon hears anything about it—" She grabbed my hand, her grip feral, strong. "Logan, please don't tell anyone."

"But—"

"If you want to help, you won't tell anyone. He'll kill me. I'm serious." There were no traces of exaggeration on her face.

"All right," I said. "I won't tell anyone."

Delilah let her breath go. Then she seemed to notice for the first time that she was holding my hand and dropped it, her cheeks reddening. "Sorry," she mumbled.

"Don't worry about it." Time for another change of subject. "Hey, how're you doing in chemistry? I am dying in that damn class."

Her face brightened a little. Chemistry was her favorite subject. "I love it. Ms. Woods is awesome." For the next few minutes, she described her chemistry project, her face animated, her hands flitting back and forth like butterflies.

She stopped when we got to the front of the supermarket and turned to me. "Wow, I can't believe you just let me babble on and on about chem class."

I grinned. "It's mostly for Daddy's sake. He's really into chem. I wasn't really listening."

She laughed. "Thanks for everything, Logan." We stood there for an awkward second before she said, "See you at school."

"See you." I made myself turn and leave instead of waiting around and watching her enter the store, which I wanted to do but would no doubt freak her out.

My mind was a whirring mess—going too fast, everything too bright and sharp-edged—as I walked Daddy back to the shelter. Delilah was in trouble. Detective Jackson was an abuser. And here I was, just another boy in love. I could feast my mind on killing him in a dozen different ways, each more gruesome than the last, but the truth was, I was pretty much powerless. And Delilah was right; accusing him was out of the question. His cop buddies would click into one giant, impenetrable wall. They'd do it even if they hated the guy; it was more about the principle of the thing. You just don't go after a cop.

When I got back to Draycott, I was too amped up to go inside my dorm room. I briskly walked past all the main buildings, through the wrought iron gate at the edge of the rose garden, and into the trees. Past the thicket of blackberry bushes and among the cedar trees, there was a little clearing. The air was suddenly different here, everything hushed as though I'd stepped into an underwater world.

Sophie had shown me this place once. Well, not shown. I'd followed her and watched as she rolled a joint with her best friend, the two of them smoking and holding it carelessly, aloof, and she looked so grown-up and worldly, it was impossible not to fall in love. Later on, Sophie would let me come here, and I'd sit next to her, watching the smoke curl out of her mouth and wishing she'd let me kiss her.

Nobody came here anymore. It was undisturbed. Even the smell was different—wild grass and overripe berries and a hint of animals.

"Hey, Soph," I said, sitting down at my usual spot. "Weird night." I breathed out and listened to the susurration of the leaves around me, like they were nodding, listening.

"I talked to her tonight," I said. "Really talked. You'd like her, I think. You guys have the same sense of humor." I took out my phone and scrolled through social media absentmindedly. I couldn't get Delilah's haunted expression out of my head. Was I destined to sit by once again while the girl I loved went through hell? Pretend I didn't know anything when she followed in Sophie's footsteps?

"Fuck," I muttered. For a moment I wanted to fling my phone into the darkness, hear the satisfying crack as it shattered against the trunk of some tree. But I couldn't let my temper mar this place, this sacred spot. I took a deep breath, listened to Sophie shushing me. This place was Sophie. The breeze caressing my skin was her soft hands, lulling me into peace. Telling me there was a way. There was always a way.

It wasn't until later, as I lay in bed watching news clips on Facebook, that I found the answer to everything.

Someone had posted a video of a police officer punching a woman and the comments were rife with anger at the display of police brutality. And it clicked, then. This was exactly what I needed. A video recording of Detective Jackson abusing Delilah and her mom.

This is it, Delilah. The whole reason you and I met. Why we ran into each other in this vast world, when all laws of probability point to us missing each other, our lives never intertwining.

Because, Delilah, I'm meant to save you, and I'm not one to turn away from destiny.

CHAPTER FIVE
delilah

Saturday morning, I sat in my room, my chemistry textbook in front of me. My eyes traveled over the same sentence for the seventh time. I still couldn't tell you what it said. It was yet another beautiful day—impossibly blue skies dabbed with wispy clouds, the air just nippy enough for the mug of hot tea cradled in my hands to taste even more delicious than usual. Not that I was in the mood to enjoy any of it.

My phone rang, and I scrambled to pick it up before the noise could irritate Brandon. He wouldn't be able to hear it, since he was in the garage blasting his shitty music, but still. Part of me was convinced he could detect the sound of my breath from across the street.

"Hello?" I said.

"Dee? You there?" Aisha was yelling over the background noise.

"I'm here," I said as loudly as I dared.

"I can barely hear you. Ugh, hang on. Lemme get outside."

I waited while she made her way out of what was presumably the school gym, smiling when I heard her snap, "Excuse you!" a couple of times.

"Phew! That's better. Dude, why aren't you here? I thought you were gonna play today!" she said.

Sourness bled through my gut. I should be in today's volleyball match. I'd been working hard on my spike, and Coach had told me I'd be able to play today. It was only a friendly match; she could afford to let the second-tier players have a go. But instead, here I was, sitting in front of my biology textbook, not reading, not playing volleyball, not anything.

"I have the flu," I said feebly. It was what I'd told Coach. The flu would be a blessing compared to how my body was feeling this morning.

Aisha knew me well enough to hear right through my lie. Her voice became heavy with sadness. "Oh, Dee. What happened?"

Oh, Dee. That was what my life had become, a sad, *Oh, Dee* said over and over. I was one of those kids that made people tilt their heads to one side and go, "Aww, poor thing."

Poor, pathetic, broken creature. Secretly, they were all think-ing, *Better her than me.*

I closed my eyes and thought of last night. I saved all those moments, to replay over and over in my head like some sick movie. I added scenes of my own, where I didn't freeze up like a fucking hamster, where I got a hammer, a kitchen knife, a corkscrew, and stabbed them into Brandon's eyes, ears, mouth, whatever.

But what really happened was that Brandon had come back in a foul mood. He hated his partner, Mendez, a.k.a. "that Mexican bitch who thinks she's a real cop." Apparently, Mendez had this silly notion that cops were meant to help everyone, not just rich white people. And she mistakenly thought that solving cases meant doing actual investigations instead of trying to get them closed ASAP. The drug case at Draycott was an itch she'd been dying to scratch for two years. She'd insisted on questioning everybody at the school again now, which was earning them a lot of disapproval from high places.

I hated Mendez. She seemed nice enough the few times we met, but she was making my life a living hell without even trying.

"The usual," I said.

"You should report him. I'll go with you—"

Not this again. Why did everybody assume report-ing Brandon would be this straightforward thing without repercussions? What would happen to me or Mom if Brandon were to get his cop buddies involved? We'd be two women who were already hated by the community making accusations about a cop. Care for a game of Guess What'll Happen to Delilah Wong, Cop Accuser? Nothing good. And Brandon? Paid vacation, he'd said. Oh, he was joking, he was always so full of jokes, good ol' Brandon, that was why his buddies at the precinct loved him so.

Paid vacation.

"I gotta go," I said.

"Dee—"

I hung up on her and let my forehead fall gently onto the table. On the bright side, Brandon didn't like to leave visible bruises. At least I didn't have to turn up at school with stories about walking into doors or falling down the stairs.

Mendez and her aspirations were giving my kidneys a run for their money. I was trying, and failing, to find a position that would make my back hate me less, and all the while I was wondering how much vacation Brandon would get if my body turned up one day, bloated and blue.

From the garage came the sound of Pink Floyd blasting on Brandon's old-school stereo. He thought old-school stereos were more authentic. There was the occasional clank as he switched tools. Brandon spent Saturday mornings blasting Pink Floyd, knocking back beer, and working on his asshole car. That was how I secretly thought of his Camaro, because it seemed like it was specifically geared toward assholes. Mom had gone to the farmers' market to buy some local salted anchovies that Brandon said would go beautifully with the pizza she was planning on making for dinner. My eyes crawled over the sentence in my textbook again. Something about stoichiometry, and why do I care about stoichiometry, literally what did stoichiometry have to do with my life?

"Dee!" Brandon's shout jerked me out of my seat, and I stood there for a few moments, my heart jumping, wondering if I'd imagined him yelling at me. Three seconds later, the shout came again, louder this time, tinged with anger. "Delilah!"

I hurried out of my room and down the stairs. It wasn't a good idea to keep Brandon waiting. When I opened the door to the garage, Pink Floyd drowned me. God, I hated Pink Floyd. I was sure Brandon only listened to them because he thought they were, like the stereo, more "authentic" than pop music. The garage was where Pa and I used to store our badminton rackets and baseball bats. Now all of our stuff was stored in boxes and shoved out of the way to make room for Brandon's shit. I walked over to where Brandon's legs were sticking out from under the hood of his Camaro. The music was so loud, he didn't hear me come in.

"Delilah!" he yelled again. I jumped again. Pathetic.

"Um—yeah?" I bent over, wincing as my back protested, and waved to catch his attention.

"About fucking time," he snarled. He pointed at a spot behind me, where four empty beer cans sat. "I'm out."

I looked at the cans strewn about the floor. That would be why he was no longer bothering with the niceties. "I'll grab you another pack."

"Get me a sandwich while you're at it. And be quick. Don't dawdle like you always do. Hang on. Hey, c'mere." He leered at me from under the car. "You think I don't know what's going on? I saw you walking with that kid the other day."

I blanched and straightened up instinctively.

"Hey! Look at me when I'm talking to you!"

I took a breath. Bent over again.

"The Chinaman might not have given a shit how you behave, but my house, my rules."

This isn't your house, I screamed silently.

"I'm not going to have you whoring around, making a fool out of me."

I'm not the one making a fool out of you, I thought.

"You get me? No boys, Delilah. I mean it. Don't make me tell you twice." He gripped his wrench hard and gestured with it for effect. "Say, 'Yes, Brandon.'"

The rage rose up, blooming, spreading out of control. *Stop that, Dee. Control it. Control yourself.* My back trembled with the effort staying bent over was costing me. "Yes, Brandon."

He held my eyes for a second longer, while blood pooled in my head, then he smiled. "All right, now go get my beer. That's my girl."

Later, when I finally had some time to let things digest, I'd pinpoint those words as the ones that pushed me over the edge. "That's my girl." Pa used to say that to me, usually followed by an affectionate noogie on my head and a proud grin. "That's my girl," he'd say when I told him how I completely destroyed my opponent during debate or how I solved the quadratic equation when nobody else could.

And hearing it from Brandon was what made me snap.

I straightened up, my brain buzzing as the blood rushed from my head. And Pink Floyd was still screaming in my ears, that hateful screech of electric guitar scratching my eardrums.

Go get my beer. That's my girl.

I stared at Brandon's legs sticking out from under the Camaro. Listened to his off-tune hum. The beer cans that littered the floor, which I would no doubt have to clean up. This was it. My life. It was to be at the beck and call of this man. Even if I were to survive long enough to leave for college in two years' time, Mom would be stuck with him. No matter how hard I tried to write Mom off, I couldn't stop playing the movie of her life in my mind. Spoiler alert: It's not a happy one. It would be a typical Oscar-winning movie—gritty, slow-moving, hard to watch. The leading actress' performance would be described as "emotionally wrenching" and during interviews she'd talk about how she had to talk to all sorts of trauma experts about various forms of abuse to really get into the damaged head of Ally Moore-Wong. He would tear at her, rip into her, peel her apart layer by bloody layer, until one day I'd come home and she'd be gone, the Mom I knew replaced by some brittle, shrilly bright housewife I wouldn't recognize. Or maybe she'd just be gone, and Brandon would be on paid vacation.

That's *my* girl.

I walked toward the back door. As I passed by the jack that was holding his car up, I swung my foot out and tripped the lever. The car sagged to the floor with terrifying swiftness. Despite the loud music, I heard the crunch as three and a half thousand pounds of solid metal sank into Brandon, crushing his bones. There was a scream, cut short as his ribs cracked and stabbed into his lungs. I stood there, frozen, reality nothing but an abstract concept. Time seemed to stop. Pink Floyd continued blasting in my ears. And still I stood there, staring at the car, registering nothing.

Then I saw it. A puddle of blood creeping out from under the car, so dark it was almost black. I watched numbly as it expanded, its edges crawling toward me. Right as it was about to touch the tips of my sneakers, I leapt back, as though I were a kid playing The Floor Is Lava. Except this puddle wasn't lava. It was blood, and it was as real as the Camaro in front of me. The Camaro that had my mom's boyfriend crushed underneath it.

Reality came rushing back in a sickening wave, an upper-cut straight to my gut. I leaned over to one side and puked. *Oh god. Oh shit. Oh god. What have I—*

I glanced back at the growing puddle and heaved again and again. I sank to my knees and wiped my mouth with the back of my hand. Oh my god. I made the mistake of looking back at the car. From where I was kneeling, I could see Brandon's arm under the car. The rest of him was bathed in darkness, a blanket of blood and shadows covering him. A scream escaped my mouth before I clapped my hands over it.

It took a while to realize I was gasping, "Oh my god, oh my god, oh my god," over and over and over. I scrambled toward the car on my hands and knees. My fingers scrabbled over the car jack, and I pushed myself back up and heaved at the lever, putting all of my weight on it. The car raised from the floor a few inches, then the catch swung loose and the car fell back down with a sickening squelch. I screamed again. From Brandon there came no sound.

Brandon was dead.

Because I killed him.

With his Camaro.

His car that crushed him.

With a bit of help from me.

Which made me a killer.

When the shock from killing Brandon stopped

overwhelming me, I staggered back inside the house and sat on the sofa. I picked up the phone and called 911.

The ghost of sirens wailed in the distance. They were soft at first, and then they were suddenly loud, suddenly here, suddenly my life was over. I stood up to let them in.

I recognized the cop who stood at the door. He was someone I'd seen when Brandon had the department over for a barbeque. Derek. Or maybe Dennis?

"Hey, Delilah. We received a nine-one-one dispatch call."

I stared at him.

"Delilah? Is your mom home? Brandon here?" Derek-Dennis peered at me. "You okay?"

I stepped aside and pointed toward the garage.

Derek-Dennis stepped inside and walked in that direction. He paused and looked over at me. "You wait there, okay?"

I continued staring at him.

He opened the garage door. Pink Floyd flooded the living room. "Brandon? It's Davian."

Ah, right. Davian.

"Brandon—oh, shit. Control, officer down, over." His walkie-talkie crackled a response. "It's Brandon Jackson. There's been an accident. He's under his car. It looks bad. I'm gonna need an ambulance." He paused. "Negative. I'm at his house. Her kid's here. She seems pretty shaken up. I don't blame her. Jesus. All right." He walked over to Brandon's stereo and turned it off.

Sweet, blessed silence. It revived me, brought me back to my senses. I blinked. Davian's words trickled through my consciousness.

"I'm so sorry you had to see that, Delilah," he was saying, and his eyes were full of pity for me. There were no traces of suspicion or anger that I'd killed one of his colleagues.

It hit me then—Davian's first assumption was that Brandon's death was an accident.

I'd assumed that when the cops arrived, they'd immediately know what had happened, how I had murdered one of them on what was pretty much a whim.

"Don't worry, the ambulance will be here soon," he said, his eyes full of pity. "Where's your mother?"

"She went to the farmers' market," I heard myself say hollowly. "To buy anchovies for Brandon—" The feel of his name rolling off my tongue made bile rise up my esophagus. I cleared my throat.

"Do you want some water?" Davian said.

My immediate reaction was to say no, because it had been so long since anyone thought to offer me something as simple as water, when I realized that yes, I did. I was parched, actually. I nodded and sat there watching as Davian went to the kitchen and looked in the cabinets for cups. I couldn't summon enough energy to tell him where they were. When he came back with a full glass, I chugged it gratefully. *Takes a lot out of you, murder.* The thought made me choke, and I coughed while Davian said, "Take it easy, you're in shock."

I nodded slowly, wondering how rotten my mind was, that it would think up something so irreverent right after I killed somebody. *I killed somebody.* Jesus. That was a reality I was going to have to live with. But the thing was...I didn't feel bad about it. I felt bad in the general sense of *oh, shit, I might go to prison*, but there was no remorse. In fact, I was just now realizing that if I had the chance to do it all over again, I would.

"You'll have to give the team an official statement when they arrive," he said when I finished coughing. "I know it's the last thing you want to do, but keep it concise and you'll be done before you know it. Have you called your mom?"

"Oh, shit. I didn't even—I totally forgot." The thought of Mom finding out what I'd done, the gruesome remains of Brandon, after everything that's happened, after Pa, tipped me over the edge. Suddenly I was crying, huge ugly sobs that wrenched their way out of my guts. They were so strong, it felt like they might rip me apart. But they weren't tears of sadness. Not over Brandon, anyway. They were tears of shock. I couldn't believe that I'd finally done it, finally broken out of my frozen, terrified hamster state and killed the asshole.

Davian patted me awkwardly on the shoulder. "I'll get your mom." He walked out to the porch, and I heard him radio for someone to contact Mom.

I forced myself to take a deep breath. And exhale. I was okay.

Right before I tripped the lever, my entire future had rolled out before me and I'd seen myself in that orange jumpsuit and I'd been okay with it. I'd really been okay. If that was the price to pay for the satisfaction of pushing Brandon out of our lives, I'd take it. But now, unexpectedly, I had so much more to lose. Now that I knew prison wasn't a given, suddenly I had my freedom to fight for. If I played this right, if I didn't screw things up, I might actually get to walk away from this.

I tuned Davian out—I was in shock, after all, he couldn't possibly blame me for being all quiet and glassy-eyed—and jump-started my mind. Sifted through the events of today with meticulous care. I had to rewrite my role from killer to unfortunate eyewitness. I had to add details—the most believable characters were given all sorts of minute detail with loving patience by their writers. All I had to do was be an unlucky teenager who stumbled upon a grisly accident that had absolutely nothing to do with her.

Right.

I was doing my chemistry homework upstairs in my room when I heard Brandon calling for me—

No. I had to change that part, because it would put me in the same room as Brandon when he died.

Okay, I was...

"I was doing my chemistry homework—something about stoichiometry—and I wanted a snack, and I thought I'd go to the store to grab some food. I went to the garage to see if Brandon wanted anything, and..." It took no effort at all for me to summon the tears. The shock of Brandon's death saw to that. The tears came in a generous rush, warming my cheeks, trembling through my shoulders. The cop who was taking my statement—her name tag read Hoffman—made a sympathetic tsk-tsk sound and shook her head.

"Take as long as you need," she said, giving me a you're-so-brave smile.

I blew my nose and continued. "I opened the door and called out to him, but he didn't answer. I thought maybe he couldn't hear me cause of the music, so I walked in, and that was when I saw the blood." The puddle of blood, growing, reaching out for my feet. I didn't have to fake my shudder. Hoffman gave me an encouraging nod. It was now safe to segue back to the truth. I told her how I'd looked under the car and saw Brandon, who wasn't moving, and I'd tried, really I did, to lever the car up with the jack, but I didn't quite know how to work it—

"Oh, honey," Hoffman said.

I sniffled; had to show some guilt at my utter failure to save the unsavable. But this was where everyday sexism came to my rescue. There were no traces of surprise on her face, because who'd expect some idiot teen girl to know how to work a car jack, right?

"—and I only ended up—I—the car—I ended up crushing him again." The sobs were real. I honestly hadn't meant to crush Brandon's body a second time.

Hoffman's mouth puckered. "And that was when you vomited?"

I nodded.

She scribbled more stuff down on her notepad and looked up. Belatedly, I heard the sound of heavy footsteps. I turned to see Detective Mendez, Brandon's partner. Ex-partner. Brandon's voice boomed through my head. *The Mexican bitch who thinks she's a real cop.* A wave of revulsion toward Brandon and his endless racism and misogyny coursed through my veins. I'd done society a favor by killing him, really.

Mendez was shaking her head grimly. "Hey, Delilah. I'm so sorry. I got here as soon as I could." She opened her arms, reaching toward me for a hug, and even though I didn't want one, certainly not from a cop, I made myself get up and fall into her arms like a toddler who'd lost her favorite soft toy. Her hug was good, maternal. Maybe I needed a hug after all.

"You've been really brave, Delilah," Mendez said. She gestured for me to sit back down. "How're you holding up?"

"I don't know. I'm as okay as I can be, given...you know," I said. I didn't even have to make my voice quaver.

Mendez nodded "Is your mom back yet?"

"She's on her way," Hoffman piped up.

"Okay. Are you done here?" Mendez said to her.

"Yep. Got her statement." Hoffman stood up and snapped her notebook shut. "I'm real sorry you had to go through that, kid."

I managed a small smile. "Thank you." *So brave.*

Hoffman walked off, leaving me with Mendez. Mendez, who was watching me closely.

"What time did you find him again?" Mendez asked. Alarm bells inside me went off—shrill peals that made me want to run away.

"Um—" I thought hard. *What time did I tell that other cop? Eleven? Eleven thirty?* "Eleven thirty, I think. I didn't really look at the clock."

Mendez nodded again, and I realized everything about her was calculated. Even the mama-bear hug had been curated to be tight enough to put me at ease and make me think she was on my side. Mendez wasn't like Davian or Hoffman, didn't automatically dismiss me as a nonthreat. *Do I not look pathetic enough to you?* I wanted to scream.

"Did Brandon seem—I don't know—has he been different lately?"

You mean like, did he lay his hands on me and Mom more often lately? Why, yes, Detective Mendez. Hey, did you know about that, btw? How often your late partner laid into us like we were pillows he had to beat into shape? You're such a sharp one, so suspicious of everything. Were you ever suspicious of him? Did you care?

I had to steer myself away from my rage and riffle through my memories. The real ones, not the one I'd written out just moments ago. If my story had me being close enough to Brandon to go out of my way to see if he needed anything at the store, I had to have been close enough to notice if he was behaving differently lately.

"Um, he..,"

Mendez nodded encouragingly.

I looked down and lowered my voice, because I was speaking ill of the dead and I was nothing if not respectful. "He's been drinking a bit more lately." It was true. Four nightly whiskey sours now, instead of his usual two. I'd never thought to wonder why, assuming it was a natural progression of the way things were. Maybe I was wrong.

"Hmm."

What does "hmm" mean?

I couldn't read her expression. I was so outmatched. I was some noob trying to play a pro-level game. All of my instincts were poised, ready for her next question.

Mendez opened her mouth. "Did you—"

"Dee!"

Our heads snapped up. Mom was home, her cheeks red, her eyes wet, and already she was flying toward me, her arms outstretched, and *what was Mendez about to ask?*

But I had to act the part. I had to call out to her in my so-glad-to-have-Mommy-back voice, "Mom!" and then fall into her arms.

"I'll leave you two alone," Mendez said as Mom and I hugged.

I watched her leave over Mom's shoulder, her last words haunting me, the unfinished question so close to an accusation.

Did you—

logan

On Sunday night, I sat in my room with my headphones on as usual, transferring the latest recordings from my hidden camera. I had quite a few videos by now, all saved in a secret folder on my laptop, and I couldn't wait to see what gems the past few days' worth of recording would give me.

There was a knock on my door a second before it swung open. I barely had time to slam my laptop closed before Matt and Josh barged in.

I pulled off my headphones. *Careful, don't show too much anger. That's not "normal."* If they noticed anything off about me and told the school counselor...

I really should remember to start locking my door.

"Remember that cop who was hanging around here?" Matt said.

"Yeah?" I said. That would be Brandon, the very guy I was trying to take down.

"He died."

Wait.

"Yep, says online he was working on his car and his jack failed." Matt brought his palms together and said, "Splat."

"You're talking about Detective Brandon Jackson?" I said. Matt nodded.

"Holy shit." I shook my head slowly. No way. "Holy shit!"

Josh, who was checking out his imaginary chin fuzz in my mirror, said, "Pretty shitty way to go. Oh, hey, isn't he some chick's dad? That Korean girl, whazzername."

"Half-Singaporean," I said. "And he's not her dad. He's just dating her mom."

They both stared at me.

Why had I said that? Under the table, my fingernails began digging into my leg. I'd never mentioned Delilah to anyone, never wanted to call attention to how much attention I paid her. Especially since I wasn't ready to make my move. She was so shy, I couldn't just—

Then it sank in: Detective Jackson was dead. The guy who was obviously abusing her, forcing her to curl up into a small, tight ball. She was free to be herself.

And she and I had made a connection. It wouldn't be long

before she realized I was exactly what she needed in her life. Why shouldn't I tell my friends that I was interested in her?

I met Matt and Josh's gazes and said, "She's cute."

"Yellow fever," Josh said, not quite under his breath. He and Matt burst into laughter.

"Shut the fuck up," I said, without any hardness in my voice, because here, finally, was my chance. I was ready. I'd regained the friends I'd lost, I had enough energy to start working out again, and the whole world was bright and glittering with opportunities. I was going to do it. Once Delilah got over the shock of what had happened, I was finally going to ask her out.

I was so beyond happy that I didn't even mind when Matt and Josh settled down in my room, chatting about which girl they were into that week and precalculus and college apps. Only a few weeks ago, their presence would've depressed me so much, I would've retreated into my shell and shut them out. I could see the relief in their eyes when I got up from behind the desk and sat next to them on the floor.

Josh frowned at my leg. "Hey, you're bleeding."

Huh. I'd scratched myself hard enough to draw blood. *Not good. Get a grip.* I shrugged and gave him the world's most casual smile. "It's nothing, just a mosquito bite."

I was fine. I was more than fine. I was fucking great.

Later, when they were gone, I quickly went through the video recording I'd collected the night before from one of my small cameras mounted on Delilah's garage window. My pulse quickened as I scrolled through the file. There he was, working underneath his car. Hah. Maybe I'd have the pleasure of watching Detective Brandon Jackson's accident. Maybe I'd—

My mouth went dry. Someone had just walked into the garage. There was no mistaking the long hair and the awkward way she hugged herself as she walked. It was Delilah. I grimaced as she bent over to speak to Brandon. I hoped she hadn't been unfortunate enough to witness the accident. It would break her, my sweet, gentle Delilah.

But even as I thought that, Delilah straightened up, and though the camera wasn't good enough to capture all the small details, I could see that her face was resolute. This was a different Delilah, one I had never seen before. A new sensation prickled down my spine, and I leaned closer. I knew something big was about to happen, though I didn't know just what it was. And then it did.

As she walked past the car, she kicked at the jack. I gasped out loud. Holy. Shit. The car sank. Detective Brandon Jackson's legs twitched once and went still. I was on my feet. I paced about for a few seconds then went back to my laptop and played the clip again. I watched again, and again, as Delilah kicked the jack. I watched as she leaned over and vomited before rushing back into the house. My sweet angel. She wasn't as broken as I thought. She was a fighter. A

Valkyrie. She was so much more than I thought she was. She was incredible.

And I loved her so much more for it.

By Monday, the entire school was buzzing. Everyone was tweeting stuff like "omg, how tragic! #prayfordraycott" as though Detective Jackson's death was even remotely connected to the school. Why should anyone have to pray for Draycott? It offended me, the fact that some attention-seeking kid had jumped on the "prayforso-and-so" bandwagon and made it look as though the entire city was under attack. But it didn't seem to bother anyone else, and the hashtag took flight.

While Josh and I walked to class, I looked out for Delilah. I'd spent hours last night watching all of the footage I'd collected of her. Now that I knew what she was capable of, everything she did became so much more nuanced, so much more complex. Words didn't do her justice. Just when you thought you'd pinned her down, just when you thought you knew everything there was to know about her, she came up with yet another layer of complexity. She was taking me by surprise, and I loved every revelation, big or small. In the end, I'd saved the file of her killing Detective Jackson in a USB drive I could wear around my neck. Something this important deserved to be on me at all times. I couldn't risk leaving it someplace where people might stumble across it. No, I needed to protect Delilah. Maybe I should delete it altogether, but it felt wrong to erase such an important part of Delilah. This was proof that my love for her was real. I loved all of her, not just the soft, lovely side of her, but the hard, jagged one, too.

I burned to see how she was doing. *Would she be haunted by what had happened? I really should be there for her. I shouldn't be here, walking along in the sunshine like it was a normal day. Delilah would be upset, she'd be in shock, she—*

"Hey, earth to Logan." Josh elbowed me.

"What?"

"Are you okay? I was asking if you're up for Saturday. Remember? The rowers are holding a party at the boathouse."

"Oh, right." I'd decided this weekend would be my first date with Delilah, and it sure as hell wasn't going to be at a boathouse party that stank of hard booze and river muck. "I can't, I gotta go to the shelter. They took in a few new dogs so they really need the extra pair of hands."

Josh grinned. "Aw, good, sweet Logan, helping the poor doggies." He clasped his hands under his chin and fluttered his lashes at me. "Oh, Logan, you are the perfect man."

I laughed. "Fuck off."

"Seriously, I don't get why you insist on spending your weekends at the shelter. It's not gonna do much for your college apps, you know that, right? If you want to make a real difference to your apps, join the robotics club. It's actually a lot cooler than people think."

I grinned at the thought of Josh fiddling with complicated systems at the robotics club. Most people dismissed him as your regular airhead jock, but he was genuinely smart. Which didn't stop him from being clueless when it came to girls. "I'm not doing it to plump up my college apps," I said. *I'm doing it to have an excuse to walk past Delilah's house*, I added silently.

"Mkay. Well, the invitation's always open. We're an inclusive club. Oh, hey, you know that cop who got crushed by his car? I heard that like, one of the wheels got him right here," Josh said, tapping his left cheek. "Squeezed his eyeball right out."

I narrowed my eyes. "Where'd you hear that?"

"Mason told me. His cousin works at the coroner's office."

"That's sick." I pushed open the double doors into Brenner Hall. It was teeming with students—boarders and day students alike—arriving, greeting one another, slamming locker doors, and making their way to class.

"Yeah! And that girl was the one who discovered him... Jesus, that's rough. How much you wanna bet she's going to milk this for all it's worth and use it to get a vacation from school?"

I was suddenly filled with an urge to punch Josh in the face. "I dunno."

"C'mon, twenty bucks says she won't show up for at least a week." Josh elbowed me again. "You scared of losing?" He clucked at me.

"No, I just don't wanna be a dick," I shot back.

"Pfft. Whatever. All right, see ya, loser," Josh said good-naturedly. He melted into the crowd.

I forced myself to smile at the students who greeted me as I made my way to chemistry. My mouth went dry when I entered the classroom. Delilah's seat was empty. Darkness bloomed in the pit of my stomach. Was she okay? Did the cops—did they do something to her? I had to make myself sit still in class instead of running all the way to her house. The last thing I needed was for Ms. Taylor to get a call about me. Delilah was probably at home comforting her grief-stricken mother. It wasn't an easy time for either of them. Right. Nothing was wrong. I replayed the videos of her in my mind, getting sicker with worry by the minute.

As soon as classes ended for the day, I faked a stomach-ache and told Coach I was going to be in the dorms. I made my way to the Eastern Gardens, where a hole in the hedge allowed us to make unscheduled visits into town. The hole was Draycott's best-kept secret. I wriggled through and jogged all the way to the nearest bus stop. Since I was supposed to remain on campus, I couldn't very well check my car out of the school garage.

Forty-five minutes later, I was strolling toward Delilah's

house, Daddy tugging vehemently at the leash. I walked slowly, cautious, unsure what I would find. There were cars parked outside her house, and it hit me then, that they must be having a wake or something. Of course. What did I expect? To be able to walk right into her house and have a heart-to-heart with her? I'd been so excited to finally get to see the real Delilah that I didn't think things through before coming here. Daddy whined, and I patted him on the head and breathed out. "You were looking forward to seeing her too, huh?"

He panted and shook his tail then tugged ferociously on the leash. Oh well. At least one of us was having a good time. I walked us to a nearby playground. As I went past it, something clattered at my feet. A pebble. I glanced up and saw Delilah waving at me from the swings. My chest expanded at the sight of her. I wanted to run to her, but I made myself walk instead.

"Be cool, man," I muttered to Daddy as we closed the distance.

"Hey," Delilah said. She smiled at Daddy. "Hey, Daddy."

Daddy rolled over on his back and stared expectantly up at her. Delilah cracked the tiniest hint of a smile, knelt on the grass, and rubbed his belly.

"Uh, I heard about what happened. I'm sorry," I said weakly. I studied her closely, trying to get a hint of how she was handling everything. Now that I saw Delilah in person, I couldn't help but notice tiny transformations about her. Was it just my imagination, or was she carrying herself differently? Did she seem more confident, more empowered? *Should I be sorry?* I wanted to say. But that would be too crass. I'd push her away.

A shadow crossed Delilah's face. "I don't really want to talk about it. I've done nothing but talk about the accident ever since it happened." She glanced up at me. "Is that okay? I'm sorry."

"Hey, you don't have to apologize. We can talk about whatever else you want."

"Thanks." We stayed silent for a while as she continued rubbing Daddy's belly.

"So... Read any good books lately?" I ask.

That got a laugh out of her. She shook her head. "I haven't had much time to read lately. What about you?"

"I'm kinda ashamed to admit it, but despite my good looks, I'm kind of a nerd." I grinned when Delilah snorted with laughter. "What, you don't believe me?"

She shrugged, the hint of a smile playing on her lips.

"I read pretty much everything. I just finished *The Rook*, and I loved that."

"Wow, you're right, you are a nerd," Delilah said.

This was my chance. I could finally put all that research, all the homework I'd done to good use. "Before that I was reading these historical mysteries set in Singapore—"

Delilah's eyes widened, and she stopped rubbing Daddy's belly for a second. "The Merlion Murder series?"

"Yeah. You know them?" Was that the right amount of surprise in my voice?

"Tan Jing Xu is one of my favorite writers. I didn't think anyone at school had ever heard of her," she said.

"Yeah, my mom brought back one of her books after her first trip to Singapore, and I was hooked. Her writing…" I shook my head, and I wasn't lying here, although maybe I was stretching the moment a bit. "I wanna say it's sublime, but I don't wanna be the sort of asshole who says *sublime*."

Delilah laughed, her eyes brighter than I had ever seen them, and god, did I ever want to kiss her. "Her writing is really great," she said. "But it's not actually why I love her books." She looked down at Daddy and rubbed his tummy again. "I've only been to Singapore twice, and even though I love the place, I always felt like an outsider. Even my own family in Singapore calls me *ang moh*. Know what that means?"

I shook my head, not daring to say a word.

Delilah gave a wry smile. "It literally means *redhead*. It's what they call white people in Singapore. Basically, they call me *whitey*. But over here, most people consider me Asian." She shrugged. "That's me—not Asian enough for Asian people, not white enough for white people. Anyway, I've always wanted to learn more about Singapore, especially after my dad—um. After his accident. And Tan Jing Xu puts in like, hundreds of hours into researching every possible thing for her books. Reading them feels like..." She shook her head, searching for the right words.

And I had to make that leap. I had to meet her halfway, show that we were operating on the same wavelength. "Like walking down Bras Basah Road in the slick tropical heat while eating kueh tutu off squares of banana leaf?" I said.

Delilah's eyes snapped to mine, and those perfect lips stretched into a smile, a real one this time, as she said, "Yes," in a voice soft with wonder. She was looking at me in an entirely different way, and in this moment, nothing else mattered.

Delilah's phone chimed, and she took it out of her pocket. Her smile melted away. "I should go. Brandon's old partner's at my house." A new expression crossed her face, turning her features into that of a stranger's. It was so different from the Delilah I knew that it took me a while to realize what it was—anger. Then she looked at me, and just like that, she was back to the same sweet Delilah. "Sorry, Logan. I should be there for my mom. Mendez is..." She shook her head. "She's persistent."

"I'm sorry," I said, my heart racing. Why was Brandon's old partner at their house? Did she know something she shouldn't? I knew by now—of course I did, I'd seen the video, hadn't I?—that Delilah was much stronger than I'd given her credit for, but maybe she was in trouble. Maybe she needed my help.

But then Delilah smiled. "Don't worry about it. It's probably nothing. I'm just being paranoid for no reason." And she gave me a smile so radiant, I forgot all about my concerns. She stood up and brushed herself off. "See you, Daddy," she said.

Daddy's butt wagged extra hard. "See you in school," I said. "You can borrow my notes for chem if you want."

"That'll be great, thanks. Bye."

I picked up Daddy's leash and tugged it lightly. "Let's go, Daddy."

There was a newfound spring in my step as I walked. I went over our conversation, going through every word, every sentence. Trying to recall the exact moments when Delilah had smiled or laughed. Drawing her face in my mind in minute detail—the angle she tilted her head to when she laughed, the way she licked her lips and how she brushed her dark hair behind her ear. We'd had a connection. She'd felt it too. The look in her eyes when I spoke about her favorite books said it all. And as soon as the fuss over Detective Jackson died down, there would no longer be a Logan or a Delilah, only an us.

delilah

The days following Brandon's death, Mom swung back and forth from hysterical to even more hysterical as she scrambled to make funeral arrangements. I jumped every time the doorbell rang, half expecting Mendez to show up and cuff me for killing her partner. She'd come 'round with the excuse of wanting "to see how you guys are doing." Sometimes she'd bring homemade empanadas, like that was all it took to make murderers fess up.

After Brandon's funeral, Mom and I ate dinner in baffled silence, both of us unsure of what to say to each other after more than a year of having all our conversations revolve around Brandon. We spoke in hushed voices at first, because that was what used to be safe. Anything louder than that and

we risked Brandon shouting at us to shut the fuck up, because
he couldn't hear the game over our goddamn chatter. Then,
one night, in the middle of a whispered sentence, Mom let
rip a huge burp, and for a second, we stared at each other in
terrified silence. One of us squeaked, and the squeak turned
into a giggle, and soon Mom and I were doubled over the
kitchen counter, gasping with laughter. Then, as suddenly as
it began, Mom stopped mid-laugh, clapping a hand over her
mouth. Tears sprang into her eyes.

"Mom, it's okay to laugh," I said. "He was terrible, he—"

A sob escaped her, and she shook her head. "Don't, Dee.
Just—don't." And then she rushed out of there, leaving me
shaking my head with disappointment. Didn't she realize
what an amazing gift she'd been given? I'd gotten rid of the
awful, abusive figure who'd been dominating us for so long.
I'd given her a whole new lease on life. Why wasn't she more
relieved? I guessed she loved Brandon at one point, but she
must've known on some level that he was a monster.

I guess Mom felt guilty about laughing so hard, because
the next day, she informed me that she'd made an appointment for the two of us to see a therapist. I rolled my eyes
and didn't say much on the drive over, but truth be told,
part of me was dying to talk to someone. I mean, holy shit.
Sometimes, the realization would strike me randomly. *I killed
somebody*. And the worst part was, I didn't feel that bad
about it. Sometimes, I tried to imagine myself back in the

garage, watching the pool of blood grow before me, just so I could feel that nauseating sense of guilt crush me, but it was getting harder and harder to get that feeling, and that felt bad. I should feel guilty, shouldn't I?

The therapist, a middle-aged Asian woman called Dr. Angie Lee, nodded and made sympathetic sounds as Mom sobbed into a wad of tissues about how abusive Brandon had been and how horrible she was now feeling because she wasn't feeling horrible enough about Brandon's death.

"I mean, I miss him, I do, but—" Mom said. She glanced at me and said, "I'm a terrible mother, what kind of example am I setting for my daughter?"

You shouldn't feel horrible, I wanted to say. *You didn't kill him. I did, and I'm mostly feeling great.*

Dr. Lee looked at me and tilted her head. "Delilah, how do you feel about Brandon's death?"

"I—" To my horror, my voice cracked, and the words came spilling out. "I'm so confused. I know I should feel really guilty and sad and whatever else, but I just—I don't. And I feel like crap about the fact that I don't feel guilty." I sucked in my breath in a quick hiss and bit my lip. Had I revealed too much?

Dr. Lee smiled kindly. "How the two of you are feeling is absolutely normal. Often, people feel responsible or guilty when someone close to them passes. And with Brandon's history of abusing both of you, you're experiencing some very complicated emotions, which is understandable.

"Abuse victims do whatever they have to do in order to survive and come out the other side intact. Feeling guilty is part of the process, but you also need to accept that Brandon was abusing you. Both of you. You've been given a second chance at life. Take it. Set aside some time to grieve Brandon's passing, but also celebrate the fact that you survived. You deserve to live your best life, especially after everything you've been through."

She was looking at me when she said this, as though she knew exactly how I was feeling. It was amazing to hear a professional say it wasn't my fault, even though the professional in question didn't know exactly what I'd done. I left her office feeling light as a bubble. She was so right: abuse victims do whatever they have to do in order to survive.

Mom still cried that night as she did the dishes. I hugged her and wondered how she could possibly grieve Brandon, of all people. But the next morning, I woke up alone. I was worried at first, until I thought to check my phone. There was a message from Mom: **Had to go to work early, have a new project to run. See you at dinner, pumpkin.**

She was back at work. Gone was Brandon's ridiculous notion that my mom, the woman who graduated summa cum laude from Georgetown, who took great pride in her job, should stay at home to serve him.

After two weeks Mom started to hum whenever she did the dishes, and I noticed that she stopped jumping every time there was a noise in the house. She even started wearing some makeup again. And though she still cried sometimes, I had the feeling she was only doing it out of some sense of obligation and not because she actually missed the guy. And I... well, I was changing too.

Now that Brandon wasn't around to tell me I was a slut for talking to boys, suddenly the guys at my school no longer seemed as dangerous. A whole world was opening up. I could talk to whoever the hell I wanted! My posture slowly corrected itself. I no longer stared at my feet when I walked. I met people's eyes. I returned their smiles. I didn't shoot up in popularity, but other kids at school were starting to acknowledge me. That was okay. Popularity is overrated. I was satisfied with the friendly but aloof smiles from my schoolmates.

The person I was dying to see was Logan, whom Aisha called Hot Logan. The nickname needed some work, but I couldn't argue with the logic of it. With his wavy, brown hair and his strong jaw and—Jesuslord, look at his abs—Logan was hot. He had this way of looking at you, this sort of dark, intense expression that made you feel like you were the only girl in the whole entire world. I probably didn't have much of a chance with him.

But a few days after I came back to school, as I was walking to the library for my shift, someone called my name.

I grinned as he walked over, then I mentally punched myself in the face and toned down my huge smile into a more normal one. How should I stand? I shifted from one leg to the other. *Argh, stop fidgeting!*

"Hey," he said.

"Hey."

"It's good to see you back at school," he said.

Is it really? my mind squeaked. "It's good to see you back at school too!" Oh my god. Be cool, damn it!

"Do you need any notes for chemistry? I could lend you mine. Mr. West's been piling on the homework."

Wow. Cute and sweet. I was in real trouble. "Yeah, that would be really great. I feel like I've missed a whole semester of work."

"I could—uh, we could study together if you want?" Logan said, with a shy smile.

I want!

I managed to stop myself from nodding frantically. "Yeah, that would be great!"

"Or maybe we could do something more fun for our first date."

"Our first date?" I squeaked. *Stop squeaking!*

Logan scratched the back of his neck, his ears turning red. "Um, yeah, I'm kinda trying to ask you out here...and doing a really bad job of it, obviously." He laughed to himself.

"No! You're not! I mean, you're not doing a bad job. I'm doing a bad job! I mean, yes. Yes!" I cleared my throat. "I mean, sure, let's go out on a date or whatever."

I couldn't be any more unappealing right now, but for some reason, Logan's face lit up, and he said, "Saturday?"

I nodded, because I couldn't trust myself to speak. If I did speak, it would be in a pitch higher than most humans could hear.

"Great! I'll see you around, Delilah." With that, he walked off, and I slumped into a watery puddle and died.

Okay, I didn't flop over. Somehow, I managed to walk away, and when I was sure he was nowhere in sight, I called Aisha and begged her to come meet me ASAP.

Aisha squeaked out loud when I told her about it.

"Hot Logan asked you out! Girl, you've got game!"

I flapped a hand in her face and went, "Ssh!" We scurried over to one of the benches in the Eastern Garden. There were many people around, soaking in the California sun and checking one another out. There were plenty of hair flips and a lot of too-loud laughter and pointed glances.

"Oh, man, I can't believe it. Do you know where you guys are going?" Aisha took a small purse out of her messenger bag and opened it. Inside was an arsenal of makeup. She carefully applied a layer of lipstick, and her eyes moved to look at me from the reflection in her mirror. "Do you know what you're going to wear?"

"Um, no. I haven't really thought about it."

"Come on," she sighed, shaking her head. "We're going to have to work on...whatever you've got going on here."

She gestured at me before turning her attention back to her compact mirror.

Aisha grinned at me and rummaged around in her makeup bag. "Dammit, I need a tissue." She pulled my bag open without asking and plucked out a packet of tissue paper. A small, clear baggie fell out, and she held it up. "What's this? Oh my GOD, are you using…drugs?"

I stared at her, openmouthed. Panic blossomed as I mentally scrambled for an answer.

Aisha burst out laughing. "Oh, man! Dee, your expression!" She nudged me with her shoulder. "Yeah, right. Sweet, nerdy Delilah Wong, taking molly!" She laughed again.

I grabbed the baggie from her and stuffed it back in my bag, my cheeks burning. "Hmph, okay, well, this happens to be aspirin, but if I wanted to, I could totally take, er—mol "

"You can't even bear to say it!" she cried.

"Mollymollymolly!"

We glanced at each other for a split second before doubling over, giggling hard. Aisha wrapped her arm around my shoulders.

"You're such a dork," she said.

My phone buzzed then. I checked the message and straightened up.

"I gotta go," I told Aisha. "You gonna be around after my shift ends?"

"I'll probably be in the lab, feeding Lucy," she said. Lucy

was the school's pet snake. Each week, students volunteered to help look after her over the weekend, which was pretty weird in my book, but whatever floated their boats. I never volunteered. I didn't even like the sight of Lucy.

I shuddered. "I don't know why you volunteer to feed that snake. It's so creepy."

She gave me a wicked grin. "Extra credit. You should come watch me feed her sometime."

"Yeah, right. Over my dead body. Okay, see you later."

She waved me off, probably relieved that something had interrupted my nagging. I briskly walked to the library.

The library was hands down the most beautiful building at Draycott. It wasn't the biggest, but it felt like the most well-thought-out—built out of sandstone, columns in a neat row, and large stained glass windows. The main entrance led to a bright, airy dome that magnified sound, so people immediately became self-conscious about every bit of noise they made. It was ingenious. I stopped by the Secrets board as usual, scanning the new posts, before making my way down the spiral steps. I pushed open the heavy steel door at the bottom and headed into the climate-controlled stacks, where Lisa was waiting for me.

"There you are," she chirped when she saw me. "How are you, Dee?" She skittered toward me—I mean it literally, the woman couldn't seem to walk like a normal person, she always took a series of tiny, dainty, quick steps. Her bird-bone arms lifted, and for a horrifying second, I thought she was going to hug me, but then she changed her mind—*phew!*— and patted me on the shoulder instead. "Oh, what happened to your stepdad is awful, just awful."

If you were to open an encyclopedia and go to the entry marked L—Librarian, you'd see a picture of Lisa. Midforties, single, wears mustard-colored knit cardigans complete with a brooch above the left breast. The brooch looked ancient, probably some sort of family heirloom. And glasses, of course. Sometimes, I tried to imagine what Lisa was like as a kid. Each time, I failed miserably. Lisa looked prepackaged, like she came into existence wearing her knitted cardigans, sensible chiropractic shoes, and argyle stockings.

I liked working for Lisa, but I hated that I knew next to nothing about her, especially since our work was so sensitive in nature. I didn't know where she lived, what she spent her weekends doing, what she liked to eat or watch or whatever. And not for a lack of effort, either. I was dying to know more about Lisa. There was so much more to her than meets the eye. But each time I asked her stuff like, "Did you do anything fun last weekend?" she'd say, "Yes. Let's get to work." I'd looked her up online once, but gave up when I realized there were about twelve million Lisa Smiths in the world.

All I knew was she owned multiples of the same cardigan and she had a pet of some sort; I sometimes saw gray strands of fur caught in her cardigan. I prided myself on the pet knowledge—that was some next-level detecting.

"I know you're supposed to have one more day off to mourn," Lisa said, "but we are so swamped here. There are new orders and special shipments and—" She shot me an imploring look. "You know how voracious the kids here are, and so spoiled too. Not you, of course. But some of the kids here... They expect everything to arrive instantly, and when they don't get what they want, they get really cranky. I'm dying. Can you come back a day early?"

"Yeah, of course," I said. I wasn't the one who chose to take time off work in the first place. Mom had suggested it, and I'd thought it looked right. It was the kind of thing people did when someone close to them died in a horrible accident. But I was keen to get back to work. Ever since Brandon took over the finances, I knew how important money was.

Some nights, as I lay in bed pressing an ice pack to my legs or my back, the only thing that kept me going was the knowledge that I was ferreting money away. Money nobody knew about. Money I would one day use to escape the hellhole I'd found myself in. And although Brandon was gone, as much as I loved Mom, I didn't trust her not to fall for yet another asshole. She was vulnerable and probably burned out after having the last two men in her life die in horrific ways. I couldn't count on her for stability.

Lisa sagged with relief. "You, my dear, are a godsend."

She hurried to the back of the stacks and plucked a folder from one of the many boxes piled up against the wall. "Here's the latest inventory. Catalog them and make sure the deliveries are safe, use the usual security protocol—oh, what am I saying? You know what to do." She paused to smile at me, her eyes shining behind her glasses. "I am so glad to have you back, Dee."

"Me. Too." I went away with my heart singing. Brandon was out of our lives, I had a well-paying job that I loved, and I scored a date with the hottest guy in my year. Honestly, it felt like the universe was rewarding me for getting rid of Brandon. If I'd known killing him was all I had to do to make everything come together so beautifully, I would've done it a lot sooner.

Saturday morning, Aisha came over to help me get ready. Her presence and the fact I was about to go on my first date revived Mom. She and Mom fluttered about me like annoying butterflies, fluffing my hair and adjusting my shirt. I rolled my eyes, but I didn't actually mind having them fuss over me. Aisha used to come over all the time, especially when she first started boarding at Draycott and got really homesick. She'd climb out of her dorm window and take the bus to my place and make Mom and Pa swear they wouldn't tell her parents, and they'd sigh and agree, but this would be the last time, okay? In the morning they'd drive her back to Draycott, and by nighttime she'd be back at the front door again, telling us Draycott kids were monsters. But over time, she started making other friends and she stopped running away to my place. And of course, when Brandon was around, I didn't allow any friends to come over. I was too afraid of what Brandon might say, too scared my friends might somehow piss him off, and too ashamed to have anyone see how afraid I was.

"Maybe you should undo the top button," Mom said as I combed my hair.

"Ew, Mooom!" I cried at the same time Aisha said, "Ooh, yeah, your mom's right!"

The room went silent as we stared at one another, and then we burst into screams of laughter.

"I am being the worst mom ever, aren't I?" Mom gave a dramatic sigh.

"Mom, stop freaking out." I exchanged an eye roll with Aisha, but we were both still grinning. Aisha reached to unbutton my top, and I swatted her hand.

"I can't help it. Look at my little baby all grown up and going on dates." Mom dabbed an imaginary tear from her eye. "I feel like I should play the part of an overly protective father. Should I greet this boy at the door with a shotgun?"

"Yes, please greet Logan with a shotgun. Pleeease," Aisha said. "I'll have my camera ready."

"We don't have a shotgun," I said.

"You don't?" Aisha said. "How unpatriotic."

"We do have an electric drill," Mom said.

"Stop it, you guys," I said, laughing. Then it hit me: the electric drill was Brandon's. Just one of the many tools he's brought with him when he moved in. The memory of Brandon made my jaw tighten and my heart rate triple in the span of two seconds. What if I got caught? I pasted a smile on my face before Mom and Aisha noticed my mood darken.

Mom cupped my cheeks with her hands. "You look gorgeous. He's one lucky guy."

I didn't look anywhere close to gorgeous, but her words made me tear up all the same. Less than a month ago, I wouldn't even have imagined being able to put on makeup without being accused of trying to whore myself out, and now here I was, about to go on a date with one of the most incredible guys I'd come across.

"Where's he taking you?" Mom said, as we walked down to the kitchen.

"He said it's a surprise," Aisha piped up with an eyebrow waggle. "But he did tell her to wear clothes she wouldn't mind getting dirty. Hence this questionable top."

Mom's eyebrows met in the middle. She opened her mouth then shook her head. "Be safe, okay?" She opened the fridge and took out a carton of orange juice. "You girls want some juice?"

I shook my head. I was about to assure her that I could take care of myself when the doorbell rang. The three of us perked up like meerkats.

"I got it!" I said.

Aisha and I hurried toward the door, but Mom made a ninja leap and beat us to it. The woman was fast. She flung it open all breathless and then stood back and stared.

"Um, hi, Mrs.—uh, Ms.—um, ma'am," Logan said. His eyes widened a little when he saw Aisha. "Oh, hey, Aisha."

"Hey, Logan." Aisha grinned at him.

I elbowed her in the ribs.

"Wasn't expecting to see you here," Logan said. His bangs flopped over one eye, and he brushed them back and then stood there, looking awkward. It was completely adorable.

"So nice to finally meet you, Logan!" Mom turned to face me with a face-splitting grin. *He's cute*, she mouthed, as though Logan wasn't right there in front of us. I wanted to crawl under a very big, very heavy rock. She turned back to Logan. "So, Logan, where are you taking my daughter today?"

"Mooom," I groaned. "Ignore her."

"Um, it's actually kind of a surprise, but I can show you the itinerary."

"An itinerary!" Mom clapped her hands. "Dee, go wait in the kitchen. I don't want to spoil the surprise." She and Aisha huddled around Logan.

I plodded to the kitchen, shaking my head and smiling—Mom and Aisha, such toddlers—and poured myself some juice. Snatches of laughter and murmurs of what sounded like approval came from the door. A few minutes later, Aisha called out my name.

"Are you satisfied?" I said to them. I walked back to the door, my insides burning. I couldn't quite meet Logan's eye.

"Very," Aisha said.

"It's very impressive," Mom added. "And Logan, remember, I have an electric drill. Okay, you kids go have fun!"

"See you Monday!" Aisha said. "Call me tonight!"

We all said a never-ending round of awkward, smiley goodbyes, and then finally Logan and I headed off.

"I am so, so sorry about my mom and Aisha," I said as we walked toward his car.

"What are you talking about? Your mom's awesome. And Aisha's funny. After you," he said, opening the passenger door for me.

I slid into the car with my cheeks tingling. No one had ever opened the car door for me. The engine turned on and music flooded the inside of the car. I turned to face Logan, my eyes wide.

"Something wrong?" he asked.

"No, it's just—you like Planet Green too?"

"Yeah, they're my favorite band. Don't tell me you're a fan, too?"

I nodded. "I've been to like, five of their concerts. I even have their T-shirts."

Logan laughed. "You like the same band I do, you read the same books I do... Have you been stalking me?"

My cheeks burned. "I swear I haven't."

"I'm kidding. Ready to go?"

I met his eyes and I felt it then, the sensation you get right before you fall, the stomach-turning loss of gravity. Everything felt amplified—the leather scent of his car, the emotastic music, the olive green of his eyes. The moment seared itself into my memory; it felt so pivotal, the time I met someone who was truly my equal, someone whose heart mine could open up to. Was this what it was like to finally fall for someone? Could it happen so fast? The sky was clear and the breeze was just right and everything had worked out fine, and I might've been falling, falling, falling for this boy who looked like he'd walked off the cover of some fashion mag. We smiled at the same time, and I wondered if this was what it was like to feel truly happy.

"Yes. I'm ready."

logan

The days leading up to our date, I put together an itinerary based on everything I had learned about Delilah in the previous weeks. And I'd learned a lot.

We stopped by Lucy's Deli, where we got subs bigger than my forearms and two bottles of locally made sodas, then I drove up to the national park. I parked at the foothill, stuffed our food into a prepared backpack, and held my hand out to her.

It seemed like a small, casual act, but anxiety prowled in the periphery, grinning with fangs, ready to pounce—*please take my hand, take it, TAKE IT*—shit, I was going to end up with sweaty palms.

Delilah only hesitated for a split second, smiling while

biting her lip—god, she was flirting with me, she wanted me, too—and then she placed her hand in mine. The world exploded into a rainbow of bright colors and music. She was mine. I swallowed, tried to regulate my breathing. Gave her a relaxed smile and reminded myself not to squeeze her hand, to hold it casually, like any normal guy would. A normal guy, on a first date, with his dream girl.

We hiked up to Strawberry Point, and the greenery swallowed us into its irresistible magic. The air was as refreshing as river water and filled with showers of birds' whistling. Gone was the city, the people, gone was Detective Jackson. In this moment, there was only me and Delilah in our own little fairy tale, and she'd dressed up just for me—a slightly off-the-shoulder green top that showed her collarbones, and her hair, usually straight, was in loose curls. Her cheeks were pink, and her lips were glossed up and begging to be kissed, and it was all for me. I could tell the magic had captured her too, because for a while, we walked without talking. We didn't need to speak; it was enough to know we were together, our fingers laced through each other's.

"This place is amazing," she said. "You gotta tell me where we're headed. The suspense is killing me."

"Don't spoil the surprise. Anyway, you wouldn't be familiar with it, because the spot I'm taking you to only sprang up like a year ago."

"Mkay. But I'm warning you, in case you're up to no good, I know jujitsu." She mimed a chop with her arms.

"Terrifying. It's right up ahead, you dope."

She grinned at me calling her a dope. She loved pet names; all of the pictures of her and her friends had been captioned with affectionate ones—dweeb, dork, dumbass. I knew calling her a dope would establish some sort of familiarity between us.

Her hand was rough and callused inside mine. As we walked, I memorized every line, every wrinkle of her palm. I was holding Delilah's hand! And more than that, it wasn't a pity handhold. Sophie used to do that, when she was in between boyfriends, when she was bored or lonely or felt my attention was wavering. She'd text me, ask me to meet at "our spot"—it was always "our" spot when she wanted me, "her" spot once she'd hooked up with the boyfriend du jour. And she'd let me hold her hand like she was the Pope and I was one of the unwashed masses who had traveled halfway around the world to touch the hem of his robes. And I didn't mind. We never dated; even after my transformation, she still didn't think I was good enough for her. But it was fine with me. Touching her, any part of her, lying next to her in our little copse, listening to her go on about her asshole exes, I knew every curve of her mind, the parts no one else did. "They're table scraps, Logan!" Mom used to say to me. "That girl's only leading you on." And I used to rage and tell

Mom she didn't know anything, that Sophie secretly loved me, that it was only a matter of time before she realized it. Now, of course, I realized Mom was right all along. But that no longer mattered.

This—what Delilah and I had—was the opposite of scraps. This was the entrée and the dessert and everything else. I could feel her pulse next to mine, we were so in sync. She was pleased I'd kept the itinerary a secret, because no one had ever gone the extra mile to plan a surprise date for her.

A shrill peal I didn't recognize sliced through the air, obliterating the magic. Delilah took out her phone. Her smile slipped, her expression becoming worried. She glanced up at me and widened her smile.

"Sorry, I gotta reply to this text. Hang on." She pulled away and turned her back on me, rounding her shoulders like she didn't want me to even catch a glimpse of the screen.

I gazed up at the trees, my hands in my pockets, trying not to appear as panicked as I felt. *What is it?* my mind screamed. I knew everything there was to know about Delilah, didn't I? So why did I not have even the smallest clue about what was so obviously upsetting her? Any moment now, she was going to tell me she had to rush back, and our perfect date would be ruined, and I would—

"Okay, let's go!" Delilah said in a voice that was determined to be cheerful.

"Everything okay?"

"Yeah. It's just work. Anyway, shall we?"

I frowned. Delilah worked at the Draycott library. Why would work need her on a Saturday? I was dying to know all about it; her work was the only thing I hadn't been able to look into, but Delilah was already walking.

It didn't take long for the allure of the great outdoors to soothe Delilah back into a good mood. The farther we went, the smoother her forehead became.

"Hey, so what sort of work do you do at the library?" I said after some time. "Is it mostly shelving books, or..."

Delilah laughed. "No! God, people always think working at the library is all about moving books around on shelves, but there's so much more than that. I do a lot of cataloging, actually. And Lisa likes to teach me to 'hustle,'" she laughed again when she said the word *hustle*. "So she gets me to call all these suppliers and pit them against one another to get the lowest possible price for the goods."

"Do you often have to work on weekends?"

I'd thought I was being really subtle, asking her about the call, but Delilah glanced at me and her eyebrows scrunched up a little.

"Not really," she said, after a moment. "Lisa was texting because she couldn't find one of our old order forms. It's really not a thing—we'll figure it out on Monday." Then we reached the clearing, and Delilah gasped. She hurried ahead of me. "Oh my god!"

I jogged to catch up with her. Her joy was so contagious. We were at Monkey See Monkey Do, an obstacle course built high in the treetops. In other words, Delilah's version of Disneyland. Even from outside the boundaries, we could see various zip lines and wood bridges crisscrossing the tall pines. Shouts and hoots filled the air, infecting us with energy. Delilah's face was that of a kid given an all-access pass to a real-life gingerbread house. I'd known she would love it ever since I saw those pictures of her with her dad, climbing trees and going on massive hikes. She reached for her wallet.

"Don't bother, I've bought us discount tickets online," I said.

"Discount tickets!" she said. "My two favorite words."

"In that case, they were fifty percent off," I whispered, taking a step toward her.

Delilah fanned her face. "God, there is nothing sexier than hearing the words *fifty percent off*." She laughed then, as though realizing how close we were standing to each other— close enough that I could see each individual eyelash—and her cheeks bloomed with red, her gaze skittering awkwardly from mine. She turned around and walked ahead without looking back.

I'd miscalculated there, gotten too close too soon. I'd known better, I'd promised myself to let her take the lead, and yet...fucking hormones, I swear. God, how could I have been this thoughtless? It had taken months to get to this point, to create the perfect date, and here I was letting my teenage-boy hormones get the better of me.

The awkwardness lingered as we strapped on our helmets and other safety gear, and I fought the increasingly violent tangle of snakes in my belly. Had I ruined the day completely? I'd been so taken in by Delilah's old pictures, swallowed by the flashes of the old Delilah, that I forgot the past two years of her life. She'd just survived an extremely abusive situation with a man twice her size. The last thing she needed was some guy coming on too strong. God, I might as well call the whole thing off. I might as well crawl into a hole and die. I—

"Hey, why so serious?"

I looked up to see Delilah waggling her eyebrows at me.

"You scared of heights? You chicken?" She put the backs of her hands on her hips and clucked at me.

The snakes in my belly evaporated and were replaced once more by feathers. I could cry, I was so relieved. I hadn't ruined everything after all. A grin melted across my face. "Let's see you put your money where your mouth is."

"Okay... Ten bucks says I beat you to the end of the course."

"Ten? Make it twenty," I said.

"Done."

"Shake on it?" I asked, and as she came close to shake my hand, I tugged on her hand and swung her behind me before running toward the first obstacle, hooting as I went.

Behind me came a laugh and a cry of "hey, no fair!"

The next hour or so was a tangle of laughter and gasps for breath as we raced each other through dizzying heights, our feet scampering across narrow rope bridges, the ground exhilaratingly far away beneath us. We screamed like toddlers high on Halloween candy as we grabbed hold of ropes and took stomach-turning jumps, the sense of free fall taking our breath away, Delilah's hair streaming behind her as she flew past me. My senses whirled; I caught Delilah's scent here and there, bewitching among the dense redwood smell that hung heavy in the air. I was finally getting to experience the real Delilah. Not Scared, Beaten-Down Delilah, not Angry Delilah, but the true Delilah, the beautiful, fearless core of her.

We went so fast that there was no room for fear, no time for doubts or second-guessing. The adventure park workers reminded us time and again to slow down, to take our time enjoying each course, to "take it all in, man," but Delilah was like a gazelle that had finally been uncaged, and all I could do was follow her lead. She beat me by a good ten seconds and punched the air with a whoop.

"I let you win," I gasped.

Delilah laughed. "Okay, old man."

We both collapsed under a tree and stayed there for a while, watching people as they went past the finish line, our breath slowly coming down from its breakneck speed. I wanted to sit closer, to feel her heartbeat slowing down to match mine, but I stopped myself just in time. *Slow and safe*, I reminded myself.

"That was amazing," she said.

I shook myself from the tendrils of anxiety and grinned at her. "I know, I'm pretty impressive like that."

She snorted. "You mean the part where you almost fell off the bridge or the part where you nearly missed the net and almost crashed into the tree?"

"Oh, okay, Miss Forgot-to-lock-the-safety-catch-and-almost-fell-to-your-death."

We mock-glared at each other for a few moments before Delilah laughed. "I think this just goes to show we're both dumbasses who would put our lives in danger to win twenty bucks."

"Fair enough," I said. I stood up and offered her my hand. "Ready for lunch?"

"Oh, man, yes please."

We grabbed our things and found a clearing right next to the river that was dotted with wooden tables and benches. I sat across from Delilah and took our sandwiches out of my backpack.

"One turkey and ham for me, and a mortadella, prosciutto, and turkey for the lady."

"I don't think it's possible to eat one of these things and still be considered a lady," said Delilah. She took a big bite of her sandwich and closed her eyes. "Oh, mm. Ee eeh oh ood."

"Lucky for you, I speak Sandwich. 'Oh, man. This is so good'?" I guessed.

Delilah's cheeks rose in a smile, and she nodded. It took an effort for her to swallow the giant mouthful, and she was left with hiccups.

"I guess you're hungry," I said.

Delilah took her time sipping her soda before replying. "I am, yeah. But it's not just that. When Brandon was around... Well, he had this thing about how women should behave. He'd tell me and my mom off if he felt we laughed too loud or ate too fast or took too big a mouthful of food or whatever other bullshit he thought women shouldn't do. Ever since he died, I can't seem to stop myself from taking the biggest possible bites when I eat."

"Sounds like he didn't want to be reminded that you all are people too."

Delilah's eyes met mine, her eyebrows slightly raised in surprise. "Yeah. That's exactly it. He only wanted to acknowledge one facet of us. Mom was his girlfriend, I was his girlfriend's daughter, and that was it. He didn't like all the other parts of us. The fact that Mom had a job that paid more than his did, that she was her own person... He hated that." Delilah took another sip of soda, her expression unreadable. She was off in a small, dark world for now. "He tried to make her quit her job." Her hands tightened around the bottle.

"I'm sorry to hear that." And I meant it, although mostly I was sorry that I didn't get a chance to wrap my hands around Detective Jackson's thick neck and feel those tendons snap under my fingers.

"Well, he's gone now," Delilah said, and her voice came out in a half growl that made the back of my neck prickle. She chewed her lip. "Sorry, that came out wrong. I didn't mean—"

"It's okay, I know what you mean." And I really did know. If only I could tell her how much I knew, how much I understood, how much I admired her for—

"What about you? I know like, next to nothing."

"My name is Logan, I'm five foot eleven, I'm a Sagittarius, my hobbies include watching movies—"

"And long walks on the beach?" Delilah laughed. "Okay, let's try this again. What do you usually do after school?"

I shrugged. "Mostly lacrosse, to be honest. I'm predictable like that."

"How long have you been playing?"

Ever since Sophie said she had a thing for lacrosse guys. "Ever since I was a freshman."

I'd never allowed myself to talk to anyone about Sophie— well, aside from Mom, but that was more of a one-way conversation. But this was Delilah. If we were going to truly connect, I had to be honest with her. To a certain extent, anyway. "I was really into this one girl, and she mentioned having a thing for guys who play lacrosse, so…"

"Aww! You started playing to impress a girl? That is so

adorable." She grinned at me from behind her ridiculously huge sandwich.

"Shut up," I groused, but I couldn't help returning her smile. "Anyway, nothing ever came out of my crush"—a flash of Sophie, dead—"but I discovered I actually did like lacrosse, so that was that."

"What else do you do when you have free time?"

"Hang out with the guys. We do all sorts of stuff."

"Really? It's not all about competing with each other to see who can sleep with the most girls?" Her voice was still casual, but her eyes never left my face. *Look who's doing a little research of her own.* She was curious about me, about my personal life. She was so into me. I knew it. I wanted to take her hand and tell her that none of it—not the guys, nor lacrosse, none of that shit—compared to her.

I gave her a solemn look. "You've been watching way too many movies about high school boys. We're really not like that. Well, not all of us are. Actually, my friend Matt has been with his girlfriend since freshman year."

"Oh, yeah—Moni. I like her."

"She's cool. We'll have to hang out."

Our conversation was everything I had ever dreamed of and more. So much more, because Delilah was right there in front of me, warm flesh and blood, and I got to see every reaction of hers, every twitch of her eyebrows, every shy smile, all the different ways her eyes lit up when we stumbled upon a subject that excited her. And it was all for me. I wasn't just an observer anymore, watching her through her window or on my laptop. I was participating directly in Delilah's life.

The drive home was too short. We never stopped talking, our conversation flowing so easily, it was like we were old friends picking up right where we left off. All too soon, we were parked in front of her house.

I'd told myself that I had to go at her pace, and so when I turned off the engine, I did not reach over to take her hand or kiss her or anything that might freak her out, even though I wanted to so badly, even though the smell of her had been distracting me the entire way home—almonds and flowers— and I could only look at her in small doses. Her lips were so plump, so kissable.

I focused on a spot right below her ear and said, "I had a great time today."

"Me too." Delilah bit her bottom lip. Then, before I could react, she reached over, caught my shirt in her hand, and tugged me to her.

Our lips met in one beautiful, heart-stopping crush. My thoughts went haywire. I was kissing Delilah. My Delilah. This was really happening. The weight of it was so intense, my throat closed up with tears. Nothing like this had happened with Sophie. Even in my wildest dreams, I never thought things would progress this well, everything clicking into place beautifully, like streams flowing downhill to join a river, everything was meant to be. I was so delirious with the touch of her, the scent everywhere around me, that I didn't realize I'd spoken out loud until Delilah pulled away from me.

"What?" she said.

It took me a moment to gather my senses. "Hm?" I mumbled.

"You said 'I love you.'" Her eyes were so wide, I could see the whites all around her irises. Her breath was still rapid from our earth-shaking kiss.

It hit me then, what I'd said, those dreaded three words that were so incredibly true. "I—I don't—"

And then the small voice at the back of my mind suddenly became a big voice, impossible to ignore. Well, why not? Why shouldn't I be honest with her? We were soul mates. Surely, after today, after everything, after the way we talked, we kissed, we connected, she'd feel the same way. I reached out and took her hand, firm, in mine.

"It's true, Delilah. I love you."

She continued gaping at me.

"I've loved you ever since I saw you the first day of school."

She recoiled. "But—that was months ago!"

"I couldn't just ask you out. I had to make sure every-thing was perfect, and the wait was worth it, wasn't it? You felt it too, I know. The way you smiled at me, the way you looked at me, maybe you don't know it yet, but you're in love with me too. Today was so..." My voice came out a hell of a lot calmer than I felt, but I had to talk slow so she'd understand, so she'd get how fucking important this was.

Her lips twitched into a smile, but it wasn't a happy one. It was an I'd-better-smile-so-this-psycho-won't-kill-me type of smile, and she tugged her hand free from mine.

"Um. Thank you for the really great day. I'm pretty tired. I think I'm gonna go in now. I'll see you at school, okay?" she said, her voice brittle, close to breaking. She reached for her bag.

I was losing her. Panic burst through the endorphin-fueled fog I'd been in since our kiss. I couldn't lose her, not now. If she got out of the car now, all I'd be left with was the faint scent of her, which would only linger for a few hours. By tomorrow, all traces of her would be gone, and I'd only have awkward glances at school and the knowledge of the most perfect relationship ruined before it could even begin.

Delilah got out, and I scrambled after her. Already she was on the pathway leading to her house.

"Please, Delilah, just... Please give me a chance." I was doing it all wrong, I knew even as I begged her. My voice was too raw, too desperate.

"It's been really great, Logan," she said. "But I think it's probably best if we just stay friends?"

"But—the date went so well. It was perfect, you know it was."

She hesitated. "Yeah, but…"

"And that kiss. There's something here, Dee. You know there is."

For a second, I thought she might relent, give in to the inevitability of us, but then her face hardened. "I'm sorry, Logan. I don't think this is a good idea. I'll see you at school."

"Wait!" I practically screamed it. *Calm. Down.* I didn't trust myself to talk again, not for a while, so I just took out my phone. Before our date, I'd saved another copy in it, aside from the one I wore around my neck. Maybe even then, part of me had known I might need this fail-safe, in case things took a bad turn on our date. I found the file I'd saved in a hidden folder and encrypted with a password, the one I'd watched over and over again the whole of last week, knowing this video would change our entire lives. Delilah as a Valkyrie, raining vengeance on the man who'd made life hell for her and her mother. I held up the phone so we could both see the screen.

Delilah was already on her doorstep, the polite smile completely gone, and I hadn't wanted to go down this route, really, but I was about to lose her, and I couldn't let that happen, not again.

"I really should go—" she said.

I pressed play. The screen lit up, showing the interior of Delilah's garage. Brandon's legs sticking out from under his car, one of his feet tapping away, probably to some music. Delilah's entire body went rigid. She turned back to face me, and her eyes slowly crept to look at my phone screen. Her mouth dropped open, but no sound came out for a few seconds.

"This is—"

I smiled sadly at her. "Yes, Delilah. This is a video of you killing Detective Brandon Jackson."

CHAPTER NINE
delilah

I could only stare, frozen, as the screen showed me the garage—my garage—Brandon's legs sticking out from under the Camaro. The sight of him was so wrong, so eerie. Then it got worse. The back door opened, and I saw myself walking in, my hands cupped around my elbows, my shoulders rounded, my head low, trying to make myself as small as possible. Bile burned through my esophagus.

"That's—stop the video," I croaked.

Logan didn't answer.

"Logan, stop the video."

I watched as I walked around the car and bent over to squeak at Brandon in my impotent, small-person voice. Oh god. In less than a minute, I would watch as I stalked back toward the house and stopped, pondering, calculating, and then, and then—

"Stop the video!" My voice came out in an animalistic scream. I swiped at the phone but Logan jerked it out of my reach.

Then, to my surprise, he tapped the Delete button and said, "I'm deleting this copy. I can't risk anyone coming across this on my phone. But I'm keeping a master copy somewhere safe." Even as we stared at each other, chests heaving hard, part of me wondered if Mom might have heard me scream. Or maybe my neighbors. I couldn't let any of them find us, not like this. We had to talk about it. I had so many questions. But where could we talk? Inside his car? A full-body shudder ran through me. No way in hell was I getting back in there with him. I gestured to Logan to follow, and we briskly walked down the street. Only after we turned the corner did I stop walking.

"How do you—I mean—why—" Coherent sentences were beyond me. I didn't even know where to begin with my questions.

Logan took a deep breath and tugged at his necklace. When he finally spoke, his words came out in a rush, his eyes shining with fervor. "I did this for your sake, Delilah. That time I talked to you, when you were on your way to the supermarket to get ice, I got the impression he was doing something bad to you, and I wanted to protect you.

Obviously if you were being abused, you couldn't report it because he was a cop, so I thought: What if I catch it all on video? They wouldn't be able to ignore it then. They'd have to take him away. I went to your house whenever I could and recorded a couple of instances of him beating you and your mom. I thought I should gather as much footage as I could, over multiple occasions, so he couldn't claim that it was a one-time thing or whatever. I was recording him working on his car that day, and…"

My head was a whirl of images. I thought of Logan skulking around the house—my house—with his camera phone brandished in front of him, trying to capture the worst moments of my life to *save me*, and I wanted to scratch him, feel his flesh peeling under my nails. "Why are you showing this to me?"

"Delilah, when I said I love you, I really meant it. This isn't some shallow teenage crush. I love you, and that means I love everything about you, even this part of you."

I gaped at him. Everything was going too fast and too slow and I didn't—couldn't—understand anything. "I don't understand."

"We're meant to be together," he said, with so much passion and belief, like a pastor making an announcement to his congregation.

"You don't even know me." But even as I said it, I knew what he was going to say. How he'd spent the last few months observing me, and—god—following me, picking up information about me to add to his sick collection.

"I do know you, Delilah. I know you better than anyone else. This video proves it."

"This video proves nothing. Aside from me—" Even now, I couldn't say it. "Brandon's death," I finished lamely.

Logan's face was shining with sincerity as he leaned close to me. "I know everything there is to know about you, and I still love you. Can anyone else say that?"

A black pit of dread had yawned open deep in my stomach, a feeling that wasn't entirely unfamiliar to me. It was the way I'd felt after the first time Brandon hit me, the sensation of standing at the lip of a crevasse, knowing monsters lurked in the deep and the dark. The sensation that things were about to get a whole lot worse. "What do you want, Logan?"

"I want you to know that we're meant to be together."

"So you're blackmailing me," I said flatly.

He looked scandalized by the statement. "Of course not. I'm not a monster. I wouldn't make you do anything you don't want to."

Despite myself, I allowed a flicker of hope to come to life. Maybe he really didn't want anything. Maybe… I shook my head. "Then why show me the video?"

"To show you we're soul mates. I don't want the love of my life behind bars."

"And if it turns out I'm not the love of your life?"

He shook his head forcefully, looking more earnest than ever. "There's no possible way we're not meant to be together. I was meant to protect you. Look how Detective Jackson hurt you all this time and I was the only one who noticed it. I was the only one who thought of a solution. You have no idea how many bad guys are out there. The world is a fucked-up place. You need me. If you left, I'd have to find you, and if I have to get the cops involved, well... I'd do anything to keep you safe, Delilah."

The hole opened up and swallowed me whole. It was hard to breathe. I sucked in a lungful of air, but my chest still felt like it was being crushed by an iron fist, as though I were drowning. I knew what drowning felt like because Brandon had once pressed my head into the pool for knocking a glass of water over his keyboard. The expression "my skin crawled" was more than appropriate here; I could practically feel my skin try to walk off my flesh just to get away from Logan. I tightened my hands into fists. I couldn't spiral back into my shell. Being trapped with Brandon, living under the crushing weight of his badge... I couldn't go back to living under someone else's thumb.

"That sounds like blackmail to me," I hissed.

Logan reached for my hand, but I snatched it away. "Why don't you give us a chance? What have you got to lose? Be honest with yourself, this was the best date you've been on. You gave me so many positive signals. You liked me. You were the one who kissed me."

I couldn't stop my upper lip from curling with disgust. A caustic retort was already fizzing its way up my throat when a small voice told me he had a point. Up until he showed me that damn video, I had regarded this as the best date I had ever been on. Not that I'd been on many, but there was a connection here, something special that made conversation between us flow effortlessly.

Yeah, that's because he's a stalker who dug up everything he could about you.

Before I could say a word, Logan spoke up. "I know right now it feels like you're being pushed into doing something you don't want to do, but over time, I promise you'll realize you need me as much as I need you. And I swear we can progress at whatever pace you're comfortable with."

"Okay," I said. "I'm comfortable with us going backward, to a time when we didn't know each other."

Logan laughed. "I knew you were going to say that."

I opened and closed my mouth, feeling ridiculously outmatched. He knew everything about me, and I knew nothing about him, nothing that could help me in this situation.

"Sleep on it," he said. "I know you won't ever find a boyfriend as dedicated as me."

I walked away in a daze, everything around me muted and slow as though I were underwater. Halfway to the house, I turned my head. Logan waved at me from inside the car, handsome face pulled into a smile fit for magazine covers. If he hadn't shown me the video, if I hadn't found out about how he'd stalked me, the sight of his face would have given flight to butterflies in my stomach. Now, it only made me sick. My skin throbbed with revulsion. And the word my mind spat out—*stalked*—sat painfully in my gut like a piece of flint, all hard, jagged edges that pierced my insides. Stalked. I had a stalker. I'd gone out on a date with him. A pretty awesome date, if I were to be completely honest. I wanted to laugh at the ridiculousness of it all. I tore my gaze from Logan and lurched away.

Mom was in the living room watching TV when I came in. She jumped up and breathed a sigh of relief when she saw me. I guess I wasn't the only one who wasn't quite used to Brandon being dead.

"How was the date?" she asked, turning off the TV. She twisted around and rested her arms on the back of the couch, smiling expectantly at me.

It was great, up until he showed me a video of me killing your boyfriend.

"It was okay."

Mom groaned. "Don't go all surly teenager on me. Come on, I need details. Tell me over a hot chocolate. I got the good stuff from Ghirardelli."

Despite myself, a small part of me whined to stay down here with Mom, sipping hot chocolate so thick that it had the consistency of melted ice cream. I wanted to spill, to sob out every single lurid detail, down to the puddle of blood reaching toward my feet from under Brandon's car. I wanted Mom to hug me and tell me it was all okay, that she didn't hold Brandon's murder against me, that I had saved us, saved *her*, and she was so grateful, and everything would be okay.

But another part was furious at Mom. It was a part that screamed, *You didn't protect us! You let Brandon into our lives, you let him strip you of your power, your strength, and reduce you into a blubbering mess with zero confidence. I killed him for our sake, and now it's my life on the line.* It took all of me to keep from lashing out at her. And I knew it wasn't fair, but I couldn't totally quiet that part of me.

I managed to choke out a nonconfrontational "I'm too tired. Maybe tomorrow?" before trudging upstairs into the bathroom. First, a shower so hot it felt like I was stripping off my skin as I lathered up. I took my time rubbing shampoo into my scalp, soaping every inch of my body, letting the suds and water scald away the grime of the day, wishing it could be this easy to wash out everything that had to do with Logan. After my shower, I felt a little bit less like I was about to explode into a million teeny shards.

My phone beeped with a message from Aisha.

Aisha [9:17 p.m.]:
How was it?????

Delilah [9:18 p.m.]:
It was ok. I'm tired. Ttyl!

I turned my phone to Silent and switched on my laptop, my head humming with thoughts of Logan, of Brandon, of Mom, of the things Logan had told me in the car. Out of habit, I opened Instagram and scrolled through it listlessly, looking at pictures of my friends blowing kisses at the camera, showing off their footwear, their food, their nails. The frivolousness of their posts jabbed at me. I wanted to put my fist through the screen.

My fingers moved across the keyboard and typed Logan's name into the search box. He and I had followed each other months ago, but I hadn't paid that much attention aside from a casual glance through some of his pictures. My skin crawled when I realized he'd been looking through my pictures with sinister purpose, digging out information about me for his sick obsession. Logan knew my darkest secret. Did he also know other secrets I carried?

No. I couldn't let my mind go there. Not right now. I'd completely lose my shit. I had to focus.

There was nothing out of the ordinary about his pictures—mostly Logan with his buddies, all of them tall, broad-shouldered, healthy, all-American types with good looks. Wholesome. Happy. I didn't even know where to begin trying to glean useful information out of this, like how the hell do I get him out of my life?

I looked through his pictures until I couldn't stomach the thought of him anymore. Slamming my laptop shut, I burrowed into my bed and nuzzled my face into my pillow. Despair sucked me in, wrapped its claws around me, and entrapped me in solid, unforgiving terror. I'd escaped from one maniac only to run straight into another. What was it about me that attracted these men, these predators? Was there something wrong with me, did I have PREY printed across my forehead? Had Pa's death broken me to the point where anyone could see I was vulnerable and ripe for the picking?

Sleep took a while to claim me. When it did, it was uneasy, a dark forest full of blood and dangerous secrets that snagged at my skin and sipped my blood. I might have screamed out loud a couple of times. In my dreams, I bit and scratched at something dark, only to find out the thing I was attacking was me, and then I wept with revulsion and lunged at myself again, claws outstretched. I was the biggest monster of them all.

I woke up more exhausted than before I'd gone to bed. I stayed in bed for a while, watching the dust motes glitter as they floated through the streaks of sunlight streaming through my curtains. No closer to figuring out what I was going to do about my little problem. I shut my eyes.

There was a hesitant knock on my door. "Sweetie, you awake?" Mom asked.

I turned my back to the door. I couldn't face Mom right now. I couldn't sit at the kitchen counter and have some bullshit girly chat with Mom about how cute my date was. I needed time to think, to let it all sink in, to get my head straight and figure—

"Detective Mendez is here, and she brought doughnuts. They're still warm. I'm making coffee. Come on, sleepyhead," Mom said cheerfully, then she padded back downstairs.

She might as well have kicked me in the chest. Mendez. I'd spent last night swimming in a lake of despair; now, all of a sudden, fear sliced through the black waters. I came fully awake, my senses painfully alert. Every alarm bell ringing. *Mendez is here!*

I shot out of bed and paced about as silently as I could. *Don't want them to hear my footsteps downstairs.* Maybe I could pretend not to feel well. But maybe that would make Mendez even more suspicious. She was obviously suspicious, otherwise she wouldn't be here with doughnuts. *What do I do what do I do what do I do?*

Calm. I must stay calm. Or must I not? How do innocent, non-cop-killing teens behave two weeks after the death of their beloved stepdad figure? Would they still be grieving? Or moving along nicely?

My mind clacked furiously as I brushed my teeth. I splashed water on my face and studied my reflection. I had the good fortune of having a near-perfect complexion—there were no dark circles nor puffiness under my eyes. I looked well-rested. Well-adjusted. *Is that a good thing?*

Then it hit me: Mom. Of course! All I had to do was follow Mom's cue. If she was still grieving, I should probably also be grieving. And if Mom was all breezy and fine, then I could probably be all la-di-da. Mom had sounded happy and relaxed at the door, so that was how I should carry myself. Okay. I got this.

Ten minutes later, I went down the stairs and greeted Mom and Detective Mendez with a cheerful, "Morning!"

Mendez was seated adjacent to Mom at the dining table. She gave me a Saturday-morning smile—bright, cheery, relaxed. But her eyes gave me a quick once-over.

I looked back at her, my face open. I'd done well, I knew I had. I'd put on a pink cable-knit sweater over faded jeans and tied my hair up with an actual, goddamn scrunchie. No one, especially not a cop, has ever been murdered by a girl who wears scrunchies with daisies printed on them. Mendez couldn't possibly find anything suspicious about me, not like this.

"Your mom told me you had a big date yesterday," Mendez said as I slid into my seat.

My skin shrank at the mention of Logan, becoming too tight for my body. *One fucking emergency at a time!* I wanted to scream.

"Yeah, it was okay," I managed to say. I'd been so focused on dealing with Mendez's questions about Brandon that I'd completely forgotten to consider what to say if she asked me about Logan. *Why's she even asking me about Logan?*

"She's been so secretive about it," Mom said. She and Mendez exchanged a look that said, *Teens, amirite?*

Mendez gave a laugh that was probably designed to sound light and breezy and very one-of-us-girls. "Where'd he take you?" She popped a doughnut hole in her mouth, her eyes never leaving mine, studying me, assessing, prickling across my skin like spider legs.

I needed caffeine to sharpen my sleep-dulled mind, so I took a glug of coffee before answering. It burned my tongue, and I coughed, almost snorting it up my nose. Oh god. I was so bad at the whole Appearing Innocent thing. "Um, we went to this like, obstacle course thingy in the middle of the woods—"

"Oooh, Monkey See Monkey Do?" Mendez said. "I love that place! Good choice. I like this kid already."

It took every drop of will not to give her a Look, not to give any indication of anything bad happening with Logan. New strategy: my date was uneventful, boring, and I proba-bly won't be seeing more of Logan.

"Yeah, it was okay," I said. I tried to punctuate it with a hair flip then belatedly realized I'd tied my hair back with a goddamn scrunchie.

Luckily, Mendez didn't seem to notice the awkward hair flip. "Your mom tells me you're thinking of applying to the National University of Singapore," she said.

I glanced at Mom, who beamed proudly at me.

"It's one of the hardest colleges to get into in the world," Mom said.

Mendez nodded. "Very impressive choice."

"Well, I haven't gotten in," I mumbled.

"You will," Mom said loyally. She turned to Mendez. "She has a 4.0 GPA, and you should read her college application essay. It made me tear up."

"I'm sure it's excellent." Mendez smiled at Mom then turned her attention to me. "How're you holding up, Dee?"

Here it comes. I glanced at Mom, took in how she was carrying herself. Bravely cheerful. Right. "Well, it hasn't been easy..."

Mendez nodded encouragingly.

"But I think Mom and I are doing the best we can?" *Should that have come out as a question?* I tried again. "We're getting by." I wondered belatedly if "getting by" sounded too much like "getting over it." I was a robot trying to pass as human. Before long, Mendez, someone who was actually paid for detecting bullshit, would sniff out my lies and—

"Good, good," Mendez said. "I'm sorry if I'm prying. I wanted to make sure you're both doing okay. I've been trying to move things along with Brandon's life insurance, but you know how insurance companies are."

I almost snorted out loud at the mention of Brandon's life insurance. It was one of the many gestures he made earlier on in their relationship to prove what a good guy he was. To prove how much he cared. "Look, babe," he'd said, present-ing the insurance papers with a flourish. And Mom had fallen for it. So had I, actually. As far as gestures went, it had been a damn convincing one.

Mom gave a bitter laugh. "I know how they are, all right. It took ages after Dee's father passed for his insurance company to pay out."

"I really hope Brandon's insurance company pays out before college. I've heard international student fees are no joke," Mendez said.

"Yep, they're brutal," Mom said. She glanced at me and smiled proudly. "But Dee here has been working really hard at her part-time job. They pay so well, much more than you'd expect from part-time work at a school!"

Mendez's eyebrows rose. "Is that so?"

My stomach curdled. The last thing I wanted to talk about right now was my part-time job. I tried a small laugh, which came out wooden. "Mom's exaggerating."

"What is it exactly that you do, Dee?" Mendez asked.

"Just boring, old library stuff," I said quickly. Too quickly? Shit. *Change the subject, quick!*

"I don't know about boring. You're helping to save up for college," Mom said. She turned to Mendez. "That's why it means so much to hear that you're following up on Brandon's life insurance. It'll help us out a lot, Detective."

"Please, call me Val." She hesitated for a second. "I

just wanted to—uh, this might be inappropriate, but, um, I know Brandon might not have been the easiest person to get along with sometimes, and I always wondered if he—um, you know—"

"Brandon was..." Mom stared into her coffee. Her voice came from afar. "I don't want to speak ill of the dead, but..." Mom said, and her chin trembled a little. Then she looked straight into Mendez's eyes and an understanding passed between them. Mendez nodded, her face registering no surprise, only an I-knew-it expression.

My stomach plunged. Mom had pretty much given Mendez the information she'd been hankering for—that we were being abused by Brandon, that we had a motive for killing him. Mom didn't care if we had a motive for killing Brandon; she thought his death was an accident. She couldn't notice the new way Mendez was looking at us. I could almost hear her thoughts whirring away, the mental calculation speeding as we sat there sipping our coffees and nibbling at doughnuts—*they both have motives, which one did it, the mother or the daughter, the mother or the—*

Mendez's gaze flicked from Mom to me, quick as a striking snake. Too fast. I was caught with my mask off. Something flickered in her eyes, and I felt the firm hand of the law closing around me, squeezing. Crushing. I saw the answer in her eyes, searing bright.

The daughter.

The rest of Saturday passed by in a haze. After Mendez left, I wandered around the house with my headphones on. They weren't plugged into anything; they were there so I wouldn't have to talk to Mom.

More texts from Aisha. **Helloooooo? Details about the date pls!**

I began to type out: **It was goo—**

Nope. Couldn't make myself do it. My stomach clenched, my teeth clashed. The thought of telling Aisha, of all people, that my date with Logan went well...

I turned off my phone instead and went back to trying to figure out how to get out of the shitstorm my life had become. But I was no cunning plotter. I knew I was hopelessly outmatched by both Logan and Mendez. Both were strategists—meticulous, able to see the big picture, patient enough to stick to the step-by-step aspects of their plans. And here I was, stuck between them.

Hah.

The same nightmares plagued me that night, and in the morning, I awoke with a start when Mom knocked on my door.

"You're gonna be late for school," she said.

"I'm up," I called out, then I remained in bed and stared at the ceiling for a while.

A delicious smell wafted through the door, tickling my nostrils. Something bready along with eggs and sausages and coffee. Despite myself, my mouth watered. What did I have for dinner? Mom had gone out with her friends, and I...had a big plate of nothing. Maybe I'd feel better after a good meal. I got dressed and bounded down the stairs. "I'll have a big plate of whatever you're making, Mom," I said, halfway down.

"Morning!" someone said. Someone who was distinctly not Mom.

Logan.

My legs forgot how to move. I stood there, staring at him, my stalker, my blackmailer, as he stood in the middle of the kitchen, holding a frying pan loaded with what looked like diced mushrooms and onions. What the hell was up with people thinking they could drop by my house for breakfast?

"Take a seat," he said.

"Morning, sweetheart," Mom said, her head popping from behind the fridge door. She took out a carton of tomato juice. "Logan brought bagels and offered to cook us breakfast. Why didn't you tell me the two of you are partners in chemistry lab?" She placed a glass in front of me and poured some juice into it.

"Mom—" My voice was strangled, small. It was drowned out by the other sounds—Mom chattering as she poured juice for all of us, the pan sizzling as Logan cracked eggs into it. Dimly, I felt myself sinking into a chair. My legs had given out beneath me. "Mom—" I tried again, louder this time, and Logan turned his head and snapped his gaze on mine. I choked on my next words. He was still smiling his easy smile, but his eyes were steel, a warning etched into the hard lines of his mouth.

"Yes, sweetie?" Mom was too busy poking inside a paper bag. She missed the look of horror that passed across my face. "Which bagel do you want? Sesame? Poppy seed? Plain?"

I tore my eyes from Logan's, my heart racing. I couldn't do it. He'd tell her everything. He'd show her the video, show her how I'd walked past Brandon's Camaro and then turned around and put my foot out and tripped the jack—

I forced a smile. "I'll have a sesame one. Thanks."

Mom winked at me when she passed me my bagel. Lowering her voice, she leaned close and said, "I like him, sweetie. I think he's a keeper."

Mom always did have the worst taste in guys.

CHAPTER TEN

logan

By the time we finished our breakfast, it was time to go. Delilah mumbled something about catching the bus to get to school, but you could tell her heart wasn't in it. We both knew I would insist on driving us to school, and her mom would tell her riding the bus was ridiculous given I had a car and was also going to Draycott. We walked out of the house with Delilah's mom telling me I was welcome at their place anytime.

Anytime, Logan, when you get tired of boarding school food.

I laughed when Delilah jerked open the door to the car. This was something I loved about her. I knew that hidden deep beneath the thick layers of shyness, Delilah had a temper that was always bubbling, constantly on the edge of erupting. It was a privilege to know this side of her, the side she'd kept hidden so well that nobody else knew about it. Nobody but me. Months down the road, when we'd be solidly, definitely, In a Relationship, we'd surely get into some passionate fights because of her temper, and I couldn't wait for that to happen, to have Delilah be comfortable enough to show me everything, all the raw, red edges she'd hidden for so long. But for now, I couldn't let that spark get the better of her. She wasn't thinking straight, what with all that happened in the past couple of weeks. It was up to me to be the rational one. If I wasn't careful, she'd end up burning both of us down.

Sure enough, the moment we were ensconced in the cocoon of the car, Delilah jabbed a finger into my chest and hissed, "Never, ever show up at my house again, you freak."

I won't lie, that hurt. I knew I shouldn't let it. People say all sorts of terrible things in the heat of the moment that they later regret, and this was obviously one of those times, but still. *You freak. Freak.*

It was something Mom called me. When she found my Sophie box—the strands of hair, the old sock I'd managed to steal from Sophie's gym bag.

It stung. I'd even brought bagels. *Deep breaths.* I wasn't a freak. I just had a bit of difficulty controlling my impulses. But as long as I understood that about myself, I'd be fine. Perfectly fine.

When I finally managed to shake Mom's voice out of my head, I forced a smile. "Dee, take a deep breath."

"Don't tell me to take a deep breath!" she cried. "I don't know what you're trying to do, Logan, but whatever it is, you are not welcome at my house, okay, you asshole?"

Christ, the girl was brutal. I tried again. *Love is patient.* "You're stressed out—"

"Hell yes, I'm stressed out! You know why? Because I freaking murdered my mom's boyfriend and now it turns out you've recorded it and I don't know—I don't understand what it is you want!"

"I want you to give us a chance," I said in calm, measured tones. *Love is kind.*

She looked at me like I'd grown another head. "Yes, but I don't get it. You know what I did. You know I'm a killer. Why would you want to go out with me? Logan, look at you. You're a real catch. You can date anyone you want."

I wanted to shake her. I hated having to sit here and listen to her say these things, because what was she really saying? "You can date anyone you want" means "Why me?" I hated how she'd been so broken by Detective Jackson that she'd think of herself in this way. How could she believe she wasn't worthy of me? Of anyone? But over time, I'd make her see I wasn't out of her league. We were perfect for each other, she'd see that soon enough. I looked her straight in the eye, unflinching, and said, "I want to date *you.*"

She stared at me like the head I'd just grown had started licking my other head. "But why?"

"When you meet the love of your life, you know. It's useless trying to pin any sort of logic to it. You might as well try to solve a calculus problem by chewing gum. And Dee, you need to know this about you: You're amazing. You're perfect. You can date just about anyone *you* want."

"Logan—" She stopped herself and took a deep breath. When she spoke again, her voice was lower, but there was a tremor in it. "You don't know me. You can't possibly know that you love me."

I wanted to shake her. Why did she keep questioning it? Questioning us? She wasn't supposed to fight this hard.

Deep breaths.

"Look, I get that it's going to take some time for you to accept that we're meant to be with each other. And that's okay. We have all the time in the world. I told you, I'm willing to go at your pace"—I held my finger up when she opened her mouth to speak—"as long as it's moving forward."

She sat there for a while, staring at me, breathing hard. My chest tightened with guilt. This wasn't what I wanted. The last thing I needed was for Delilah to fear me the way she feared Detective Jackson. I had to make her see I was nothing like him.

"Just spend some time with me," I said kindly, and my heart ached because Delilah wasn't used to kind, wasn't used to being handled with tenderness. "You'll see it's really not as bad as you think."

She didn't answer, merely turned her head so she was looking out the window. I started the car and turned on the stereo. Her favorite song came on. She glanced at me, her forehead clearing for a split second, and I smiled, hopeful. Then she scowled and punched the Power button on the stereo.

"You probably didn't even know about Planet Green until you stalked me," she snapped.

She turned her back on me once more. I had to laugh. That fire inside her. Unbelievable. I was so glad Detective Jackson hadn't managed to stamp it out of her. She was still my Delilah. When we got to school, Delilah sat sullenly and watched as kids streamed into Wheeler Hall.

"You ready?" I asked.

"They're gonna see me coming out of your car," she said flatly.

I waited for her to continue. When it became obvious she wasn't going to, I said, "And?"

"They're going to think we're together."

"Is that such a bad thing?"

Delilah glared at me. If looks could kill, I would be flayed and chopped into at least ten different chunks before being flung to wild animals, and honestly, I could kiss her for being such a firecracker. When she finally spoke, she said the words slowly, enunciating each syllable as though I were a complete airhead. "I do not want to be in the limelight at school. Surely you can understand that, given my circumstances."

I took her hand, ignoring the curl of her lip when our skin touched. "Our relationship will be the perfect cover. Nobody is going to be thinking of Detective Jackson." Then, just as an incentive, I added, "Not unless you want them to." Damn, I felt like a total asshole, bringing that up, but I had to remind her of what a huge secret I was keeping on her behalf, what a big deal it was that I'd seen what she did and loved her in spite of it. Maybe I loved her because of it as well.

She paled, her jaw tightening. "Whatever. I'm going to be late for class."

"I'll see you at lunch," I said, trying not to stare at her lips, trying not to freak her out even though they were begging to be kissed.

She paused. "We don't sit at the same table for lunch."

I grinned. "We do now."

I parked the car, and we headed out into the sunshine together. I walked next to her casually, the way a friend would, and I didn't stare at her with naked adoration the way I wanted to. I walked benignly, sexlessly, and I waved bye to Delilah when we got to the lockers. Didn't even walk her to her class, *look at that self-restraint.*

Then I headed to my own class and shrugged and smiled and fielded questions until the bell rang, and how could I concentrate, when the thought of Delilah was so real, so fresh?

Someone hit the back of my head with a balled-up note.

R U and Delilah a thing?

I turned around to see Josh grinning and waggling his eyebrows at me. But then I noticed how strained his smile was, and how hard he was staring at me. Josh was one of the few people who knew what happened with Sophie, how into her I was. He'd called it "an obsession," and he was the only student who knew about my suicide attempt after Sophie died. Everyone else thought I'd just gotten really sick and had to take some time off, but Josh knew. He was the one who found me in the glade, after I took all those pills.

And now here he was, good old Josh, worrying about me again. I gave him the world's most casual shrug and turned back to face the board. After class, I launched into a discussion about the lesson, hoping that would distract him, and it did, for a while. But when I paused for breath, Josh said, "So, about Delilah…"

"Yeah?" I said casually.

"Um, are you guys a thing?"

I shrugged. "Sort of."

"Cool, cool." He scratched the back of his neck. "Only, um, I didn't want to mention it before because it—I don't know—seemed a bit weird or whatever, but she kind of really looks like Sophie."

"Really? I haven't noticed." I put on an expression of blank curiosity.

Josh frowned. "Okay." He didn't look entirely convinced, but luckily he had to rush off to geography, so I was spared the rest of his concerned speech.

When the bell finally rang for lunch, I stood outside Delilah's class waiting for her. I spotted her as soon as she came out, even with her head tucked down. Seeing her sent a burst of joy rushing through my chest. Not so for Delilah; her face soured when she saw me. I tried not to let it bother me. She'd come around. I fell easily into step next to her.

"How was class?" I asked.

She gave me a look.

"I am genuinely interested in how your day went."

Delilah looked up at the ceiling then at me and said, "It's been terrible. Okay? And you know why it's been terrible? Because, as it turns out, I have a stalker who wants to ruin my life." She was near tears, her eyes shining, her voice shrill.

This was the worst part, knowing I was doing this to her, causing distress to my girl. *But it'll pass*, I reminded myself. I caught her hand and led her out of the building into the bright sunshine. "Take a deep breath," I said kindly.

She did as I said before glaring at me. "I hope you enjoyed that. You're even controlling my breathing now."

I sighed. "You know it's not like that. I just want you to give us a chance. Let's go have lunch. You'll like my friends."

"I like mine just fine," she said.

She was so stubborn, she couldn't see that I was trying to save her. Sophie was like that too. Anyone could tell she didn't have the right friends. Sure enough, as soon as she ran into trouble with her class, her so-called friends melted away. A couple of them stuck around long enough to watch Sophie spiral into depression and frantic desperation before posting all about it on Draycott Dirt.

"Give it a chance," I said again. I didn't wait for a reply before taking her hand, gently but firmly, and leading her toward the cafeteria.

Noise spilled out, almost deafening, and Delilah instinctively clutched at my hand. I gave her a reassuring squeeze and said, "Just keep walking. You'll be okay."

Even on normal days, the cafeteria was a lot to take in—the air boiling with students yelling, babbling, laughing over some text or picture or video on their phones, and the scent thick with the smells of hot food and last night's dinner. Delilah was so pale, I started to worry she'd burst into tears or puke or something. But I knew her. She was strong. She'd make it. Halfway there, she stumbled and would have fallen if I hadn't caught her. The voices around us became excited murmurs, an almost physical cloud that clung to us like a sickly mist.

"Breathe," I whispered.

She took in a shaky breath and kept going. When we

neared the center table, my friends looked up and the conversation lulled to a halt.

"Hey, guys," I said.

Their eyes moved from my face to Delilah's to our hands, still linked tightly together. Another flash of concern from Josh. Had I been wrong about him? Did he tell everyone about my thing for Sophie? My unfortunate incident?

Moni was the first to break the silence.

"Hey," she said, smiling. She always was the sweetheart of the group. "I'm Moni."

"I know," Delilah said. "You're in Mrs. Holston's class too."

"That's right! You always have the best answers. C'mon, take a seat." Moni slid over and patted the spot next to hers. I wanted to sag with relief. I gave her a silent nod of thanks as Delilah let go of my hand and went to sit next to her.

Moni's invitation broke the ice. The other two girls in the group leaned across the table, and soon Delilah was swallowed up in their conversation. I took my seat next to Josh.

He leaned close and lowered his voice. "So it's official, huh?"

We glanced at Delilah, caught up in conversation with the girls, and Josh said, carefully, "She seems...cool."

"You have no idea."

delilah

As much as I hated to admit it, lunch with Logan and his friends wasn't actually terrible. I'd always assumed that Josh and Matt would be the worst, but they turned out to be pretty nice. And the girls were great. Despite my wariness, despite my lack of interest in becoming one of them, I felt as though Moni, Hannah, and Tonya were genuinely welcoming me into their group.

"Maybe Delilah can resolve it," Moni said when I'd settled in my seat and was comfortable enough to open my bottle of organic elderflower and apple juice. Everything at Draycott was organic. Four months in and I still wasn't used to it.

"Resolve what?" I asked, instantly nervous. My first test. Tonya sat up straight. She was a natural storyteller, the leader of the trio. She leaned in close enough for me to see the lack of pores on her skin and smell her perfume. Something expensive and very grown-up. She smelled like a woman, not a girl. "Hannah has a hot date this weekend with an older guy—a freshman from Stanford," she said, solemnly.

I was impressed. Hannah didn't strike me as the kind of girl who'd get asked out by a college guy. She was sweet and quiet, with a smooth, brown complexion that blotched red whenever she got embarrassed. "How do you know him?"

"He's a friend of my brother's. We met over the summer. It's not really a date. He said they're having a party at his frat house this weekend and invited me to go." Her gaze flicked up for a split second, long enough for me to catch it—something I was very, very familiar with. Hannah was scared. Of what, I wasn't sure, but I knew that look, the quiet panic of prey.

"But she doesn't want to go." Tonya delivered the line with triumph; the final twist in her story.

"Which is bananas," Moni said. "I mean, it's a college guy. From Stanford."

"Ooh, Stanford!" Josh sang, his hands clasped under his chin.

"Shut up, Josh," Moni said without looking at him. "C'mon, Hannah, we're pushing you for your own good here. You need to live a little."

Hannah sighed and slurped up a noodle with a small shrug.

"Is your brother going to be at the party?" I asked.

She shook her head, her corkscrew curls bouncing. "He's doing a semester abroad in Paris."

"Her brother is like, so protective over her," Tonya said. "He'd probably microchip her if he could, so he'd know where she is all the time."

Hannah bit her lip to stifle a laugh. "Stop, he's really not that bad."

"Oh, yeah, he is," Moni said. "So now that he's away, it's time for lil' sis to go out and play. Right, Delilah?"

Three pairs of eyes rested on my face. I looked at them, my mind flailing wildly. How the hell would I know? I was about to mumble something about not having a clue when I realized I did have something to say. Hannah was shy and retiring. You could tell she'd been brought up on a steady diet of "girls should be seen and not heard." Every time she laughed, she covered her mouth, as though laughter had to be hidden.

And some guy thought it was a good idea to invite her to a frat party, a place where she'd be outmatched and alone in a house full of strangers. I didn't even know the guy and already I wanted to punch him in the face.

"Actually, I think the party's a terrible idea." My voice came out like a spoon clanging on crystal—too sharp, too noticeable. *Tone it down.* But I couldn't. I couldn't tone it down after Brandon, after Logan—I glanced at him, two seats down, laughing with his buddies, and something inside me hardened. "Frat parties are basically a cesspool of horny guys drunk on privilege and booze trying to get girls dead-drunk so they can take advantage of them. I mean, sure, that's a stereotype, and I'm sure some frat parties are nice and some frat guys respect women or whatever, but this guy is asking a high school girl to come on her own to a place where she'll be completely surrounded by his friends. I don't think you should go. Not without a shitload of pepper spray and a couple of Tasers."

By the time I finished my speech, they were all staring at me with mouths open. Crap. I'd gone too far. I shouldn't have said all those things.

Moni let out a bark. It took me a second to realize she was laughing. My face burned, until she reached out and gave me a one-armed hug.

"Delilah, that was fucking awesome!" she said.

Even Tonya was nodding, her mouth stretched into a grudging smile. "I have to admit, when you put it that way, it doesn't seem like such a great idea." She leaned closer to me. "Hey, anyone ever told you that you look a lot like So—"

She was quickly shushed by Moni, who glared at her. "I'm sorry," Moni said. "Ignore her."

I was about to ask who Tonya was about to say I looked like when Hannah said, "Thanks. I really like him, but like, I didn't feel good about the invitation and I couldn't put my finger on it. You said it perfectly."

"Damn, now I feel bad for pushing you to get with him," Tonya said.

"Aww, no, don't feel bad!" Hannah said. She leaned into Tonya. "You just don't want me to miss out on life experiences."

"You can miss out on this one," Tonya said, and the two of them laughed, and Tonya reached out and gave me a fist bump.

I couldn't hold back my smile. I'd never wanted to join the cool crowd, never coveted a spot at this table.

But the girls' approval gave me a surprisingly sweet burst of joy. *They like me, they really do! They think I give good advice!* I wanted to bite my lip and giggle and tell Aisha—

Aisha.

What with Mendez's surprise visit and then Logan's surprise visit and then being forced to sit with his friends for lunch, I hadn't had a chance to think of Aisha. I twisted in my seat to look at my usual lunch table. I caught Aisha's eye, but she turned away as soon as our eyes met.

Logan was watching me with a little smile, smug and secure in the knowledge that his friends would charm me into a false sense of acceptance. My gaze flicked to Tonya, Moni, and Hannah, now discussing their college applications. Every move they made, every hair toss, every laugh, every hand wave became suspicious. *Do they know? Do they know Logan's blackmailing me?*

"Which colleges are you applying to, Delilah?" Moni said.

Like hell I would tell any of them anything. "Um, the usual. The UCs and maybe Stanford, I don't know," I muttered and kept my eyes on my food so no one would be interested in talking to me.

I hated them all, the fun guys and the cool girls, even sweet Hannah. They must know. They'd been his friends for years. Part of them must be aware what he was capable of. But the way they interacted with one another over lunch was so easygoing, so casual and light, like everything was sunshine and flowers...which only made it worse. They all thought Logan was a Nice Guy. They loved him, you could see it from the way they shifted their bodies to face him slightly when he sat down, the way they watched him when he talked. They were under his spell. I couldn't blame them. Logan was fizz and fireworks. Beneath the model good looks was a brain bursting with brilliance. Delicious sharp-edged wit, an intense stare that made you feel like he was truly listening to what you were saying. Irresistible. I knew what it was like to be under his spell, to be sucked into the Logan vortex.

I stood up abruptly. Conversation around me ceased. "Sorry, I just remembered I need to um—I have this assignment for world history. Anyway, I'll see you guys around." Logan started to get up. "No!" I snapped. *Oops.* I tried again. More sugar this time. "I really need to finish my essay. Thanks for, um—thanks for this." I gestured at the table. "Bye!"

As soon as the doors swung shut behind me, I let out my

breath. The noise was sliced off, the smells of cooked meat and ripe fruit no longer as rich and cloying. Thank god. I could think clearly again. I sent Aisha a text: **Hey can u come out? I need to talk to u.**

I paced around for a bit outside, checking my phone every five seconds. **Aisha, come on, I need to talk to u.**

Still no reply. Argh. I shook my head and headed out of the building and toward Brenner Hall, where my next class was. Aisha was in world history with me, so if I got there early, I could try to ambush her before class. I passed by the track field, where the really dedicated athletes had chosen to spend their lunch hour jogging under the blazing California sun. In between the shadows of the trees, my scalp prickled with the heat. I sifted through the events from my weekend, discarding things I couldn't share with Aisha. Which was all of the things. Literally all of them. Crap. Somehow, I had to explain to Aisha why I'd ditched her during lunch without actually telling her anything.

The minutes crawled by as I stood outside the classroom, shuffling my feet awkwardly, trying my best to look inconspicuous as more and more students filed into the building. I pretended to be interested in the bulletin boards and a poster about Earth Day and why honeybees were so important to the ecosystem, just what I wanted to read.

I heard a muttered *tsk* and turned to see Aisha heading my way.

I hurried up to her and tried to look as pathetic as I knew how, which was very pathetic indeed. "Aisha, I'm sorry I couldn't sit with you all at lunch, I—"

"You couldn't. Really." She cocked an eyebrow at me.

"Yes, really. I wanted to, but—"

"That's funny, because all I saw was you hanging on to Logan and ignoring me."

The red rage inside me leapt up. This was all Logan's fault.

"That's not what happened. You don't understand. Come on, don't be so mad at me. It was just lunch..." That was weak. You don't ditch your best friend at lunch to sit with some guy.

Aisha snorted. "It's not just that, okay? You were all excited about your date with Logan, and I get it, he's a hottie. I was super excited for you too. I mean, I helped pick out your outfit and everything. And then you had your date, and it's like, boom! Later, Aish! You didn't even care enough to update me on how it went. I sent you messages asking you about the date and you ignored all of them." Aisha glared at me for a few more seconds then sighed. "We can talk later."

Relief flooded me. "Okay. Yeah. After school?" Then I remembered that I had to work after school. "Or tomorrow?"

Disappointment crossed her face. "Yeah, I guess."

Aisha whooshed into the classroom, leaving me alone in the corridor. I let my head fall against the wall and stayed there until a cough made me look up. Mr. Francis, the world history teacher, had arrived and was frowning at me.

"Everything okay, Delilah?"

"Yeah." I skulked into the classroom. Aisha sat sullenly in her seat. I sank into mine and willed myself to become invisible, to melt into the air, to stop existing. I gripped my pencil so tight, my hand went numb, and still I couldn't make my heart slow down, couldn't stop the hole from opening up and swallowing me.

The rest of the day was more of the same. Everybody had seen me sitting with Logan and his posse. There were a few curious smiles thrown my way, one or two people—kids who would never otherwise give me a second glance—came up to me and said hi, tried to dig out more information about how I snagged Logan when he'd been so unattainable. There were even more sharp glances, lips curled into a sneer, snatched whispers like, "Why would he choose *her*?" Every stare, every quiet comment, weighed heavily on my shoulders, until I found myself hunching once more, my hands cupping my elbows. The way I used to when Brandon was around.

The realization sliced through everything. The air around me thrummed. I'd gotten rid of Brandon just to replace him with Logan. And the rest of my time in high school would be spent playing by Logan's rules, having to sit with his friends at lunch instead of Aisha, asking in a very sweet, very sad voice, could I please sit with Aisha today, him smiling indulgently at me. We'd go to school dances as a couple, and he'd decide that we should dance, and all the while what I had done would hang over me.

A hot kernel sat deep in my gut, getting hotter by the second, until my entire being was filled with its heat. I had to fight back. I'd call him out on his bluff. If he claimed to love me as much as he did, he wouldn't want me behind bars. Probably not, anyway. It was worth a try.

My resolve lasted throughout my shift at the library, where I channeled some of my frustration into packaging orders.

"Wow, someone's being really productive today," Lisa said, from behind her laptop. She had a state-of-the-art computer from the school to keep up with the cataloging, but she chose to use her clunky laptop to keep all her records.

I made a noncommittal grunt and continued wrapping packages with a vengeance. There was a knock at the door, and my head snapped up. Lisa and I looked at each other, wide-eyed. Nobody ever came down here.

"Hello?" came a voice. Even though it was muffled, every hair on the back of my neck stood straight up. "I'm looking for Delilah? I was told she'd be down here."

Oh. My. Fucking. God. It was Logan.

"Why are you taking visitors down here?" Lisa snapped, her cheeks red.

I could kill him. Thank god the door was locked.

"I'm not. Sorry," I whispered to Lisa. "I'll get rid of him."

I swept my table clean and then unlocked the door and slipped out, closing it tight behind me.

"Ready to go?" he said, flashing me his trademark sweetheart smile. The smile that stole hearts. I wanted to scratch it off his face. "Your shift was over fifteen minutes ago. I was waiting outside, but—"

"Don't you ever come to my workplace again," I hissed.

He looked surprised but recovered himself and nodded. "I'm sorry, Dee. I guess I got impatient. I just wanted to see you so badly. Anyway, are you done? Should we go?"

"I'm taking the bus home," I said.

"No, you're not," he said easily. "Come on, I'll drive you."

I inhaled, ready to roar at him, shove him back, tell him to get the hell out of my life, when the door swung open and Lisa walked out. She cocked her head to one side when she spotted me and Logan.

"What are you kids still doing here?" she chirped in her tiny, sweet librarian voice. My heart thudded at how angry she must be right now, though she was hiding it very well.

"I came to pick Delilah up," Logan said.

"I didn't know you had a boyfriend!" she said. "That is so cute."

I have her a weak smile.

"Delilah's told me so much about her job and how great it is working for you."

"She has?" Lisa's eyebrows disappeared into her hairline.

I shook my head quickly. "He's exaggerating." I imagined stabbing Logan right in the head. How dare he come here, and talk to my employer, and invade the only space that's mine, and—

Lisa laughed. "Okay, sorry to cut this short, but I have to rush off. You kids have fun!" she said before walking off, her skirt swishing in time with her ponytail. Only I caught the glimpse of coldness in her eyes, and the sight of it twisted like a knife in my guts.

"Let's go," I growled and headed out of the library without waiting for him.

I refused to look at him throughout the car ride. I stared straight ahead, ignoring all of his attempts at making conversation. I'd show him what a miserable asshole I could be when I put my mind to it. I frowned when he pulled up in front of a supermarket but refused to give him the satisfaction of asking what we were doing here.

"Come on, we've got a bit of shopping to do," he said.

I closed my eyes for a moment, drawing from that kernel of rage, letting my anger get good and hot, then turned to face him. "Cut the crap, Logan. I'm not playing your game anymore."

His eyebrows knitted together. "But Dee—"

"I'm not. It's over. You can go to the cops or whatever. I'd rather be in prison than do this with you." The last two words were spat out, dripping with revulsion. I leaned back, every inch of my skin prickling, battle drums throbbing through my veins.

Logan blinked and ran his fingers through his hair. "I mean... I don't know what to say. I thought things were going so well. You got along really well with the girls, and—"

"I don't have a problem with 'the girls.' I have a problem with you!"

Logan shook his head, his face a mask of sadness. "I'm really sorry you feel that way, Dee. Fine. All right."

I could have leapt up, punched my way through the car roof and clouds and through the atmosphere. I called him out on his bluff and it worked! I was going to be free of this nightmare.

There was a click—Logan had unbuckled his seat belt. I watched for a second, bemused, as he got out of the car and walked across the parking lot toward the supermarket. He stopped at the old pay phone out front, took out his wallet—

I scrambled to unlock my seat belt, shot out of the car—too slow, too fucking slow. Images flashed through my mind as I ran—the red and blue flashes of cop cars screeching into the parking lot, everybody watching, phones flashing as I got cuffed and pushed inside a cop car, me in an orange jumpsuit, Mom sobbing, "Why, Dee, why did you do it?"

His fingers moved across the buttons, pushed three numbers. He glanced up, saw me running, and smiled apologetically.

I reached him just as he said, "Yes, I'd like to report a murder. The murder of Detective Brandon Jackson."

I grabbed his arm, tried to wrench the phone out of his hand, but he was a lacrosse player, and I might as well be made of marshmallow. Weak, soft. I couldn't budge him. I could only whisper, "Sorry, I'm sorry, I didn't mean it, please hang up now, please please please." A couple of shoppers came out of the store, glanced at us, and kept going.

Logan watched me in silence for a moment, while the operator said something.

Just as I thought my heart would tear itself out of my rib cage, Logan smiled, showing a flash of beautifully straight teeth, and said, "Oops, sorry, I was mistaken. Thanks for your time!" and hung up.

For the next few moments, there was no sound but the roar of blood in my ears, my heart pounding, pounding, a mad beast. Then, his eyes wide with sincerity, Logan took my hand and squeezed it.

"I'm sorry I had to do that, Dee, but I need you to know I'm serious about this. I'm serious about us."

All I could do was gape at him. Everything had blurred into fuzz behind him—the shoppers streaming in and out, the cars driving past, the sounds and the smells, it all felt unreal. Logan was the only thing that was clear-edged and sharp, and though he spoke quietly, his words were so solid that they were almost physical.

"I want you to give us a chance. A real chance," he continued. "Come on, Dee, we deserve this, you know? We're going to be so, so good, I swear."

Every cell in my body writhed with revulsion. He was delusional, completely and utterly. I wanted to spit in his face and tell him to go to hell. But I couldn't do it to Mom, it would destroy her.

Patience.

Pa was always telling me to be patient, to work my way out of problems slowly, patiently.

I saw myself at NUS, walking across campus in the sticky tropical heat, surrounded by students speaking Singlish. A place where no one knew who I was, the bodies I'd left behind, the secrets I'd buried. There was hope. I had to suck it up and pretend to be Logan's girlfriend for the rest of high school. That wasn't so bad. I was planning on applying to NUS, anyway. That meant I'd only have to keep up this charade for another year or so, and then I'd be out of here. It was a familiar goal, one I'd kept turning to whenever Brandon's fists found their way onto my body. It felt like returning to an old friend. College, where I would finally be free.

I closed my eyes and said, "All right. Fine."

I could do this. I could be patient for a year in exchange for a lifetime of freedom.

logan

Joy has a particular flavor to it—liquid gold, like honey champagne. It bubbled through my veins when Delilah finally saw sense in what I was proposing and agreed to give us a go. I wanted to pull her close and kiss her, but no, I'd already promised I wouldn't make her do anything she didn't want to do, and I was a man of my word.

"This calls for a celebration," I said.

"No parties," Delilah said, rather snappishly, I thought, but I let it slide.

"I wasn't going to suggest a party." She wasn't ready to go to parties with me, which was fine. Parties were so impersonal. "I'm going to cook for you and your mom."

She goggled at me. "Why?"

"Would you rather we go to Freddy's instead?"

Freddy's was the local diner. It used to be your typical diner—metal and faux leather booths, greasy burgers and soggy fries, '50s music. But it was recently bought by some wealthy hipster and now it was all gentrified. The booths were ripped out and switched to boxy wooden chairs, the walls were bare brick, the menu was written on a giant chalkboard behind the bar, and the drinks came in mason jars. The place became an overnight sensation. Every other Draycott kid had been in there and taken a selfie under the naked light bulbs and hashtagged the pictures with #freddysdraycott. We were bound to run into people we knew.

Delilah gave me a death glare. "No, I would not." She took a deep breath and unclenched her fists. "Fine, you can cook for me and my mom. But you are leaving right after dinner. I have a ton of homework."

"Deal," I said and held out my hand for her.

She glared at it like it was a poisonous snake waiting to strike. I cocked my head to one side and raised an eyebrow. She shuddered as she put her hand on top of mine, which made me laugh again. Who would have known Delilah would have such a taste for theatrics? Honestly, I would probably be slightly disappointed if she wasn't fighting me so hard. I loved scrappy, feisty Delilah.

"You know, if you supposedly care for me, you shouldn't enjoy my suffering," she said as we walked inside the store.

"I'm not. I'm just laughing at how stubborn you are."

Delilah snatched her hand out of mine and grabbed a basket before I could comment. "Sorry, can't hold hands because basket," she said, waving it around with both hands.

"I'll carry that." I caught one of the handles and held tight when she predictably tried to yank it back.

"Fine." She reached for another basket, but I stopped her.

"We only need one."

We stood there glaring at each other, neither one of us willing to let go of the basket, until someone cleared his throat. It was an elderly man.

"You kids mind getting out of the way?" he asked.

Delilah flushed and stepped back, and I took the chance to claim the basket. When I offered her my free hand, she took it without comment. Thus began the most delightfully infuriating grocery shopping I had ever done.

"What are you going to make for me and my mom tonight?"

I grinned at her. "My signature pasta dish."

"I hate pasta."

Oh, Delilah. "Oookay. I'll make my famous spicy garlic pork instead, then."

"I hate pork," she snapped.

"I can make it with chicken."

"I hate chicken."

I almost laughed out loud then. God, she was so feisty. "What do you not hate?"

"Food that isn't cooked by my stalker."

"Pasta it is."

She scowled but didn't say anything.

Despite Delilah's insistence on being contrarian, I noticed after the first couple of aisles, we fell into an easy step with each other. Her hand was no longer curled up tight in mine, as if to ensure minimal skin contact. Instead, it hung nicely loose, like holding each other's hands was the most natural thing in the world. I had to bite the inside of my cheek to stop the huge grin from taking over my face.

I paused at the cookie aisle. "One of my vices," I said.

She shrugged and scanned the shelves. I pointed at a box of chocolate-flavored rabbit cookies.

"Ever tried these?" I asked.

A long-suffering sigh. "No."

"You're going to love them." I popped a box in our basket. *Our* basket! "I started eating these because of Jade Rabbit."

Delilah actually sneered at me, which made me love her even more. "What's that, like some Asian fetish version of Jessica Rabbit?"

"What? No!" My eyebrows were up. "You've really never heard of Jade Rabbit?"

Another shrug.

"Jade Rabbit is—was—China's moon rover. It was launched in...um, twenty thirteen or twenty fourteen or something, and it was supposed to explore the moon. They named it after Chang'e's pet rabbit."

Delilah stopped scowling. "I grew up listening to stories about Chang'e," she said, and for the first time, her voice didn't have any barbs.

"You'll have to tell me about Chang'e sometime. Jade Rabbit landed successfully and everything seemed fine, but then it turns out it couldn't go into its dormant state, which it needed to do to survive the super-cold lunar nights. Its machines started to break down, and China could no longer control its movements. Basically, Jade Rabbit was slowly freezing to death. But the worst and best part was that Jade Rabbit started tweeting about its oncoming demise," I said.

"The rover tweeted?" Delilah arched her eyebrows.

"Well, some people in charge of Jade Rabbit's social media accounts tweeted. But the tweets were amazing. I actually saved them, just 'cause I loved them so much. Hang on..." I took my phone out and located them. I cleared my throat. "'*Although I should've gone to bed this morning, my masters discovered something abnormal with my mechanical control system. My masters are staying up all night working for a solution. I heard their eyes are looking more like my red rabbit eyes. Nevertheless, I'm aware that I might not survive this lunar night.*'"

Delilah looked the way I felt when I first read Jade Rabbit's message, like she was being pulled between laughter and tears.

"Just like any other hero, I've only encountered a little problem while on my own adventure. Good night, planet Earth. Good night, humanity." My voice trembled a little at the end, but I could be forgiven for that; no one could possibly read Jade Rabbit's dying message the whole way through without getting a little wobbly.

Delilah looked at me like she was finding a whole new way of thinking of me, because none of the old ways worked, and she had to shift her whole perspective. Something jumped in my stomach, sending warmth shooting through my chest. She must've seen it, she must have felt it in my voice, in my story; the beauty of *us*.

"Dee—"

"That was the stupidest shit I've ever heard," she said flatly, grabbing a box of Goldfish crackers.

I shook my head, and god, I loved what an asshole Delilah could be. I couldn't wait to laugh about this with her months down the road. I'd pull her close and remind her what an absolute brat she was to me in the early days and she'd grin and tell me it was worth it, and then our lips would meet in a kiss as hungry and sweet as the kiss we had after our first date.

Back in the car, Delilah retreated once more into a shell. I didn't push her. We had all the time in the world, and the silence wasn't entirely uncompanionable. When I pulled up in front of her house, she started to open her door then stopped with a sharp intake of breath. She stared out the windshield, her mouth slightly open, her face pale.

"What is it?" I asked.

She pointed to a car parked on the curb across the street. "That's Mendez's car. Brandon's ex-partner," she added when I didn't reply.

"I take it she doesn't often drop by unannounced?"

Delilah clenched her jaw. "Not before he died. Now she likes to drop by with doughnuts and all these questions about Brandon—" She swallowed and looked at me, her eyebrows knitted together. "What if she suspects something about Brandon's death? He was always complaining about how she could never leave things alone. What if she's been digging and she knows—"

"Hey, calm down," I said, taking her hand. Delilah was so scared about Mendez, she didn't even recoil at my touch. "I won't let anything bad happen to you."

Her eyes narrowed, and the curl appeared again in her upper lip. "Right, my seventeen-year-old stalker is going to protect me from the big bad cop."

"Dee—"

"Whatever, it's fine. I'll be fine." She took a deep breath. "All right. I'm okay. Let's go find out what the hell she knows." She got out of the car and wiped her palms on her jeans.

We walked slowly, the distance from the car to the house stretching impossibly long. Delilah's anxiety was contagious;

I half expected cops to jump out of the bushes and pounce on us.

Delilah unlocked the front door and led the way in. "Mom?" she called out.

No answer. She turned back to me and shrugged, closing the door. "Maybe I was wrong, maybe that wasn't Detective Mendez's—"

As though the very mention of Mendez summoned her, there was a knock on the door. We stared at each other, then Delilah frantically motioned at me to hide in the kitchen.

"Why?" I mouthed.

"Just go!" she hissed. She watched as I left and hid behind a corner. Once I was out of sight from the front door, she took a deep breath, brushed down her top, and plastered a halfway-decent smile onto her face. I slunk behind the wall so I wouldn't be seen.

"Detective Mendez, hi," Delilah said.

"Hi, Delilah."

A slight pause, then Delilah said, "Can I help you with anything?" the same time Detective Mendez said, "Is your mom in?"

"She's still at work," Delilah said.

"Right. Well, that's okay. I'd like to speak with you, actually."

The note of fear was sharp in Delilah's answer. "Me?"

I closed my eyes. Her voice came out too high, brittle with fear.

"Yeah, we got a call earlier today claiming that Brandon's death wasn't an accident, and I was in the neighborhood, so I thought I'd stop by, see if you might have heard anything..." Detective Mendez's voice trailed off. It was an old trick that begged the person you were questioning to fill up the silence.

Delilah fell for it. "Oh, wow. Do you know who made the call?"

My hands tightened into fists. I hated having to listen to my Delilah being tricked into making mistakes like this.

"That's not for me to disclose." Meaning she didn't know. I breathed a sigh of relief. "Do you have any idea who might have done anything to Brandon?"

"Well, he was your partner. Your guess is as good as mine."

I rolled my eyes to the ceiling, squeezing my pendant with frustration. Now Delilah sounded defensive. She was really bad at this. Was it just me, or was her distaste for Brandon painfully obvious? If she revealed Brandon had been abusive, Detective Mendez would know Delilah had a strong motive for killing him, and from there, it wouldn't take long at all for her to piece together what happened.

"Did he tell you what he was working on before the accident?" asked Mendez.

Silence. I could only assume Delilah either nodded or shook her head in answer.

"You were here the day he was killed, right?" Mendez pressed.

"I—yes. I was upstairs. I've told the cops everything—"

I closed my eyes. Come on, Dee. She was too rattled, too defensive. I could see the hole she was digging for herself. It was a deep one.

"Do you recognize this?" Mendez said, taking out a photograph from her back pocket. From my vantage point, I couldn't tell what it was, but Delilah's face paled visibly. "I found it in Brandon's car," Mendez said. "It matches one of the drugs we traced back to Draycott."

"I—I don't do drugs, you can ask—" Delilah squeaked.

"I know, Dee, you're a good kid," Mendez said. "Tell me, what do you know about what Brandon was looking into before he died? I think you know something."

Delilah opened and closed her mouth, but nothing came out.

"Let's go over the day of the accident again. Did you see or hear anything before you came down to the garage? Anything out of the ordinary?"

I didn't think twice before stepping out from the kitchen. "Hey, do you have any oregan—oh, sorry, am I interrupting something?"

Delilah glared at me like a caged tiger, frightened and angry. Probably wondering what the hell I was doing, why I was out here. Probably thought I'd make things worse. I ignored her and walked up to Detective Mendez and shook her hand.

"I'm Logan. I'm Delilah's boyfriend." Delilah's boyfriend.

The title slipped out as easily as an eel wriggling out of a fisherman's grip. So natural, the way it rolled off my tongue, as though I'd always been her boyfriend.

"I didn't know you were dating somebody," Detective Mendez said to Delilah.

Delilah schooled her expression into a smile. Good girl.

"We're keeping our relationship on the down low," I said. "Nobody else knows we've been dating for months. Detective Jackson—was—kinda protective, so…"

"Gotcha," Detective Mendez said. "Well, it was nice meeting you, Logan. Would you mind giving me a minute with Delilah?"

"Sure." I turned around then stopped. "Actually, I sorta overheard your last question and, uh, we didn't wanna get in trouble with our parents, but…" I glanced at Delilah. "I think we should tell her, Dee." Sincere, that was what I was going for. Sincerity, tinged by the slightest bit of hesitation, the way any teen would feel.

"Tell me what?" Mendez said.

I ignored Delilah's frantic, confused face and said, "The day Detective Jackson died, I was upstairs with Delilah. She'd let me in the night before, and we were, uh, you know, um, messing around—"

Understanding dawned on Delilah's face the same time it did on Detective Mendez's. Mendez turned to Delilah and said, "Is this true?"

Delilah nodded. "I was scared, I didn't want to tell anyone because I'd get in so much trouble, and with Mom going through so much already, I didn't want to tell her I was upstairs with a guy. I kept thinking, Brandon would have a fit. I mean, I know that makes zero sense because he's, you know, gone, but still." She lowered her head. "I'm really sorry about lying."

Detective Mendez gave us both a kind smile. "Don't worry about it. I know what it's like to be young and in love."

To her credit, Delilah managed not to look revolted at the L word. She merely simpered at the detective and took my hand in hers.

Joy pounded through my veins. We were holding hands because she wanted to, and now it was no longer her against the cop, it was Us against the cop.

"This means you were here at the house during the time of the accident," Detective Mendez said, and now her attention was completely on me.

It was unnerving, to be under that stare. Detective Mendez wasn't the type to pluck her brows into delicate arches; they sat atop her eyes like two fat, angry caterpillars.

"Yeah," I said, after a half beat.

"When did you leave?" she asked, and suddenly her notebook was out of her pocket. Then came her pen, shining like a little sword.

I shuffled through my memory of that day, when I'd hid

in my usual spot, deep in the backyard, my camera aimed through the gaping back door of the garage. When would have been a good time to leave?

"About eleven, I think?" Delilah said, coming to my rescue, what a champ, what a perfect girlfriend she was. "Brandon called for—" She paused, stumbled.

I didn't understand why Delilah halted, why she looked like she could burst into tears, but Detective Mendez did.

"Brandon called for you?" she said, the two caterpillars now trained on Delilah. "Didn't you say you went down to see if he wanted anything from the supermarket and found him that way?" *That way*. Even now, even when she was homing in for the kill, Detective Mendez was well-mannered enough to say "that way" instead of dead.

"Yeah, well, it took quite a while for Dee to get downstairs, because we had to, you know, get dressed and stuff, and then she snuck me out, and the accident probably happened then," I said.

"I'm so sorry for not telling the truth," Delilah said, and if I didn't know any better, I would've believed her. Everything about her was steeped in regret—her eyes shiny with tears, her mouth twisted with sadness, her voice wavering but brave. "I can't stop thinking about it. At night I lie in bed and I ask myself, 'If I'd come down sooner, could I have stopped it? Could I have helped? If I'd learned more about cars and jacks and all that stuff, maybe I could've lifted it, maybe…'"

I pulled Delilah close, rubbing my hand up and down her arm soothingly.

"Hey, no, don't do that to yourself," Detective Mendez said, all sympathy now. "It's no one's fault. It was an old jack, and Brandon hadn't maintained it well. There was nothing you could've done."

Delilah nodded, taking a deep breath.

"Well, it was probably just a prank call," Detective Mendez said.

"People do that? To cops?" Delilah asked, her voice tinged with anger. "About someone who died?"

"All the time," Detective Mendez said. "Normally I wouldn't even be here, but like I said, I was in the area and I thought I'd drop by, see how you and your mom are doing."

"Thank you," Delilah said. "That's really nice of you." She sounded like she meant it.

"All right, I should get back to the station. You kids stay out of trouble now." She gave us a quick smile and strolled back toward her car, giving the garage a couple of glances along the way.

Once the door was closed, Delilah snatched her hand out of mine and sagged against the wall. "God," she whispered. Then she turned to face me and I got that jolt again, because her eyes were no longer bright with anger or wide with fear. "You gave me an alibi," she said.

I resisted the urge to hold her hand. *Careful, tread gently, this is new territory.* "I was serious when I told you I love you. I won't ever let anything bad happen to you, even if it means sacrificing myself. Look, Dee, our fates are tied to each other's now. If you go to jail, I go down with you as an accessory. Doesn't that tell you how serious I am about us?"

Curiosity flared in her eyes, another new emotion. "What is it you like about me?"

Careful. This was my chance to really get her to see, to understand why we were meant to be with each other. "You know those old couples who have been together forever? When you ask them how they met, they'd say something like, 'I saw her walking inside the library where I worked and that was it. I knew.' This is exactly like that. I saw you and I knew."

"Well, that's a load of crap," she muttered, but there was no sting in her voice. There was something else, something dawning, wary, but there. A new understanding.

"It's how I feel about you." I took her hand, and she didn't fight it. I could leap to the skies, I was filled with so many bubbles. Delilah had let me save her. All along, she just wanted someone to save her, someone to be on her side. And I'd shown her I was that someone.

"Feelings change."

"Mine won't."

"We're seventeen," she said. "Our feelings change from minute to minute." She wanted to be convinced, to be courted, to not be an easy kill.

"Mine won't," I said, again, pulling her close. I caught a lock of her hair gently, tucked it bchind her ear, and leaned in. My lips brushed her cheek, soft, and I whispered in her ear, "I promise."

CHAPTER THIRTEEN
delilah

As expected, Mom was totally enamored by the dish I insisted on calling Stalketti Carbonara when she wasn't within earshot. Logan had sighed when I came up with the name while he was cooking it, but then he smiled and told me my sense of humor was one of the many things he loved about me. I had given him the finger, then, in the name of humor.

Dinner conversation flowed so easily, I started to forget to be awful toward Logan and had to go to the bathroom and remind myself what a disgusting creep he was. It was incredible; he'd basically shoved himself into my life, but part of me was beginning to actually enjoy his company. Clearly it was a part of me that needed to be strangled and dumped into a vat of toxic waste, but it was still part of me. Maybe it was a "like attracts like" thing. Who was I to judge Logan so harshly, after everything I'd done, everything I was doing?

"Gosh, Logan, you are really spoiling us!" Mom said after she finished her second plate of Stalketti.

I glowered at her.

"You both deserve it, after everything you've been through," he said.

Ugh.

I stood up and started gathering the plates noisily. "Yeah, thanks for cooking, Logan. You should go back to school. Wouldn't want to miss curfew."

"Delilah! Don't be so rude," Mom scolded, but the bite in her words was blunted by all the carbs she'd stuffed in her face. "But I agree, Logan, as much as I love having you around, I don't want you getting in trouble."

"Oh, don't worry about that, ma'am," Logan said. He made a big show of looking at his watch. "Still got another forty minutes before curfew, and I've finished most of my homework."

Mom's eyes widened. "Wow! Dee, this boy is amazing."

Seriously, Mom?

"It's so rare to find someone so well-adjusted. Your parents must be very proud of you," Mom said.

"They're okay, yeah," Logan said, smiling shyly.

This might be what I hated most about all of this. Seeing Logan charm Mom into trusting him, unable to do anything about it. And that tiny, traitorous part of me was falling for it, getting charmed, batting its eyelashes at him and going, *Gosh, isn't he just amazing?*

"All right," I said loudly. "Logan may have finished his homework, but I'm far from finishing mine, so…"

"Okay, hon. I get it." Mom stood up and winked at Logan. "She's been worrying over her grades ever since she decided to apply for early admission to college."

"Early admission?" Logan's voice was totally calm, but I caught the flare in his eyes. Panic pounded through me.

"Yes, to the National University of Singapore. It's her father's alma mater, and—"

"There's no need to bore him with all that stuff, Mom," I said quickly, my heart thumping out a new rhythm so hard, I could feel my fingertips throbbing: *shitshitshitshitshit.*

Logan was nodding his head thoughtfully at me. I could practically read what he was thinking: *gotcha.*

"Pick you up at seven," he said, standing up.

"You don't have to," I said. Still beating the same rhythm: *shitshitshitshit.*

"No, but I want to."

And that tiny part of me fluttered. I tightened my lips into a sexless, matronly smile. "Thanks. See you." As soon as I closed the door, my breath released in a tired exhale. *Shit. He knows about NUS.* I could cry, I really could. It was too much. Everything was too much. But surely even Logan wasn't invested enough to change his entire life plan and move to a foreign country for a girl. Right? There was hope. And I'd prepared so hard for NUS. I'd read up on everything I could find on Singapore, and not even just Singapore, but the entirety of Southeast Asia. Plus, it was my dad's alma mater. I had a better chance of getting in than he did. Things were bad but not catastrophic. I slouched toward the kitchen to start doing the dishes, but I found Mom there, pouring hot water into two mugs. She handed me one when she saw me, and the scent of tea with orange peel wafted out of the mug, sweet and soothing.

Mom gestured at me to take a seat.

"I should go up and get a start on my schoolwork," I said, not quite meeting her eye, not quite able to forgive her for loving Logan so quickly, for not being wary, for failing me yet again.

"I know, this won't take long." She smiled and tucked a stray strand of hair behind my ear. I stopped myself from shuddering at the memory of Logan doing the exact same thing only hours ago. "Sweetie, I have to ask, are things between you and Logan okay? I mean, he seems like a nice boy, but you seem a bit...*off* around him, and admittedly, I haven't been the best judge of men, so I'm asking you now, is everything all right?"

There it was, my chance to open up the door, my chance to let everything spill out of me. Mom would be able to assess the situation and tell me what to do to minimize the damage. My insides pushed at me to do it, to vomit out the truth that had been festering deep inside me. It would be such a relief to get it out. I opened my mouth, the words teetering on the tip of my tongue.

Mom sighed, and suddenly there were tears in her eyes. "I'm sorry, you must think I'm a hypocrite, asking you a question like that when I'm the one who invited Brandon into our lives. You're so much wiser than I am, in many ways, and I should give you more credit."

"That's not—"

"I just—when I think of how stupid I was, letting Brandon move in and run our lives like that…and to think of how he treated us, how he treated you, I—how could I have let that happen? I used to be so strong, Dee. I believed I could do anything."

"You can, Mom," I said. "Look at you, you're a powerhouse at your company—"

Mom snorted. "I'm a woman working in tech. I had no idea how much that was affecting me. I spent years making my skin thick, so all of the comments and snide remarks about how women are ruining tech wouldn't get to me, but… it all adds up. And I was so scared of losing yet another man after your dad…" she said in a broken whisper. "I've failed you, Dee. I should have been strong. I should—I don't know what I was thinking, what happened to me."

"It's not all your fault, Mom," I said, tasting tears at the back of my throat. I'd been angry at her for so long, blaming her for Brandon, but now, I realized I meant what I said. "What Brandon did, it's not on you. He was the perfect gentleman just long enough for us to trust him, and then…"

We lapsed into silence for a few moments, both of us lost in the past. I was reminded of how insidious Brandon's abuse had been, at first. How it didn't feel at all like abuse, how we both mistook it for concern, for love. By the time he raised his hand against us, it was too late. His poison had seeped under our skin, twined itself like roots around our hearts, making us believe in him, believe that the wall of blue would shut us out and protect him. Worst of all, by that time, he had stripped us both of our sense of self-worth, so much so that Mom, who was a grown-ass adult, had been turned into a trembling, watery mess. And me, who knows what he'd turned me into? A broken thing, monstrous—a killer.

Mom gripped her mug white-knuckle tight. "I used to wonder why battered women would stay with their asshole husband or boyfriend. There are so many resources out there. Use them!" She snorted. "I was so ignorant. It never crossed my mind that what Brandon was doing was wrong. I mean, I knew it was wrong, but I didn't think it was enough to report him over, you know? I felt like I was making a fuss over nothing more than a spat. That was what he'd say: 'God, why do you have to make a big deal out of everything?' And part of me even felt like I deserved it. I'd tell myself he was doing it because I was being a bitch—"

The word jolted me, and I snapped, "Mom, you were never a bitch toward him. You were never a bitch to anyone." Using the word alone made me angry. The number of times Brandon had used it against Mom and me, the way it reduced us, the way it was meant to knock the wind out of us. How effective it had been. "It was his way of keeping us obedient."

"I know, and I hate that it worked. I hate that I let it work. And if Brandon hadn't had his accident, who knows how long I would have allowed him to stay in our lives?" Mom shuddered then locked eyes with me, her voice dropping to a whisper. "You know, a large part of me is almost glad that he had that accident." She covered her mouth as soon as she said it, looking somewhat startled, as though she hadn't allowed even herself to think the thought.

I bit my lip, nodding.

Mom sniffled and blew her nose into a kitchen napkin. "Anyway, I wanted to say I'm sorry. I haven't been a good mother, but if you let me, I will try my best to make it up to you."

I put my hand over hers, snotty tissue and all. "We were both pretty messed up after Pa's death." *And only one of us emerged a killer.* "Don't be so hard on yourself."

Mom laughed. "All right. Promise you'll tell me if

anything's wrong? If Logan or any other boy does or says even the slightest thing that makes you feel less than—"

"I will," I said. I couldn't let her carry on. The temptation to break, to reveal everything and shed the load was becoming way too great. "Thanks, Mom." I kissed her on her cheek and went upstairs.

I sat at my desk for the longest time, considering my options. The talk with Mom had refreshed my memory. I had forgotten the subtlety with which Brandon had wormed his way into our minds and hearts. Now, with bitterness, I recalled how I used to find Detective Brandon Jackson charming. I couldn't stop my upper lip from curling into a disgusted sneer at the memory of the three of us laughing together, Brandon putting a meaty arm around my shoulders and giving me a fatherly hug, how good that had felt, his hand on my shoulder so firm and warm, how nice it had been to see Mom's eyes light up after Pa's death. And, to think, I had almost allowed Logan to do the exact same goddamned thing, worm his sick way into my life like Brandon did. I really was the most gullible person alive.

Deep breaths, I reminded myself when my breath became rapid with self-hatred. What do we know about manipulative assholes like Brandon and Logan? They're charming, overflowing with charisma when they put their minds to it. They're like a mind-altering drug; they keep you from thinking clearly. I had to keep reminding myself that whatever he said, Logan didn't truly love me. His version of love was warped, corrupted. And the only reason our first date had been so amazing was because he'd stalked me online and crafted a date based on what he'd discovered.

The thought of Logan trawling the web for information about me was a chilling one. I turned on my laptop and looked through all my social media accounts. I'd never stopped to think about how many accounts I had across platforms, but now I saw the painful truth: I was so exposed, so easy to find, my life so quick to map out. I clicked through Facebook, Twitter, Instagram, Snapchat, Tumblr, Goodreads. Every picture I had up, every post I'd made, now felt tainted, dirty. Logan had read every word, stared at every picture. My finger hovered over the Delete button. I wanted to erase every trace of me that was on the internet.

Instead, I opened up a new tab and did a search for *stalker in love*. I got plenty of hits for some novel, but one of the results was an article on something called *erotomania*. I Googled it, and when I clicked the first hit, my heart clenched in my throat.

Erotomania is a type of delusional disorder where the affected person believes that another person is in love with him or her.

I clicked on *delusional disorder*.

Delusional disorder is a mental illness in which the patient presents delusions. Apart from their delusions, people with DD may continue to socialize and function in a normal manner and their behavior does not necessarily generally seem odd.

A flash of Logan, laughing easily with his friends, none of whom seemed to have an inkling that something was off with him.

I scrolled down to *symptoms.*

The patient expresses an idea or belief with unusual persistence or force.

I recalled the intensity in Logan's eyes as he told me, over and over, that we were meant to be.

That idea appears to have an undue influence on the patient's life.

Him following me everywhere. Turning up at the library. Turning up at my house.

Despite his/her profound conviction, there is often a quality of secretiveness.

As far as I was aware, no one else knew about Logan's obsession with me. Everyone else seemed to think we were just a normal couple. And yet he'd been stalking me for weeks, watching, making videos of me...

I scanned the rest of the page, my stomach sinking when I came to the part about treatment and how challenging it was to treat delusional disorders. Could I report Logan to the school admin? Maybe file an anonymous report on how he was harassing a female student?

No. I couldn't take that risk. He'd know it was me. I read through the list of symptoms again.

An attempt to contradict the belief is likely to arouse an inappropriately strong emotional reaction, often with irritability and hostility.

What if he were confronted by the principal and reacted badly? What if he told her the truth about me? And what was worse, did he know all of my secrets? Did he know that killing Brandon wasn't my only secret? That I had another one, which was perhaps just as bad, if not worse than that?

Did he know I was Draycott's drug dealer?

The thought of it made me ill. No one, not even Aisha, would ever think me capable of such a thing.

I'd known, when Lisa first approached me, that the new job was bad news. But the legit librarian job wasn't paying much, and with Brandon around, I'd needed all the money I could get. I needed to save every cent to ensure I could get out of the house once school was over, instead of being beholden to Brandon. He'd taken over Mom's finances by then, and he'd started grumbling about how expensive college would be, which terrified me. I needed a way to survive, and Lisa had offered that. And, like Lisa had pointed out, drugs were already part of Draycott life. Part of the scenery. It wasn't like I would be creating them. She just needed help sorting out the inventory. Just a...a desk person. Inconsequential. With or without my help, the business would continue to tick over in the background. Without me, the students of Draycott would still get their manicured fingers on drugs some other way.

Then she'd told me I was the best worker she'd ever had and offered me a raise for more responsibilities, and all I could think of was college and getting as far away from Brandon as I could...

If Logan knew—

No. I couldn't think of that right now. He didn't know. He couldn't possibly. Lisa and I had always been so careful. And if he did, he would've told me he had that over my head as well. I had to focus. With a deep breath, I pushed all thoughts of my secret job aside and forced myself to look at the computer screen once more.

This was ridiculous. I was being an armchair psychiatrist.

I had no idea if this was at all relevant to Logan, and even if it was, I couldn't do anything with it.

I closed the tabs and opened my college apps folder instead. Working on college apps always calmed me, all the way back to the dark Brandon Days. I opened up my personal essay. There were four versions of it. I still couldn't decide on how personal NUS wanted me to be. Should I be honest about the latent anger festering deep inside my belly, both at Pa for blowing himself and others up, and at Mom for being so weak? Or should I not mention Pa at all and present myself as another hopeful student with nothing weighing her down? Everything I read said colleges liked to hear that you have overcome some sort of strife in your life, but how much strife was too much?

Out of habit, I turned to my phone and clicked on Aisha's name.

Delilah [9:17 p.m.]:
Hey

I watched the three dots appear in the chat box as Aisha typed a reply. It took forever, the dots disappearing and then reappearing, before she finally replied with a single: **Hey.**

Delilah [9:20 p.m.]:
What's up?

Aisha [9:21 p.m.]:
Not much. Homework. U?

Delilah [9:21 p.m.]:
Same

Aisha [9:22 p.m.]:
So...what's going on with you and Logan?

Now it was my turn to type and delete and retype a message. What should I say to her?

Delilah [9:24 p.m.]:
We're just hanging out.

My phone rang with a call from Aisha. I quickly hit answer and smiled when her face filled my screen. "Hey, Aish—"

"'We're just hanging out'?" she demanded.

"What?"

"How long have we known each other, Dee? Nine years? Ten? This is your first ever boyfriend and all you tell me is that you're 'just hanging out'? This is bullshit."

I blanched. "I'm sorry, I don't know what else to tell you, I—"

"How about details like how your date went, and all

the usual stuff about, I don't know, like shouldn't you be squealing and giggling and telling your best friend every goddamn thing?"

"I—yeah, of course."

"Okay, so start with the date. Tell me everything."

I gaped at her as my disastrous first date with Logan flashed through my mind. The way he'd told me he loved me. The way he'd brandished his phone at me, showing me that video. How dirty I'd felt for kissing him. A lump formed in my throat. "It was—um, it was okay."

Aisha merely shook her head at me, hurt showing clearly on her face. "Whatever, Dee."

"Aisha, wait—"

She hung up, and my phone screen went dark. I tried calling back several times, but each time, the call was rejected.

I flung my phone onto my bed and flopped down in front of the computer again. Thanks to Logan, my best friend was no longer talking to me. I massaged my temples. Admittedly, it didn't sound that bad when I put it that way. In fact, it sounded trivial, ridiculously childish. I couldn't even bring myself to feel too bad about it. Once I left for NUS, what were the chances Aisha and I would keep in touch?

The thought of that kept me from losing it and bursting into tears the rest of the night. Instead, I busied myself by doing work inventory. I went through everything carefully, making sure the spreadsheet was flawless before arranging our next deliveries. Lisa was going to be so pleased. By the end of it, I felt somewhat better. I was a hard worker, not brilliant, but scrupulous. I would be okay. I'd leave all of this behind, make new friends, build a brand-new life where no one knew me or this mess I called home.

In the morning, I grumpily got into Logan's car and glared when he said, "Guess what?"

"It's too early in the morning to play a guessing game with my blackmailer," I snapped.

Logan laughed and started the car. "Not a morning person, I see. All right, well, I'm applying for early admission to NUS."

I considered strangling him then and there. Already I could feel his neck muscles giving way under my fingers, hear the satisfying crack of his neck snapping.

Who was I kidding? I wouldn't be able to pull it off. He was taller and stronger. He'd probably laugh and tell me to stop tickling him. Maybe I could stab him? If only I had the foresight to walk around with a knife on me. I looked at his handsome face and wondered if I could gouge out his eyes with my thumbs. I would relish the feel of his eyeballs squelching against my thumbs, hear his shrieks as I stabbed all the way through to his brain.

"It'll be great," he was saying as he drove. "Have you ever visited the campus? My mom said it's really big, and very high-tech, of course."

He said it all casually, in the tones one might say, "I'll have a double cheeseburger, hold the pickles."

"Your mom was there?" My head whirled. "What for?"

He gave me a smile that was condescending as hell. "Oh, Dee. You've forgotten? I told you before, she works at Duke, remember? She's one of the people overseeing the Duke-NUS program. She'll be able to put in a good word for us."

A good word for us. I didn't miss the little hint, that snide reminder: there will be a reward at the end, Dee, but only if you behave like a good little dog, only if there's still an us at the end.

"Isn't this great?" he said. "I mean, I can't guarantee that we'll get in, but every little bit helps, right? It is NUS, after all. Competition is tough." He slid into a parking space smoothly. The move represented everything about Logan's life. Everything he did went smoothly.

The rest of my life played before me like a silent movie, the scenes going clack-clack-clack. There I am with Logan, flying to Singapore. There we are, taking a cab to campus, fanning ourselves in a constant battle against the tropical weather. There I am, coming out of class, and there's Logan, waiting outside for me, what a sweet boyfriend. There's Logan, charming my Singaporean relatives. What a catch, they say, so handsome and sweet. There I am, begging Logan to let me go, to end this farce, and there he is, explaining to me kindly, slowly, like I am a child, that we are meant to be.

I felt it again, the out-of-body sensation that took over right before I tripped Brandon's jack. Rage flooded through me. My hand shot out like a snake and grabbed Logan's sleeve.

"No!" I cried. "Logan, this isn't a game, okay? It's my life! My fucking life!"

He looked shocked and more than a little hurt, like my outburst was a complete surprise. "Dee, you're not thinking clearly—"

"Don't tell me what to think! You're not coming to Singapore with me, Logan. You're not. I don't love you, Logan. Get that through your head. In fact, I fucking hate you. I can't stand looking at your face, knowing what you've done."

He started to say something and stopped. The surprise melted away from his face and was replaced with something else. His mouth turned into a thin line, his jaw tightened. Beneath my hand, his arm muscles knotted, turned hard as granite. And suddenly, I was afraid.

Belatedly, I recalled what I'd read last night. *An attempt to contradict the belief is likely to arouse an inappropriately strong emotional reaction, often with irritability and hostility.*

"Dee, this is so disappointing," he said, and there was no warmth in his voice. He looked at me like I was a broken toy. "You don't mean that, do you?"

I snatched my hand back, or tried to anyway. Logan caught it and squeezed. Hard.

"Logan, you're hurting me—"

He didn't let go. "Why is it so difficult for you to get that we're soul mates? I'm only trying to protect you. The world is so dangerous. I would do anything to keep you safe. Anything."

I tasted fear, sharp and metallic. A familiar taste.

"If I can't be around to protect you, I'd have to—well, I don't know what I'd have to do. I can't lose you, Dee. I'd have to save you from yourself."

Bile boiled its way up my throat. "What do you mean, save me from myself?"

—arouse an inappropriately strong emotional reaction—

"Dee, you don't get it. I have to be around to protect you. You're so incredible, so luminous. You're perfect. You're like this...priceless work of art. It's my job to make sure nobody, not even you, can ruin this perfection."

I opened and closed my mouth. "You're saying if you can't have me, no one else can?" I whispered.

"Let's not find out, okay?" he said pleadingly, like he really thought he didn't have any other choice.

I wish I could say I punched him in the face or did something equally badass, but I was frozen in place. Brandon had been dangerous, but his brand of danger was at least predictable; after a while, you learned which things would piss him off and avoided doing them. Logan was different. He was completely, wholly volatile. And he might actually end up killing me.

CHAPTER FOURTEEN

logan

I paced my room like a caged animal. I was fuming. Boiling, really, thoughts bubbling and popping everywhere. How could Delilah say those things to me? Tell me it was her "fucking life," like I didn't know, like this wasn't *my* fucking life that I was putting on hold just for her. Did she not realize how much I'd done for her? How much I'd lost? She didn't get it, she didn't understand just how dangerous the world was, how many predators there were, how many sickos just waiting around the corner for the right target before they pounced. She didn't understand that I was put in this world to protect her, like those guards protecting the Mona Lisa.

How could I make her see that? How?

Pain exploded from my hand, and I realized that I'd just

slammed my fist into the wall. "Shit!" I gripped my fist with my other hand and hopped around in pain. Jesus, it felt like I'd broken all of the bones in my hand. I practically bit through my lower lip as I fought the urge to shriek like a baby.

After what seemed like an eternity, the pain abated enough for me to draw in a few short breaths. I held up my trembling hand and surveyed it, prodding at it gingerly to make sure nothing was broken. The knuckles were split and bleeding, but aside from that, I was pretty sure the bones were still intact. I breathed hard. I'd lost control there. Not good, Logan. Gotta get a grip. I couldn't afford to lose my shit, not like that. What if I'd done that in front of Delilah? It would scare her so badly, she'd never ever be able to trust me. And I couldn't have that. I needed her to see that I was good for her.

But I couldn't stay in my room and do nothing either. I had to—

Had to what? What else was left for me to do? Why did she keep fighting me? Fighting us? The anger simmered again, but before it could come up to another boil, I jumped up, grabbed my hoodie, and strode out of the room. It was dark outside, the air cool and pleasant. I broke into a run. It felt good to run like this, to feel the ground being pounded by my feet, miles being eaten up by my strides. My lungs were bursting, my calves burning in the best possible way, but best of all, my thoughts were finally, blessedly silent. No more whispers at the edge of my hearing, telling me I was doing everything wrong with Dee, that she would never love me back. In fact, I wasn't even thinking about Dee at all, which was amazing. The past few weeks, life had been about Dee this and Dee that, and though I felt a bit guilty to admit it, it was refreshing to not be so hung up on her. Maybe I was getting a tiny bit obsessed, maybe I shouldn't—

I slowed to a walk to catch my breath and stopped short, looking around me with wide eyes. Oh, shit.

I was around the corner from Dee's house.

Come *on*, subconscious. Just when I was congratulating myself for taking a healthy distance from Dee. Dee, who didn't appreciate how much I'd done for her. Dee, who would most definitely lose her shit if she found me here. How the hell did I get here, anyway? I tried to sift through the last few minutes. I'd been on such an endorphin high thanks to the sprint, I'd reached a meditative state where I wasn't really aware of my surroundings. But my feet still carried me closer, to the back of the house, to a low fence that would be easy to climb over. But I should go.

I was very definitely about to make my way home when a light from inside the house caught my eye. I couldn't help myself. I scaled the fence to investigate. I walked closer to the side of the house, making sure to keep away from any windows, and peeped inside. My heart was beating so fast. I'd never been in here, not like this. Someone moved into view, and I froze. It was her. My vitamin Dee. God, she was beautiful.

She was carrying a bowl of food with chopsticks and a spoon stuck in. Her mom followed behind with her own bowl. I loved everything about Dee and her mom. They didn't bother with frills like setting the table. I watched as Dee tied her hair back so she could slurp her noodles without any strands getting in the way. I watched the way she made her mom laugh without even trying.

Then I inched away but not toward the gate. I went around the corner, and there I hit the jackpot: there was a wall trellis at the back of the house that went all the way up to the second floor. My blood roared in my ears. Surely this was an invitation. Fate was telling me I should take this chance. Climb up. Go inside. Which I shouldn't do...

And yet, I found myself doing exactly that, praying that the wood trellis would be enough to hold my weight as I climbed up, and up. Before I knew it, I was at the top, reaching out to pull the nearest window, teeth gritted in anticipation of it creaking. It didn't creak, which surely went to show how I was meant to climb in undetected. With a deep breath, I grabbed the windowsill and heaved myself up. I landed on a bathroom counter and clambered forward until my legs were through. My heart was beating so fast, I felt sick. What if one of them came in here and found me like this, half hanging from the window?

But neither one did, and, soon enough, I was inside Dee's house. No, not just that. I was on the second floor, inside her bathroom. I'd never been upstairs, never been allowed, even though I clearly deserved to come up. Whenever I'd been over to her house, it was always with Dee shooting dirty looks at me and the knowledge that I had to behave a certain way so I wouldn't scare her mom off. Always with that little voice in my head telling me to be careful, to act normal. It was like having to hold my breath. But now I was here—upstairs!—and neither of them knew about it. I was free to really observe without the fear that I was being observed. Above the thudding of my heart, I caught little snippets of her voice, her laugh. I scanned the bathroom counter, looking at the bottles of face cream and toner and other beauty products I didn't recognize. Were they Dee's, or her mom's? I picked up a bottle of moisturizer and opened it. Immediately, my senses were flooded with the image of Dee. This was very definitely hers. The label read: Rose Garden. God, this was so her. I inhaled deeply, closing my eyes.

Footsteps, coming up the stairs.

Everything inside me shattered. Shit, shit! I jumped as noiselessly as I could into the bathtub and hid behind the shower curtain just as the bathroom door swung open.

I didn't dare breathe. Whoever it was came inside and turned on the tap. A second later came the sound of an electric toothbrush being used. I was dying to know if it was Dee or her mom, but I didn't move a single muscle, just stood there with my back against the tiled wall. At least the whir of the toothbrush meant I could draw in little sips of air without the person on the other side hearing.

Please, please be done with the brushing soon. Please. But no. After she brushed her teeth, she started washing her face, lathering for what felt like hours before rinsing. Bottles were picked up, sloshed around, and put down. Cabinets were opened, various products slathered on. This was getting ridiculous. How long could someone's nightly beauty routine possibly take?

Then a terrifying thought struck me: What if the routine included a bath?

What would I do?

The sink turned off. My thoughts cut short in my head, and I waited for the curtain to be yanked aside, for the shriek to come. But instead, the person left the bathroom. I sagged against the wall, my muscles turning into water. God, that had been way too close. I had to get out of here right now. But not without a souvenir. I slipped the bottle of moisturizer into my back pocket and climbed back out the window and down the trellis. Outside, I crept past the house and unlocked the gate. I made sure to wiggle the lock shut behind me; I didn't want some creep to get into Delilah's house. Then I walked briskly away, checking once or twice to make sure no one had followed me.

My heart was singing. I'd just gone up to the second floor of Dee's house. Been in the bathroom at the same time as she was. I knew her nightly beauty routine now. Well, I supposed there was a chance it was her mom's nightly beauty routine, which took the wind out of my sails a little. But still. Then a chill crept down my spine. They were so careless. So fucking clueless about how unsafe their house was. Look how easily I got in, without even breaking anything. I could've been anyone. I could've been a burglar, slinking into the house with a gun, rifling through their stuff while they stood, terrified, at gunpoint. The thought was unbearable. *Oh, Dee. You really should be more careful.*

But it was okay. I was around to protect her. I took out the moisturizer, unscrewed the bottle, and took a deep inhale. Everything would be okay, because I was here, and I was never going to leave her.

delilah

I set my alarm to go off inhumanly early on Saturday. As soon as I'd washed and dressed, I grabbed my wallet and coat and ran all the way to the bus stop, where I paced restlessly until the bus arrived. The rest of the week had been a continuous march of Logan shoving his way into my life. He'd wait outside of my classrooms whenever his classes happened to be nearby and walk me to the library for my shifts whenever he could. Lunches were always spent with him and his friends, whom I couldn't help but like, while Aisha shot me death glares from our usual seat. And even though Lisa squeaked, "How sweet!" whenever she saw Logan, I could tell his presence made her nervous, which in turn made me even angrier. On top of everything else, I couldn't afford to lose my job. On the bright side, at least Detective Mendez had stopped her surprise visits. One could only hope she'd moved on to bigger, more exciting cases.

I came up with half a dozen plans to deal with Logan, each one flimsier than the last. I spent all of my free time trying to look up information on Logan that I could use against him, but I always came up empty.

It surprised me how much I missed Aisha. Seeing her at school and not talking to her was killing me. I needed her now, more than ever.

By the time I got off at Draycott, all of my fingernails had been bitten into ragged stubs. I wrapped my arms around myself as I walked across campus. The atmosphere on a weekend was completely different. This early, the school was off-puttingly silent. When I got to the girls' dorm, I hung around outside, pretending to text someone. I couldn't ask Aisha to let me in since she'd been ignoring my messages. Luckily, a couple of girls wearing running gear came out, laughing over something, and I was able to slip inside before the doors closed.

The first time I visited Aisha's dorm, I'd paused in the foyer, my mouth falling open at how grand the place was. An elaborate chandelier hung in the center of the wood-paneled room, giving the place a soft, rich glow. My footsteps were immediately muffled by a thick, green carpet. Paintings of important women throughout history smiled down at me. I'd never felt so much like an impostor as I did then.

Aisha had taken me to the common room, which was bright and sunny with high ceilings, picture windows, and overstuffed couches and beanbags. We'd hung out there for hours, stuffing ourselves with cookies and hot chocolate and talking about everything and nothing. The memory of that afternoon brought tears rushing into my eyes. I shook my head and hurried up to the second floor. Each room had a whiteboard next to the front door. Aisha's board had a doodle of her licking an ice cream cone. I knocked on the door.

There was some muffled sound and then silence. I knocked again.

"Aisha, I know you're there. Open up."

A bump, then footsteps. The door was wrenched open, revealing a half-awake Aisha, grumpy with sleep, wearing her blanket like a cloak. She peered at me and scowled. "What're you doing here?"

Tears rushed into my eyes. I hadn't realized how much I'd missed her. "I need to talk to you. Please?"

I could see she wanted to snap at me, but she must have sensed my desperation, because she hesitated, started to say something again, hesitated again. Then she sighed, swung the door wide open, and cocked her head at me. "What're you gawking at? Get in."

And I burst into tears.

Later, forever later, or maybe minutes later, we both sat on the floor, leaning against Aisha's bed. I had a mug of hot chocolate cradled in my hands and Aisha's arm around my shoulders, and I had never felt so comforted.

"You know what you need right now?" Aisha said. "Breakfast."

I lifted my mug of hot chocolate. "I already have this."

Aisha sniffed. "Please, those instant cocoa mixes are basically corn starch and sugar. Gimme that." She plucked the mug out of my hands. "Come on. We're going to Liberica. My treat."

I was about to protest when it hit me that breakfast actually sounded good. Now that I'd cried myself empty, I was too exhausted to even begin to tell Aisha what had happened. Liberica's breakfasts—which featured stacks of pancakes so big, the edges flopped over the sides of the plates and breakfast burritos the size of my calves—were just the thing I needed to jump-start the conversation. The whole way there, Aisha linked arms with me, like old times, and filled me in on the latest gossip, as though she knew I wasn't quite ready to share what had happened.

Half an hour later, we were seated at a table loaded with a ridiculous amount of food. How do you reveal to your BFF that you crushed your mother's boyfriend with his car and you were now being coerced into dating some creepy stalker who'd caught the whole thing on camera? Being made to date Logan sounded so absurd when I went over it in my head. Yeah, I'm being forced into dating one of the hottest guys in school. Part of me was convinced if anyone knew, they'd roll their eyes and go, "Oh, poor you. You have to go out with Hot Logan, a guy you were lusting over, who has promised not to touch you unless you want him to. Let me play you a sad song on the world's smallest violin."

"Oh, man, I needed this," Aisha said, stuffing a heaping forkful of pumpkin and candied pecan pancake into her mouth before chasing it down with a gulp of red velvet Oreo milkshake. "The food at school is bullshit. Know what we were served for dinner last night?" She didn't wait for me to guess. "Organic microgreens with a side of free-range chicken breast. Sans hormones, sans chemicals, sans flavor. I don't even know what their deal is with microgreens. Does being micro somehow make it better for you or something?"

"The food at lunch isn't that bad," I said, laughing.

"That's 'cause the boarders pay a lot more than day students do, so the school thinks it should save up all the pretentious food for dinner. You got lucky, my friend." She attacked the burrito and crammed what looked like a fistful of it into her mouth.

As the carbs and sugar hit us, the conversation flowed faster, easier. We complained about our classes, bitched and laughed about our classmates, and chatted about the latest celebrity scandals. I felt almost like my old self again, pre-Logan, pre-Brandon, even pre-Pa.

Aisha dropped her fork on the plate and leaned back,

groaning. "Ugh. I ate too much again. Why didn't you stop me?" She pushed the plate toward me. "Argh, get this away from me. I can't even look at food right now."

"Want me to get them to clear the table?"

"No! I might want some more."

I laughed.

"You love me."

"Yeah, yeah." I rolled my eyes, but I was still grinning.

"So." Aisha leaned forward, her face suddenly turning serious. "Tell me, what happened with Hot Logan?"

The syrupy pancake turned to mealy cement in my mouth. I put my fork down and pushed the plate off to one side. I glanced around the room. The diner was filled with people— townies, tourists, but no one from Draycott, thank god. I guessed it was still too early for students, even with the lure of giant pancakes. Nobody was paying any attention to us. It was time. I had to tell her. I needed somebody on my side. I swallowed, clenched my hands together. "Um, something happened. Something...bad."

Aisha's eyes widened and she straightened up in her seat. "Shit," she muttered. "I didn't think Logan would—shit." She reached out and grabbed my hand. "Dee, I'll be by your side a hundred percent, I swear, no matter how bad it gets. These things... There will always be assholes who blame the victim."

I stared at her. "What are you talking about?"

Aisha scanned the room before whispering, "Did he

force you to do something you didn't want to do? I should've known. I'm so sorry I didn't realize it sooner—"

"What? No! No, it's nothing like that," I cried.

"Oh, thank god." Aisha sighed. "Then what is it? You're acting so weird."

"It's really hard to explain. But, um, Logan has something on me."

"Something on you. A...crush? He has a crush on you?"

"No, something bad. I did something"—my voice cracked, and I had to take a deep breath before continuing— "something really, really bad." The last bit came out in a strangled whisper, my eyes rushing with tears.

For the first time, Aisha didn't make any smart-ass remarks. She only squeezed my hand and nodded, encouraging me to keep going.

"It's really bad, Aisha," I whispered.

"What is it?" she pressed.

"Promise me you'll never tell anyone?"

Aisha nodded furiously, her eyes wide and trusting.

I took a deep breath. "It's a video of me, uh...cheating on the chem test."

Aisha's mouth dropped open. "Whoa. Jesus." She blinked a few times, as though she'd just gotten punched. "Seriously? You cheated on a test? But Dee, you're—" She flapped her arms wildly, gesturing at me. "You're you! You'd never do something like that."

Good grief. If this was how badly she reacted over something like *cheating*, I couldn't even fathom how she'd react if she ever found out the truth. "I was desperate," I cried. "You know what Brandon was doing to me, and I couldn't focus on anything, I was living in fear. And I couldn't afford to flunk it. If I did, Brandon would get so angry."

The expression on Aisha's face melted from shock into sympathy. "Oh, Dee, of course. Yeah, I get it. That was an impossible situation for you." She grabbed my hand. "Okay, what can I do to help?"

Relief rushed through me. I wanted to hug her so tight right now. Instead, I wiped at my eyes, taking a couple deep breaths.

"Anyway, Logan knows about it, and he's kind of—well, not kind of, he is blackmailing me into going out with him."

Aisha gave a bark of laughter, then she saw my expression and stopped abruptly. "Oh. Oh! You're not kidding. Holy shit." She sat back and gazed out the window for a while, tapping on her teeth with a meticulously manicured fingernail. "Wait, but you said he didn't touch you."

"He didn't."

"But he's using this…whatever he has on you, to get you to sleep with him. That's rape."

"No, he's not. He's only using it to be my boyfriend."

"Without sex?" Aisha said, her tone incredulous.

"Yeah. He said all the physical stuff can go at my own

pace." Even as I said it, I realized how ridiculous it sounded. My cheeks reddened.

"Huh. That's weird. So he just wants to be your boyfriend, but without benefits. Why? He's hot and rich. He could get any girl he wanted. I mean, no offense, you know I love you and I think you look great, but..."

"I know! He says he's in love with me, but we barely know each other!"

"Aww," Aisha said, twirling a lock of hair.

"Aisha!" I wailed.

"Okay, okay, not 'aww'. Okay. Seriously, that is some weird shit." Aisha went still for a second and then suddenly gasped. "Oh my god! That explains the weird-ass conversation I had with him!"

"What conversation?" I asked, my skin prickling.

"The other day I ran into Logan and he was like, 'Yo, Aisha, how's it going?' and we started chatting, and then he asked which colleges you and I are planning to apply to, and I thought it was really sweet that he was so interested and—" Aisha took a sharp inhale and bit her lip. "I told him all of your college choices." Her face was twisted now. "Shit, I'm so sorry, Dee, I—"

"It's okay, you couldn't have known," I said. All the food I'd just eaten sat heavily in my stomach. I wanted to throw up. The past few days, I'd been surviving, consoling myself with the thought that I could simply go to some other college.

I didn't have to go to NUS. I liked Berkeley, I loved the green-ery, the way it was tucked in between the hills in an off-beat city full of vegan restaurants and graffitied walls. Push came to shove, I could give NUS up. But now, as it turned out, not only did Logan know about NUS, he knew all of the schools I'd listed as my backups. "I think he has this condition called *delusional disorder*." I gave Aisha a quick rundown on the symptoms.

"Okay…" Aisha said. "That means you can report him, right?"

"No! He has something on me, remember?"

"What if I made the report? Like, say I noticed something off about his behavior and went to the school counselor 'cause I'm a good citizen… Would that work?"

Would it? I toyed with the idea for about a second before I immediately shut it down. Too risky. Who knew how Logan would react? What if he somehow linked it back to me? I shuddered at the thought.

"If it makes you feel any better, it's not you. It's him," Aisha said.

"What do you mean?"

"It's not the first time Logan's become obsessed over a girl. When we were freshmen, he was totally in love with this junior. He followed her around like a little dog. She thought it was funny. We all thought it was harmless."

Ice prickled down the length of my body. "Was it Sophie?"

"Yeah," Aisha said, straightening up. "You know about her?"

"Sort of. I'm fuzzy on the details."

"Nobody really knows what happened. All I know is she was expelled and then she died."

For a second, my mind crystallized into something solid and jagged. "She—died?" I choked out. "Did someone—"

Aisha shook her head. "No! Sorry, I should've been clearer. She killed herself. I guess she couldn't handle getting expelled. She got all messed up on drugs and then overdosed."

Overdosed? My stomach turned. Lisa had told me about an old assistant of hers who'd started sampling the product and gotten addicted. She'd fired the girl immediately. "Never, ever sample the product," Lisa had said, her eyes drilling into mine, and I'd nodded. Now I wondered if Sophie was that girl.

"How did Logan react?"

"How do you think he reacted? He was super in love with her. He had to go on antidepressants or something, but people didn't really pay much attention to him 'cause that year was like, bonkers."

I nodded. "I heard about the mess with the teacher and the cops. Brandon mentioned it before—um, before, you know. He said there was a lot going on at school, like really shady stuff."

"Right, so when Sophie died, no one really noticed Logan or anything, and he went off the deep end. He was so broken."

Despite myself, a tiny part of me ached at the thought of Logan, mourning the death of the girl he loved all alone, while all around him, his peers chattered excitedly about the latest scandal. If Sophie hadn't died, would he have won her heart in the end? Or maybe she would've gone to college, leaving him to get over her gently. And then maybe he wouldn't be in my life at all, and my biggest worry at this moment would be normal school stuff instead of how to get rid of my blackmailer.

"And he hasn't gone out with any other girl since Sophie?" I said.

"Not that I know of. That's why I was so excited when he asked you out."

"But why me? I don't get it!" I wailed.

"Okay, Whiney McWhinerson," Aisha said. She tilted her head and narrowed her eyes at me. "I never thought of this before, I mean, I was never close to her or anything, but you sort of look like her. I think you do, anyway. I don't know, I've forgotten how she looked, exactly. She was two years my senior."

"He likes me because I remind him of a dead girl," I said flatly.

"How creeptastic," Aisha said, grinning.

"So what do I do? Be as different from her as I can be? I don't even know what she was like."

Aisha took her cell phone out. "Let's do a preliminary

check." She scooted over to sit next to me and paused, her lips pursed. "Is it sick that I'm kind of excited about this?"

"Yes." Although to be perfectly honest, I was also somewhat excited about it. No, excited wasn't the right word. I was filled with a sick sort of anticipation, the way it feels to be at the very top of the roller coaster, right before that stomach-lurching plunge. And when Aisha typed in Sophie's name and called up pictures she'd been tagged in, the fall was so much worse than I'd been expecting.

"Dang, girl," Aisha said.

Yeah, I wanted to say, but I couldn't speak.

Sophie...Sophie was...me.

I'd been prepared to identify Logan's obsession as a fetish, like maybe he thought all Asians looked the same, but holy shit, the resemblance.

Sophie was me, but on my best day, after I'd spent ages applying makeup like a total pro. Her skin poreless and porcelain smooth, her eyes lined in a very wicked, mischievous way, her lips painted into a startling red heart, her hair silky and tousled. Like Aisha so kindly pointed out before, I was nice to look at, but I wasn't what you'd call stunning. Sophie was. Hauntingly so. There was something about her that shone even through the pictures, that made you want to reach out and cling to her. There was an aura, something almost otherworldly about her.

I didn't want to blink as Aisha scrolled through the

pictures. I didn't want to miss a single shot, she was so heart-stoppingly beautiful. She'd been popular; most of the pictures were of her with other people, most of them laughing. A few were selfies—Sophie pouting or smiling, posing with some of her favorite makeup, her favorite perfume. Some of them were candids—not the posed sort of "candid" that featured a carefully angled face looking away from the camera, but actually caught without Sophie knowing about it. In one she was laughing unabashed, her mouth full of half-chewed food. In another, she was calling out to someone in the distance, her hand raised in a wave. She was so full of life.

I realized part of me had expected something that showed death looming over her. Muted pictures with a vintage filter of Sophie looking depressed. But these images showed that, if anything, death had come as a surprise for her.

And, sick as it may sound, looking at these pictures of Sophie was giving me an idea. That maybe what happened to her could be a way out for me.

I shuddered. No. I couldn't possibly do that, not even to someone who was blackmailing me. Not even when he was threatening to ruin my life. Could I?

———

When I came home, I trudged to the kitchen, where last night's dirty dishes were piled up in the sink. Our countertop was filled with trash collected throughout the week—empty wrappers, paper cups, wilted leftovers. Mom was working on a big project, and I hadn't seen her for a while now; by the time she came home, I'd already be in bed.

I still couldn't let go of the idea that had started to form earlier today. An idea that had to do with drugs, and my easy access to them. But the very thought filled me with revulsion. I paced about for a while then decided to at least spend my anxious energy doing something useful.

I grabbed a trash bag and went around the house, picking up all of our crap. Soon, the bag was full, and I lugged it over my shoulder and headed outside.

"Howdy, neighbor!" someone called out from across the street.

Mr. Chan was the only person I knew who actually said the word *howdy*. He was a fifty-year-old man who'd immigrated here from China thirty years ago. He prided himself on watching a ton of old Westerns and southern cooking shows to make himself sound more American. He was always saying stuff like *y'all* and *fixin' to*. It was sweet and heartbreaking at the same time, because all that effort he put into sounding less Asian reminded me of Pa. I had a soft spot for Mr. Chan, and right now, he was the only person who wasn't involved in any way with the train wreck that was my life, which made him a welcome sight for sore eyes.

"Hi, Mr. Chan," I said, walking over to him.

"It's been a while, Dee!" He patted my shoulder affection-
ately. "How you doing, you okay? You shore do look tired."

I bit back my smile at the Southern pronunciation of *sure*.
"I'm okay, I'm coping."

"You're a brave lil' dumpling, you are." Mr. Chan shook
his head and sighed. "It's terrible, what happened to Brandon.
He was a good guy."

I gave him a polite nod and a noncommittal smile. "Yeah."

"Bad way to go, that. Gruesome." He shuddered. "I don't
know why his pardner's so keen on watching it."

The non-smile froze on my face. "Sorry?"

"Yeah, you know, the tall one? Latina, I think? Or maybe
Hawaiian. She could be Hawaiian…"

I wanted to scream at him to focus. "Detective Mendez?"
I said.

"Yeah, that's the one. She came by yesterday, real nice,
she was, and asked if she could get the footage from my
security camera," he said and pointed up at his garage.

The world crumbled under my feet. Mr. Chan had a
fancy-looking security camera mounted on top of his garage
door, pointing in the direction of my house.

"I got a few of these babies after the Underwoods' shed
got broken into last year," he said proudly. "You like it? It's
state-of-the-art, very high-tech, can zoom in real close. The
cop lady was very impressed by it, you know."

"That's—it's very—big," I croaked. "So you can look

right into my garage with that?" Did my voice sound as panicked and close to tears as I felt?

Mr. Chan shrugged. "Who knows? I've never bothered to watch the feed. But the cop lady thought it was worth checking out. What a beauty, eh? I got it fifty percent off because my brother-in-law owns the store—well, he doesn't actually own it, but he's the senior manager—"

I barely heard anything he said. I couldn't tear my eyes off the camera. It seemed to jeer at me with its all-seeing eye.

"Are you okay, hon? You're looking a bit pale," Mr. Chan said. "Wanna come inside? Priya is making chai."

I recovered enough of my senses to shake my head. I blinked at Mr. Chan, my lovely neighbor who'd unwittingly set up my downfall, and it took everything to stop myself from bursting into tears. "I have to go," I managed to say, and then I ran across the street.

Back in the privacy of my own room, I paced about, biting my fingernails ferociously, *shitshitshit, what's going to happen, what do I do, what do I do?* I picked up my phone, scrolled through my contacts—nothing useful. I hurled it at the wall with an animalistic scream. While I spent the past few days worrying about Logan, Mendez had been working on this case, gnawing, digging at every angle. Did she know I was Brandon's killer? Did she suspect that there was a link to the drugs business? Had she put two and two together? Did she realize I was a two-for-one deal—Draycott's dealer and

Brandon's murderer? This was something else, something on an entirely different level. Logan was bad; Mendez getting hold of potential footage of me killing Brandon was catastrophic.

Calm down. Calm. Down!

I dashed down the stairs to the garage. I turned on the lights and paused. This was the first time I'd been in there since the accident. Mom had gotten the floor professionally cleaned, thank god, so there were no stains on it. She'd also gotten rid of the Camaro. In fact, aside from a few of Brandon's old work tools, there were very few signs of Brandon having been in the garage. Still, a wave of nausea rolled over me, and I had to take a few deep breaths before going in. I retraced my steps on the day of the accident and looked out the window. From where I stood, I couldn't see Mr. Chan's camera; it was blocked by a tree. Did that mean his camera wouldn't see me, either?

My heart beat out a desperate, hopeful rhythm as I made my way out of the garage and back across the street. I knocked on Mr. Chan's door and plastered on a neighborly smile when he opened it.

"What's up, Dee?" he asked, his expression mildly bemused.

"Hi, Mr. Chan. Um, I was thinking about your security camera and like, I was thinking of asking Mom to buy a few for our house. I mean, it's just the two of us ever since

Brandon died, and I'd feel a lot safer with cameras around. Can I take a look at the video feed? I just wanna check the resolution."

Mr. Chan beamed with pride. You could tell he'd been dying to share the stuff with anyone who would listen. "Of course! Come on in."

Moments later, I was seated in Mr. Chan's study while he powered up his computer. He'd been talking nonstop about camera specs for the past few minutes. "I can probably get your mom a discount, too. Maybe not as much as the one I got, but you never know!"

"Wow, that's great," I said, doing my best to sound halfway enthused.

"Okay, here we go…" He waved me over and pushed the monitor toward me. "Look at that image quality. Crystal."

"It's very good," I mumbled, my stomach sinking. His camera really was excellent. Everything was shown in high definition, down to the paw prints of some cat that had walked across the pavement before it had completely set. My garage was partly hidden by the tree in front of Mr. Chan's house, but through the gaps between the leaves I could see inside the top garage window.

"Um, could you rewind to like, a few minutes ago?" I said.

Blood roared in my ears as Mr. Chan clicked open a menu. This was it. It would either reveal me as Brandon's killer, or…

The video played. My breath hitched, my eyes glued, unblinking to the screen.

And there I was, on the screen. Or rather, there was the very top of my head.

"Could you zoom in?" I said.

I leaned close as the image enlarged. My face wasn't visible from the vantage point, especially since it was obscured by a tree, but it was clear there was somebody moving around inside the garage. The knot inside my stomach tightened. Mendez would know someone was inside the garage. But maybe this checked out with my story? After all, I'd told them I'd gone down to see if Brandon wanted anything from the store, and then tried to lift the jack…so maybe not all was lost. Except I hadn't run around all panicked like an innocent person probably would. I'd walked slowly toward Brandon, talking to him, and then bent over…

Dimly, I heard myself thanking Mr. Chan for his time. My mind churned nonstop as I walked home, twisting all sorts of different scenarios into shape. So many possibilities, ranging from Mendez completely missing the top of my head (unlikely) to Mendez zooming in endlessly, using some fancy image-enhancing software until she had irrefutable evidence that the person walking around in the garage right before Brandon died was me (more likely).

I was a bone caught between two dogs. If Mendez got her way, I'd be locked up for good. If Logan got his way, I'd be at his beck and call for the rest of my life or at least until he got bored and discarded me for his next obsession. I was nothing more than the passive object of their interests. All that time when Brandon was around, I'd cowered and tiptoed and tried to make myself as tiny as possible so he wouldn't notice me. And I'd hated myself for being so weak, so docile, so power-less. But hadn't I proven I wasn't entirely helpless? Hadn't I shown I had the strength and cunning to take charge? My life was diverging into two of the worst possible outcomes— Mendez or Logan, prison or blackmail. But maybe it was time I forged a change. Maybe it was time I carved out a new path for myself. Mendez was itching for a suspect. Logan was pining for a dead girl. Maybe, if I played it right, I could give them both what they wanted.

PART TWO

girl loses boy

CHAPTER SIXTEEN
delilah

The kitchen was a whirlwind of dirty pots and mixing bowls and flour and cocoa powder and spilled batter. It also smelled heavenly. I carefully crushed a few pills under a spoon and then poured the powder into a mixing bowl with whipped butter and sugar. Buttercream frosting, with a sprinkling of MDMA and Ambien. Just in case Logan might be able to taste the bitterness of the drugs, I heaped two more spoonfuls of powdered sugar and a shot of espresso into the mix before whipping it all up into a light, fluffy mass. The coffee should mask anything suspicious. I'd worked with Lisa long enough to know just how many pills would be enough to have the desired effect.

With any luck, Mom wouldn't wake up until noon, and by the time she came downstairs, the mess would be—

"Baking again, are we?" she said, popping her head around the doorway. She was still in her pj's.

I jumped a little then composed myself and gave her a sheepish grin. "I'm sorry, I'll clean it all up, I promise."

Luckily, Mom was still too sleepy to notice my little jump. "What are you making this time?"

"Rocky Road cupcakes. Marshmallow?" I pushed an open bag of marshmallows across the kitchen island.

Mom poured herself a glass of orange juice and sat down at the counter. "Sounds yummy. What's with the hardcore baking sessions nowadays?"

"I've been watching these cooking videos on Facebook, and some of the recipes look so delish."

"So they have nothing to do with wanting to impress Logan?" she asked, grinning at me.

"Ew, no!" My cheeks grew warm, and I turned to look at the oven so Mom wouldn't be able to see my expression. She'd think I was blushing because I was shy. The truth was, I was turning red because I was practically boiling with rage. I was on a mission, the most important quest that would make or break the rest of my life: I was going to drug Logan, keep him off balance until I could find some way of escaping this nightmare, and my own mother was so clueless she thought I was just doing this to impress my boyfriend. Unbidden, Brandon's voice rose to the surface, like a bubble floating up a dank swamp, bursting, releasing its noxious poison fumes. *Stupid bitch*.

I shook my head, trying to clear it. I shouldn't be angry at Mom. None of this was her fault. Okay, some of it was her fault. But most of it was Logan's. All of my pent-up rage, my cold fury, should be directed at him. I took a deep breath.

Mom laughed. "It's okay to want to do nice things for your boyfriend, Dee. Mmm, they really do smell good."

I turned around in time to see Mom reaching to dip her finger into the frosting bowl. "No!" I leapt across the counter and smacked her hand.

"Ouch! Heeey!" Mom said, frowning and rubbing her hand.

"That one's got peanut butter in it," I said, taking the mixing bowl away from her. "I don't want you to break out in a rash."

"Ugh. What's with all the peanuts you're using in your baking?" Mom grumbled. "Last time it was caramel peanut butter cookies, and then the time before that it was banana peanut butter muffins, and now—"

"I knew you'd say that, which is why I've got a peanut-free batch in the fridge."

Mom brightened up. "Really? Best daughter ever." She pinched my cheek like I was all of two years old and walked out of the kitchen, humming to herself. I didn't want to wait around to have a chat with Mom about baking and impressing the boyfriend I was desperate to get rid of, so once the second batch was out, I washed all the dirty dishes, separated the cupcakes into various Tupperware containers, and zipped out of the house.

On the bus to Draycott, I did what I'd been obsessing over the last few days: I ruminated on how the hell I could get myself free of Logan. Step One was easy: throw him off balance so I could plot the next step. Step Two: um…

I caught a corner of my thumbnail between my teeth and yanked hard, ripping the tip of the nail off. The pain snatched me from my dark thoughts, and I watched the blood welling from my thumb. It made me think of Brandon's blood. I licked it off and squeezed my thumb, watching as more blood trickled out.

Before I knew it, I was at Draycott.

Aisha was still grumpy with sleep when she opened the door to her room. "Why do you always insist on meeting so early?" she grumbled, slouching back in and slumping down on her bed.

"Uh, it's almost noon, and I brought cupcakes." I held up a container of frosting-free cupcakes, and she snatched it from my hands.

She inhaled deeply and sighed. "Mmm, real sugar. Frikkin' Draycott. Everything here's made with agave nectar or some other bullshit healthy sweetener. You know, before I came here, I was whatever about sugar. Now I legit crave it. This place is gonna give me an eating disorder, I swear." She took a big bite and leaned back with a happy grunt. "This is so good, Dee."

"It's just a boxed cake mix. All I had to do was add eggs and oil to the mix."

"That's why it's so good." She ducked, laughing, when I took a swipe at her. Then her expression turned somber, and she leveled her gaze at me. "How're you holding up?"

I sighed. "I don't know. I still don't know how I'm going to get out of this."

"Well," Aisha said, "I've been thinking about it, and you said he has a video he's holding over you. What do you think of breaking into his room and looking for it?"

My mouth dropped open. I was about to tell her that the idea was completely nuts when my mind caught up with my mouth and closed it. Why not? Step Two: find the video of me killing Brandon. Once that was gone, Logan would have nothing to hold over me. And where else would it be if not his room? But the thought of breaking into Logan's room made my stomach twist in a way that stole my breath. "I don't know. How would I even do that?" I may be a drug dealer, but when it came to breaking and entering, I was as clueless as they come. Also, it sounded dangerous as hell. "If I got caught, I'd be expelled—"

"Okay, first of all, I think you mean how would *we* do that."

"Aish, I can't make you do that. It's so dangerous. We could get in so much trouble."

Aisha snorted. "Dude, I've been a model student all my life. I'm dying to break some rules before I graduate. Plus, it's for a good cause. I hate the thought of some asshole guy blackmailing you. Even if he is hot."

I hugged her tight. It felt good to have Aisha on my side. I really didn't deserve her. She and Mom were the only two people keeping me going.

"Okay, okay!" she said, laughing. "Oh, shit, what time is it?" She glanced at her phone and scrambled to her feet. "Crap, I need to go feed Lucy. This feeding day happened to fall on the weekend—total bummer."

"That's what you get for volunteering to feed the bio lab snake," I said.

Aisha sighed. "I thought it would look good on my college apps. I don't know what I was thinking. Anyway, you wanna wait here, or you wanna meet me somewhere?"

"Actually, can I come watch?" I said. Ugh. Why did I just say that? Who the hell wants to watch some poor rat being fed to a snake? But even as I thought that, I realized I did. In a hide-behind-a-cushion-and-squeal sort of way.

Aisha paused in the middle of putting on a pair of jeans and stared at me. "You wanna come watch me feed Lucy? Oookay. Don't blame me when you pass out."

"Asshole," I muttered, elbowing her gently.

Weekends at Draycott gave me an unshakable feeling of being out of place. The vibe was so different—students were in casual wear instead of the gray or blue blazers we were required to wear on schooldays. We walked into Wheeler Hall, and the eerie silence of the inside of the building pressed in on me. Our footsteps rang loudly down the corridor, and I wanted to turn around and run back out into the sunlight but for a small part of me that found itself inexplicably drawn toward the idea of watching Lucy eat.

Aisha unlocked the biology classroom and headed to the back of the room, where the rats were kept. I perched at the edge of a table in front of Lucy's tank and watched as Aisha picked out a large rat—a white male with a black spot on its head. She unlocked a small window at the top of Lucy's cage with practiced efficiency and dropped the rat in without hesitation before brushing her hands off.

"All right, let's go," she said.

My eyes were glued to the tank. The rat had sensed danger and was perfectly still, one front paw slightly raised, haunches rigid.

"Hellooo, earth to Dee," Aisha said, waving her hand in front of my face. "Come on, let's go get lunch."

"Can we stay?" I muttered. The coil of vivid colors was moving. Lucy had sensed prey.

"Uh, who are you and what have you done with my best friend?" Aisha asked.

When I didn't reply, she stepped right in front of me, blocking my view. "Dude, it's pretty gross stuff. You sure you're up for it?"

It took a surprising amount of effort not to push Aisha aside. I willed myself to give her a reassuring smile. "Yeah, I'm really curious."

Aisha stared at me for a few seconds, biting her lip, before shrugging and moving aside. She sat down next to me, took out her phone, and started scrolling through social media.

Lucy's head had popped out from under the coils of her body, and she was moving with aching slowness, her tongue flicking out now and again to taste the air. My skin crawled, although I wasn't sure whether it crawled to get away from Lucy or to move toward her. The rat's whiskers twitched as Lucy slithered close. It raised its front paw ever so slightly, the two creatures moving slow and silent as molasses. Then the rat started, and Lucy's head darted forward, impossibly fast.

I was still watching the spot where the rat had been when I realized it was no longer there. Lucy had the front half of the rat in her mouth. The rat's back legs scrabbled madly, its tail swishing like it had a mind of its own. Lucy ignored all of its movements, continuing to swallow it, and as more of its body slid down her throat, the rat became limp. Soon, only its tail remained visible, and then that, too, was slurped up. As Aisha and I walked out of the classroom, I took one last look at Lucy. She was back in her favorite corner, her head tucked into a hollow log. Of the white rat with the black spot on its head, no traces remained.

The rat was me. Or rather, it used to be me. But not anymore. I wasn't going to let Logan corner me and swallow me whole like I was some helpless prey. Step Three: be the snake.

CHAPTER SEVENTEEN

logan

"—man, hey, you okay? Logan?"

I blinked, and Josh's face swam back into focus. It was wearing a very familiar expression—concern, tinged with uneasiness. I forced my voice to come out casual. "Yeah, what's up?"

I could practically see the weight leaving Josh's shoulders, the tension melting from his features. "The game, remember? Against those assholes from Applewood?" He rubbed his palms together, and the noise grated in my ears.

"Stop."

Josh looked down with a surprised frown and that was when I realized I'd reached out and grabbed his hands, tight. So tight that my knuckles were white. I released him quickly and tried for a simple, harmless grin. Except I thought the grin came out looking manic. What the hell was up with me? The last few days, I'd felt really weird. I wasn't sure how to describe it; but sometimes I'd feel incredible, like I could sprint and fly up and touch the fucking sky. Sometimes, the world felt like it was in the palm of my hand, ripe for the taking. And then suddenly I'd come crashing down, like now, and I just wanted to lash out at anyone who had the misfortune to be near me. "Sorry," I mumbled to Josh.

"It's fine," he laughed, lying through his fucking teeth. I could punch those perfect white teeth straight out—

Whoa. Seriously, what the hell was going on with me?

My phone beeped with a text.

Delilah [2:47 p.m.]:
I'm swamped at the library. Rain check on our study date? xo

Warmth flooded through my chest. Nowadays, her messages were often punctuated with *x*'s and *o*'s. We still hadn't kissed, but we were slowly getting there, we really were. I knew just what I needed. I needed Dee. The past few days, she'd been so different. She was opening up to me. Like a flower slowly blooming. After classes ended, I'd gone to my locker to find that Delilah had left me a surprise: a red velvet cupcake she'd baked. I'd eaten it then and there, grinning like an idiot the whole time. She'd been baking so many cupcakes lately, and either left them in my locker as a surprise gift or gave them to me in person, watching with an affectionate smile as I ate, asking me sweetly if they tasted okay. Whenever she was around, I felt invincible, like I could literally move faster than the speed of light. And then she'd go to class or go home or whatever, and the weight of the world would crush me. I needed her.

"Logan?" Josh said, frowning again, but his voice was coming from a distance. I supposed that wasn't weird; we'd been drifting apart for a while now. I tuned out his meaning-less chatter for a while, until he said, "—Delilah?" and suddenly, he was right next to me again, his voice coming in at a normal volume.

I snapped back to reality. "What?"

"I said, is that Delilah?" Josh pointed to a girl across the quad, walking with some guy. Though their backs were turned toward us, I knew from the way the girl moved and the way she tilted her head just so that it was her. My Delilah. But I thought she was busy at the library. The guy said something and she laughed, the sound of it carrying crystal clear even from this distance. It stabbed through my guts and twisted like a goddamn knife. And I thought things had been going so well with her.

I blinked, and I was halfway across the quad. Part of me registered that Josh was somewhere behind me, running after me and calling my name. I blinked again, and I was right behind Delilah and the guy, this fucking prick whose head I was going to bash in. I reached out to grab his shoulder—

"Logan!" Josh shouted, and the couple turned.

It wasn't Delilah. This girl wasn't anything like her. I vaguely recognized her as some sophomore.

"Not her," I muttered.

"Heyyy," Josh half gasped, half laughed as he caught up. "How're you guys doing? You okay? Great, ha ha." He waved at the confused couple and led me away by the arm like I was some misbehaving toddler. "What happened there, Logan?" His voice came out low and serious. Gone was Meathead Josh. Now it was Concerned Bestie Josh, and there was honestly no one I hated more than Concerned Bestie Josh who thought he knew what was best for me. I'd had enough. I knew what was best for me. It was Delilah. Delilah was everything I needed. I walked away from Josh, ignoring his stupid whines about stopping and having a chat. I had to get out of there, get some air.

I didn't remember walking off campus, but I must've, because when I next blinked, I was standing outside of Dee's house again.

What the fuck?

I knew I shouldn't, but I wanted to be close to her, in any way I could. So I climbed the trellis again and eased myself inside. And this time, there was no one home to trap me in the bathroom.

Maybe it was fate. Maybe it was meant to be. I didn't mean to, but now that I was here, how could I ignore the opportunity? Clearly I was meant to be here, if not by my own design, then by some cosmic interference. I was in Delilah's bedroom. Her inner sanctuary. With no one holding me back. I could look all I wanted, touch everything I desired.

I swallowed. Forced my breathing to even out a bit. And then I looked. Really looked. And god. *Delilah, your room is so, unapologetically, beautifully you.*

I'd only ever seen it from outside, spying on her from across the street while she was working at her computer, nibbling at her fingernails, and bopping her head along to some music, or when she was drying her hair. I'd only caught glimpses of it. But now, the sense of her was overwhelming. I had enough presence of mind to check the time on my phone, at least. 3:28 p.m. She was still at work. She was so hardworking, my little worker bee buzzing away at her job. Her mom was also still at work. She worked in tech; their hours were brutal. So. This was really a gift from the universe, rewarding me for being such a good boy, for being ever so patient with her. I'd never even tried to kiss her, not since our first date. I knew that had to be her move.

I remained respectful, even though yes, Universe, I heard you loud and clear, and I was grateful to be led here. I walked around carefully, trailing my fingertips across her things.

Her wall was plastered with all sorts of decor: there were photo frames that had been taken apart and turned into jewelry organizers, a sign in cursive that said *Good Vibes Only*—which, okay, kind of basic, but I supposed no one was perfect—and photos. So many photos. I took my time looking at each one. So many of her dad, laughing, one of him at work, looking serious. She was such a daddy's girl. A handful of her mom, who was a stunner back in the day, and then dozens of Dee and her old friends. When I was done with the pictures, I went to the jewelry organizers, touching each trinket, delighting in the knowledge that they had been on her skin, warmed by her body heat. I couldn't help taking a souvenir. Just a small aquamarine earring she would not miss; she had so many of the things, over two dozen pairs at a glance. She'd understand that I did it because I loved her, because I couldn't have enough of her.

Then came the drawers. I didn't steal her panties or bra or anything like that. I wasn't that person. I respected Dee. I worshipped her. I didn't even touch any of her underwear, even though I wanted to. But no. I moved on. I pulled out a pair of flannel pajamas and pressed my face into it, engulfing myself in the beautiful scent of her. The pajamas were pink with pineapples on them, and fuck, I bet Delilah looked absolutely adorable in them.

I sat down on her bed. I lay down, my head right where hers was every night. I imagined her right there next to me, going to sleep. I'd watch her eyelids fluttering as she dreamed, and I damn near burst into tears because I wanted that so badly. I clutched her earring so hard that sharp pain sparked up my arm, and I started. The back of the earring had pierced my palm. These things were dangerous. She shouldn't be wearing them. Why did she wear jewelry, anyway? She didn't need to wear jewelry or makeup, she looked beautiful as she was, and she didn't need to be attracting any other guy.

Another guy. The thought of the couple Josh and I had run across earlier flashed through my mind, and even though that girl had turned out to not be Delilah, my stomach lurched sickeningly. Bile rose, and I had to fight to keep it down. The last thing I wanted was to puke in Delilah's room. But the thought of her with some other guy...

No. I couldn't let myself even think of that possibility.

A small voice whispered, *Yes, but that happened with Sophie, didn't it? She left you for some other guy. Or guys, rather. She couldn't have enough of them. And now with Detective Brandon Jackson out of Delilah's life, maybe she'll want to date around for a bit.*

I put my hands over my ears and squeezed my eyes shut, willing the voice to shut up. But it wouldn't. It kept whispering, getting louder and louder until it was shouting, filling my entire head with its hateful words. *She'll never love you the way you love her, she'll leave you, she'll find a way, and you'll never see her again.*

I jumped from her bed and paced her room, muttering at the voice to shut up. I wouldn't let that happen. I'd—

What? I'd what?

Well, I didn't have to do anything. I had the video. She'd never dare leave me, not while I had the video of her killing Detective Jackson.

Yes, but the video is also the reason she won't ever love you. Not truly. Because you're blackmailing her into being with you.

I shook my head. Not true. She was in love with me, I could tell. Those XOs she left at the end of every message, those cakes…

Just a ruse. No, see, she doesn't understand how cruel the world can be. She doesn't know, even after the way Brandon hurt her, she doesn't know that you're her only sanctuary. It's hopeless. Without you, she'll only get hurt again. She'll run into another bad guy. If you want her to be truly yours, forever and ever, you'll need to make sure nothing bad ever happens to her. Her life is so chaotic right now. It needs order. It needs saving. And to save her, you need to take it, take her life—

"NO!" I shouted. Everything shattered into silence. No, no. I couldn't go down that route. Not again. Not after Sophie.

But that's just it, isn't it? You didn't do it with Sophie. You didn't save her, and when she died, she was alone, and she died hating you.

Tears coursed down my face. Sophie did die hating me. In those final days, her last words to me had been a hushed: *Just go, Lolo. Nobody understands.* I did. I understood. But she wouldn't, couldn't believe me. I still remembered that day so clearly. I'd climbed up the tree outside her window, moving like a goddamn monkey. I'd done it dozens of times before, though she didn't know it. I knew which branches to go for, which ones were cracking and had to be avoided. I was so happy. I'd bought a first edition of her favorite book, *Alice in Wonderland*, and I was sure she'd finally smile at that, she had to. I finally reached her window, and there she was, my princess, my Sleeping Beauty. She was lying so sweetly in her bed. I pried the window open and climbed in noiselessly. Placed the book on her study desk. I walked closer, heart thudding so fast and so hard. I just wanted to touch her hair. And I did. So soft and silky, like a feather. I couldn't help it. I touched her cheek. And stopped. That was when I knew. She was no longer breathing. Something imploded inside me then. I moved like lightning. I practically jumped out of her window. I twisted my ankle when I landed, but I barely felt it. I sprinted all the way back to campus and shut myself up in my room and waited for the news of her death.

I couldn't let the same thing happen with Dee. I couldn't stomach it if I lost her the same way.

Blink.

"Logan?"

I was—where the hell was I? It took a second to recognize my surroundings. I was outside of Delilah's house. And of course, Detective Mendez was right in front of me, her concerned gaze piercing my skin.

Seeing her was like having a bowl of ice water flung in my face. I brushed myself off and blinked a few times, trying to clear my head.

"Hi, Logan," she said. Her gaze darted from me to my schoolbag, and then to my tousled hair, which I belatedly realized had broken twigs and leaves in it. How the hell did I get all this crap in my hair? When I touched my face, my fingers came away greasy. Jesus. When was the last time I washed my face? Took a shower?

"Hey." I should say something else, try to charm her or whatever, but my thoughts were all scrambled, harried and panicked and, above all, coated with a thick layer of rage. She'd come to my sanctuary, violated this place that belonged to Delilah and me. I wanted to reach out and shake Detective Mendez hard, hard enough to make her head flop back and forth like a rag doll.

Somewhere, deep in the tangled forest of my mind, a warning bell was ringing. This anger, this sudden rush of red rage, wasn't normal. Was it? How did anyone know what was normal and what wasn't?

"Everything okay? What are you doing here?" That came out a lot more accusatory than I'd intended. I swallowed and tried to smile.

"Oh, I just came by to see Delilah's mom. Is she in?"

"No. No one's in," I said, quickly. Too quickly.

Confusion crossed her face. "No one's home? What brings you here then?"

Shit, shit! I tried to come up with something viable, something not at all suspicious, but my mind was glue. "I just wanted to surprise Dee." Which was normal, right? Boyfriends surprised their girlfriends all the time, especially when they were really into said girlfriend.

But instead of looking mollified, Detective Mendez looked even more concerned, her frown gouging deep into her forehead. "Did Delilah give you a key to her house?"

"I..."

"You came out of the house. I'm guessing you had a key?"

"Um, yeah, she lent me her key."

"So she knows you're here? I thought you said it was supposed to be a surprise?"

Jesus, won't this bitch just let up already?

"Yeah, um, the surprise was something I was leaving for her inside. Flowers," I added before she could ask.

"That's so sweet," Detective Mendez said, smiling. The smile did not reach her eyes.

"I'm going to be honest with you, Logan. I'm looking into a drug case. Know anything about that?"

I didn't have to fake my surprise. What with Delilah and Detective Jackson and Sophie, drugs were the last thing on my mind. "Drugs?" I asked.

"Come on, you must have heard something about it. Seems like every other kid at school knows where to get recreational drugs."

I shrugged. "I've seen a couple of kids smoking pot, but I don't know where they got it."

"I'm not just talking about the occasional pot, Logan. I'm talking about hard drugs. Ecstasy, cocaine, maybe a few prescription drugs."

My eyes widened. "Er—you got me there. I really don't know anything about that." I frowned. I was being entirely honest here, but Detective Mendez was staring at me like she'd just caught me with white powder all over my face. "Hang on, I thought you're in homicide. If there's a drug case, shouldn't it be handled by the DEA or something?"

Detective Mendez snorted, a bitter sound. "Not in a small town like ours, not until we have hard evidence." She looked me straight in the eye. "I know someone here is dealing. We had a problem with it a couple years ago, but then it died down and we lost the trail. Now someone's selling again, and I'm betting you kids know more than you're letting on. You always do."

"A couple of years ago? That would be around the time…"

"That girl passed away, yes."

Sophie's words sliced through my mind. *"Nobody can help me, Lolo. I'm all alone."* I couldn't help wincing. The memory of Sophie in her darkest hour physically hurt. I forced myself to take a breath.

"What was her name?" Detective Mendez mused.

"I—I don't know—"

"Sylvia, was it? Sarah?"

I couldn't stand it, couldn't listen to her butchering Sophie's name. "Sophie," I blurted.

Detective Mendez gave me a long look. "You knew her?"

"No. I mean, I knew of her. She was someone I'd seen around, that's all. Said hi a few times." Flashes of me and Sophie sitting in our glade, my hand on hers. Me willing my palms not to sweat, reminding myself not to stare, not to talk too much, not to do anything that might irritate Sophie. Me taking in her presence, her fragrance, all of her.

"Really sad, what happened to Sophie, wasn't it?"

I shrugged. I couldn't look at Detective Mendez. If I did, she'd see the anger leaping inside me. *Don't say her name like that, like she's nothing but a case number, you fucking bitch, you fucking—*

"Detective Jackson was looking into the drug case before he died," she said, and there was something new in her voice, something like disgust or resentment, something bitter and sharp. She was looking at me intently, like a shark that smells blood. "Funny timing, that," she said. "He told me he'd found something, a clue, and he was going to show it to me. But then that terrible accident happened, and now I'm left wondering what he was about to tell me. And of course there's that pill we found in his car…"

Realization dawned with sickening weight. Everything clicked into place, and the world looked different. Detective Mendez suspected foul play was involved, but for a completely different reason. She thought someone had killed Detective Jackson (true) because he'd come too close to cracking a case (so not true). And I didn't like the way she was studying me. I didn't like that at all.

I wanted to grab her arm, hard, dig my fingers into her flesh, and tell her Brandon Jackson had died because he was a massively misogynistic abusive asshole whose hobbies included working on his car, drinking, and beating the shit out of his girlfriend and girlfriend's teenage daughter. She must have known what a monster the guy was. Did she never suspect what he got up to when he was at home? Or, worse, did she know and choose to turn a blind eye to it?

Not that I could say any of that, of course. All I could do was shrug and say, "I don't know anything about that. I didn't even know you guys were looking into a drug case here."

Detective Mendez nodded slowly, her eyes never leaving mine. "Okay, Logan. This has been…illuminating. Well, take it easy. And say hi to Delilah for me." With that, she turned and walked back toward her car, leaving me alone in front of Delilah's empty house.

delilah

Poor, sweet Logan. He wasn't doing well. Fidget, fidget, fidget. I wanted to slam my hand on the table and snap, "Sit. Still!" like he was a squirmy five-year-old on a sugar rush. But patience. Oh, patience. My plan required it in spades.

We sat at one of the large wooden desks in one corner of the Creighton Reading Room, a large, modern addition to the library. This space was made largely out of glass and metal, sticking out of the brick and mortar building like a glass foot. Sunlight streamed through the windows in golden shafts, and as you worked, you could gaze out of the great glass panes and look across the green expanse of the Western Gardens. White and yellow flowers were in bloom at the moment, frosting the landscape. Pa would have loved

Draycott. He would've been happy to know that his death had at least allowed me to go to school at a place like this. The thought of Pa made my throat tighten, and I cleared it and shook my head. I glanced at Logan, who was frowning at a spot a couple of inches above his laptop and scratching his neck and, of course, fidgeting.

"You okay?" I asked. It was obvious he wasn't, but I had to keep up appearances.

He shrugged.

"Only you weren't at lunch today..." Not that I minded, of course. Him not turning up for lunch meant I didn't have to sit with him and his freakishly upbeat friends. I'd actually had a pleasant lunch with Aisha, where we'd discussed ideas on how to break into Logan's room.

He glanced at me like he was seeing me for the first time. "Oh, yeah. Something came up. Sorry." His face was creased with some unfamiliar emotion.

I watched him out of the corner of my eye, imagining him as the little rat being dangled over Lucy's cage. How would he react if the tables were turned and I was the predator and he was the prey? Probably not very well. I went through the list of adverse effects he should be feeling from all the MDMA I'd been dosing him with. Increased anxiety, check. Restlessness, check. Paranoia, check. Those were all side effects he'd get when he came down off the drugs. I'd also helpfully added some Ambien to help with the anxiety. I didn't want him to be too restless, after all. I could barely keep up with non-drugged-out Logan. The last thing I wanted was for him to spiral out of control before I was ready.

I glanced at the online application on my computer and sighed. I'd suggested working on our early admissions application for NUS together, but there was no way I could focus on that right now. Instead, I took out a Tupperware container and opened it. Logan looked like he could use a bit of a high right now. The smell of chocolate filled the air.

"Brownies?" I asked, holding the container out to Logan. "Baked them last night."

Some of the sadness leaked away from his face, and he smiled. "You're too good to me," he said, taking a piece of brownie. He gazed at me with such adoration, it made me want to punch him in the throat. The brownie went down nice and easy. Probably didn't even taste anything, he was so far removed from here.

He took another piece, and another. Uh-oh. An image of the unfortunate mice I'd experimented with flashed through my mind. The two that died did not go gently into that good night. I couldn't afford to let Logan overdose here, as tempting as that was. I closed the container and stuffed it back in my bag. "I think that's enough for now."

"Huh? Oh, heh. Can't help it, these are really good." He stuffed his third piece in his mouth. Fidget, fidget. He really wasn't looking well.

"Have some water," I said, handing him a bottle.

Logan gulped down the water and sighed. "I'm sorry, it's so hard to focus on my essay with all this shit going on."

"What's going on?"

"It's…stuff from my past. It's not important."

The only stuff I knew from his past had to do with Sophie, but saying her name out loud to Logan felt all sorts of wrong.

"Okay, well, if you ever wanna talk about it…" Not that I cared, but it might give me some information I could use.

"Thanks, Dee." He smiled, and for a second, he was the old Logan—charming, golden, healthy. Only for a second, though. He resumed shifting and squirming and running his fingers through his greasy hair. "Anyway!" he said suddenly, clapping loudly. "College apps. Let's do this!" He rubbed his hands together. I resisted the urge to reach out and smack them so they'd stop flying everywhere.

"I heard from Aisha that you guys had a college prep thing over the summer where they taught you the basics of what to include in your college essay," I said.

"Yep. They pretty much guided us through everything. I actually wrote my college essay then and there."

"Wow." I chewed my lip. An idea was taking root. Could this be my chance to stop Logan from following me all the way to NUS? "Can I take a look so I have an idea what colleges are looking for?"

"Anything for you." He slid his laptop around to face me, took out his cellphone, and began tapping on it.

"Thanks." I skimmed the first page, my heart beating in my throat. This was it. My chance to keep him from NUS. I sighed theatrically. "You've got quite a few grammatical errors in here. It's driving me bonkers."

Logan focused his eyes on me and grinned. "Who would've known that you're the grammar police?"

"I'm gonna edit this. Don't worry, I'll use Track Changes."

"Thanks, babe. You're so sweet."

Babe. Ugh.

I started typing so he'd stop talking to me. I was almost all the way through Logan's essay, which was annoyingly well-written, when he got up.

"Gonna go to the restroom," he said.

I froze. He was actually going to leave me alone with his computer. I wasn't sure if pre-drugged-out Logan would've been so careless. I waved him off as casually as I could, still typing and making changes to his essay. As soon as he was out of sight, I minimized the document window, clicked on the computer icon, and called up a search. I went through the list of words he might've saved the video under.

Delilah.

Brandon.

Jackson.

Wong.

Camaro.

No luck. I looked through his recently opened files. Still no luck. I opened the internet browser and looked at his search history. Sweet Jesus. He'd not only done an extensive search on me, he'd also done his homework on Aisha and Mom and Pa. *Sick, sick fuck. When I finally get rid of you, I'm going to—no, focus.* I scrolled down the list, chewing on my lip. Where could he have hidden the file? He wouldn't stick with the one copy he had on his phone; he must've made several copies. I'd planned on finding them and deleting them all, but here I was, unable to locate even one.

I was so engrossed in looking for the video I almost didn't hear Logan coming back. He was at the desk before I noticed, and I started, barely having time to close the browser before he leaned over and took a peek.

"Doing a little snooping, are we?"

"Um—" *Thinkfastthinkfastthink!*

"That's okay, it's only natural to be curious when you like someone." The kindness in his voice grated.

Fuck you.

"Is that what you told yourself when you stalked me? That it's only natural to be curious?" The words slipped out before I could catch them. If I could only cram them back in my mouth. But he'd said it with such confidence, such smugness like, *See, stalking is natural. Stalking happens.*

He didn't seem to notice, anyway. He practically bounced

into his seat, his eyes shining with a sick light. The drugs were working. He was well on his way to another high. "How's the reading going?" His mouth visibly trembled as he spoke, then broke into a manic grin.

"It's great," I said, and damn if I wasn't being honest. His essay really was good. "I think it's ready to turn in. I'm jealous."

"Are you serious?" He bounced again.

"Yeah. I mean, aside from the grammar stuff, but those were easy to fix."

Logan laughed and rubbed his face hard, leaving pink blotches on his cheeks, and let his head fall backward. "You have no idea how glad I am to hear that. I'm so fucking sick of this essay." He jerked forward, swung his laptop to face him, and skimmed the document. The entire time his fingernails drummed a maddening beat on the tabletop. He gave a couple of clicks and then slammed the laptop shut. "Perfect. I accepted your changes. I'm gonna send it in tonight."

"That's fast," I said.

"Gotta move fast, babe." He beat out a rhythm on the table with his palms until I reached out and caught his hands.

"We're in the library," I whispered with a strained smile. "I think it's probably time for us to go, okay?"

"Yeah, yeah."

I stole glances at him as he packed his stuff. His behavior was definitely off. Erratic, manic, with an intense look in his eyes and a greasy sheen to his whole...self. I wondered if anyone else noticed. I thought again of the rat freezing as the snake approached, one paw raised in vain. What would Logan be like if he were faced with a snake? Would he freeze as well or try to scramble up the smooth walls of the snake tank? Not that it mattered, of course. Either way, the snake always wins.

Halfway to the front door, I stopped and said, "I forgot I still have to update some stuff at work. You go on ahead."

Logan frowned. "But it's late."

"Yeah, I've kind of let things slide around here. You go back to your room, you look like you could use the rest."

"I'll stay and drive you home," he said.

Like hell I'd let him drive me after three pieces of my brownies. He'd probably end up killing both of us. I made my voice firm as steel and said, "Logan, go."

He started, confusion flashing across his features, then he gave me a toddler's trusting grin and said, "Okay. I'll see you tomorrow."

I watched him bounce off like Tigger before I turned around and went down to the stacks. I sighed as I unlocked the office and settled behind my desk. It felt great to finally be free of Logan, if only for the moment.

"Good study session?" Lisa asked. I jumped and dropped my folder and books. She had the softest footsteps.

"It was okay."

"He seems like a sweet kid," she said, helping me gather all the papers that had spilled from my folder.

I snorted. Yeah, he sure *seems* like a sweet kid.

Heavy footsteps clopped down the stairs. Lisa glanced up at me, looking as bemused as I felt. Before we could say anything, someone called out, "Hello? Excuse me?"

My stomach tipped sideways. Mendez.

"Yes?" Lisa said in her high-pitched librarian voice. She straightened up, brushing herself off and adjusting her glasses before unlocking the door.

The old anger resurfaced. First, Logan came bumbling down here. And now here was Mendez. Why couldn't people just leave my workplace alone?

"I'm Detective Mendez. You must be Lisa Smith."

"That's me, Lisa the librarian," Lisa said, shaking Mendez's hand. "This is Delilah, my assistant. She's also a student here."

I forced a smile.

"I know Dee."

"Oh, right." Lisa smiled back and pushed her glasses up. She was laying on the librarian act nice and thick. *Look at me, I'm Lisa the librarian! I wear glasses! I couldn't possibly be the mastermind behind Draycott's drug ring!* "Can I help you with anything, Detective?"

"Yes, actually, I'm looking for a...some sort of message board?" Mendez took out a slim notebook and riffled through the pages. "A message board where students post their secrets?"

There was a beat, and then Lisa chirped, "Of course! Yes. The Post Ur Secret board. Right this way." She ushered Mendez out of the office, chattering the entire time. "What are you looking for at the board? Ooh, don't tell me if it's something awful, I have a very weak stomach. Maybe you could give me a hint, though." God, she was such a pro. No one could possibly suspect this version of Lisa of doing anything remotely illegal. She absolutely radiated helplessness; someone who'd turn herself in if she so much as ran a red light. Someone who fainted at the sight of blood. I should be taking notes.

Mendez laughed. "I'll know when I see it. Tell me about this board."

The two of them seemed to have forgotten about me, which was just fine. I trailed along quietly, trying to look calm, trying to keep all of the little broken pieces of me from falling apart. I listened closely to Mendez's voice and studied her every move. Was anything off? Was she looking at me differently, like she knew something I didn't? What had she heard about the Post Ur Secret Board? Worse still, what would she find?

By the time we got to the board, every nerve inside me was thrumming.

"This is it," Lisa said, with a flourish. She stood to one

side with her back to the board, her eyes studying Mendez studying the board. You'd catch the cold calculation behind Lisa's deferential expression only if you were looking out for it.

"Whoa," Mendez said.

"It is quite a lot to take in," Lisa agreed.

No kidding. The first time I'd come across the board, I'd been swept away by the sheer size of it. So many secrets pinned together to make one giant flock, so many voices whispering, so many emotions, all of them extreme—elated, excited, some enraged, others sorrowful, none of them peaceful. It was like plunging into the deep end of the ocean. I stood on the other side of Mendez and scanned the board. She'd never find anything in this—

"Aha!" Mendez cried.

Lisa and I jumped. I twisted to look at Mendez and found her gaze locked not on the board but on me. Every inch of my skin turned cold. This was a trap. She didn't care about the board. She'd just used it as a way of catching me out—

"What is it? Did you find something?" Lisa said, her voice just the right mix of excitement, wonder, and fear.

Mendez tore her gaze from me and glanced at Lisa. "Hmm? No, I thought I saw something, but I was mistaken."

Lisa frowned. "Well, maybe if you could give us some sort of clue as to what you're looking for, we'd be able to help…"

"Sorry, Lisa, I need to talk to Dee for a second."

Lisa's mouth dropped open. "But—"

Mendez took me by the arm and led me, gently but firmly, out of the library. *This is it, then. This is how it all ends.* All of my planning was for nothing. *How much does she know?* My legs turned to water, and I would've fallen if Mendez's hand weren't wrapped around my arm, steadying me. With each step, I had to remind myself to breathe deeply, slowly.

Outside, Mendez turned to me. "Okay, Dee, you need to be honest with me."

My voice was gone. I could only nod wordlessly as I waited for her to say the words that would end my life. "I've told you everything I know about Brandon's acc—"

"I'm not here about that," she said. "Well, it's sort of related to that. I'm here investigating the drug ring at your school." That was not much better. I'd thought it would be Brandon's murder that got me in the end, but apparently, I was mistaken. "Remember that pill I found in Brandon's car?"

Oh god, here it comes. Just tell me you know it belonged to me. It must've fallen out of my bag. Rip off the Band-Aid already. Tell me you know, tell me!

"I've told you—I don't do drugs," I said weakly. "Honest. You can ask anyone here—"

Mendez sighed. "Dee, I know that. I've been talking to people here. They all say the same thing about you. That you're the last person who'd know anything about drugs."

She gave me a sad smile. "You're a good kid, Dee. But maybe a bit naïve."

My head whirled. What was she saying? Okay, she just said I was a good kid, which meant she didn't know about Brandon's murder or my role in the drug ring. But then she said I was naive... "I don't understand," I said.

"Dee, I know relationships in high school can be intense. I was so in love with my high school boyfriend when I was your age. I would've done anything for him."

"I—what?" I said.

Mendez leveled her gaze at me. "How well do you know Logan?"

My mind drew a blank. Of all the questions I'd braced myself for, this was not one of them. "Um, I don't know—" At some point she was going to notice how I was answering everything with "I don't know" or "I don't understand." I had to come up with something more tangible to satisfy her. Something that wouldn't tip her off. "We haven't been dating that long..." I said.

"Long enough to have him over to meet your mom," Mendez pressed. "Have you noticed anything odd about him? Is he particularly secretive when it comes to say, his phone?"

I shook my head. "I haven't tried to steal his phone or anything, so I wouldn't know. He seems okay to me? Normal, I mean."

Mendez's eyes drilled into mine. "Really? That's very interesting, Dee, because apparently you're close enough to give Logan a key to your place."

"A...key?"

Mendez's eyebrows rose. "You didn't? I ran into him yesterday outside your house, and he said you'd given him a key. He said he left a surprise for you at the house."

My thoughts shattered into a million galloping, shrieking questions. He was at my house? He broke in? He left something? Some sick, twisted thing, no doubt. God, how I wished I could tell Mendez the truth about Logan, reveal to her what a sicko he was. But then what would happen? She'd catch him, maybe question him, and who knew what he'd say to her? I couldn't let that happen.

Through some superhuman effort, I managed not to move a single facial muscle. I stretched my mouth into a smile. "Oh, yeah! Yeah, I did...do that, yes."

Mendez sighed. "Look, Dee, I know you're in a relationship with him, but there's something really off about that kid, okay? When I saw him yesterday, he didn't look so good. Kind of twitchy. Sweaty sheen to him. Eyes all manic."

That would be the drugs I've been slipping into his food, Detective. I wanted to scream with nervous, sick laughter. My plan was working a little bit too fast for my liking. "He can be a bit intense, sure—"

"Dee, between you and me? I know drug addicts. I've

caught them, I've questioned them, I deal with them a lot more often than you think. And Logan—he's on drugs, Delilah. You really haven't noticed anything off about him?"

"I'm sorry!" I cried. "I don't know—yes, maybe, he's been a little bit more frantic. I didn't think much of it, I didn't—"

"Hey, listen." Mendez placed a firm hand on my shoulder. "You're a bright girl, Dee. But when it comes to Logan, maybe you're not quite thinking clearly. You need to be smart about all of this, okay? I have a bad feeling about Logan. You need to watch out for him. Understand?"

What else could I do but nod wordlessly? Mendez said a few other things, but I failed to register any of them. After she left, I stood there watching until her silhouette turned into a small blip, and I wanted to fall into a hundred thousand little pieces. Things were moving too fast. My plan—my unfinished plan—was unraveling. For god's sake, I'd only completed Step One so far. I hadn't even carried out Step Two, and Step Three was still just a vague idea. I hadn't counted on Detective Mendez coming so close to the truth so fast. What if she gathered enough evidence to arrest Logan? He'd spill then, he definitely would. He'd be like, "Why are you wasting your time looking for a drug dealer when there's a killer right under your nose?" He'd cut a deal with them for immunity. He may have thought he loved me, but I wasn't too eager to find out how long that "love" would last when he's facing potential jail time.

And Logan, that sick, twisted boy, had broken into my house. I couldn't even register just how violated that made me feel. And, as I stood there, feeling increasingly cold, I realized that I also felt fearful. That maybe I wasn't the snake after all, that maybe I was always doomed to be the rat. Always the prey, always one step behind. Tears stung my eyes. He'd been inside my house. My safe place. He'd been in there, doing god knows what, and I didn't even realize it. How many times had he broken in without my knowledge? Which of my things had he rifled through? My books? My clothes? Bile rose. My underwear?

"Everything okay?" Lisa asked.

I started again then gritted my teeth and forced myself to smile. "Yeah, just a few routine questions."

"Hmm." Lisa didn't look convinced. She chewed on her bottom lip for a bit. "You'd tell me, wouldn't you?"

"Huh?"

"If you're in any sort of trouble," she said.

The concerned librarian act isn't fooling me, I wanted to scream at her. *Not when I know who you truly are. What you really are.*

Then it hit me. She wasn't asking me because she was concerned about me. She was concerned about how it might affect her and her business. Resentment coursed through my stomach, souring it. I kept my face still, though my insides were writhing and twisting. If she cut me off…hung me out to dry…

I'd take the whole fucking place down with me, Lisa included.

And that was when I realized what Step Three was. I had known a while ago that Step Three was about me being the snake, but I didn't know what that entailed, exactly. Now I did. And I needed all of the resources I had to do it.

I gritted my teeth and said, "I'm fine." Well, I wasn't, not yet. But soon I would be.

CHAPTER NINETEEN
logan

The first few months after Sophie died, I'd had a bit of trouble digesting the news. My brain refused to register it, and for weeks after, I'd see Sophie everywhere. I'd be standing in line at the cafeteria and I'd hear her laugh and turn my head just in time to catch her turning a corner. I'd drop everything—tray, food, and water crashing to the floor, heads turning in my direction, people whispering, but it didn't matter. Nothing mattered. All that mattered was me running, running, calling out her name. But I was never fast enough. By the time I turned the corner, she was always gone, dispersing into thin air like a breeze.

It took months for it to finally sink in, for the neurons in my brain to finally relay the message to my consciousness:

Sophie was dead. She was gone. She'd been alive, and now she no longer was, and all I could do was keep going, keep living, while the memory of Sophie lurked under the surface.

Except now she'd been called up again, shaken out of her slumber. I'd be talking to Delilah, watching her perfect mouth move as she spoke, and suddenly her lips would turn red, her eyes lined in that dramatic way, and I'd be talking to Sophie, and it was like old times, so perfect, and I could reach out and touch Sophie, my Sophie. She flinched when I pulled her close and tried to kiss her.

"Logan, you promised, no physical stuff unless I'm okay with it," she said.

I blinked, and it was no longer Sophie standing before me. Right. I was with Delilah. I let go of her and squinted into the sunset, trying to clear my head. "Sorry, I—"

She was watching me with concern, which made my heart beat faster, golden heat spreading across my chest, drowning out my anxiety. That's right, Sophie was dead, she was still gone, but I wasn't alone anymore. I had Delilah, and she was falling in love with me. She'd stopped fighting me. She'd stopped scowling whenever I met her for lunch, and our dates no longer consisted of her trying to pick fights over the smallest things. The other day, she actually plucked a stray leaf from my hair. I'd almost died when she reached out and her fingers brushed my forehead. Yes, things were definitely looking up with Delilah. Which was why I had to get myself together. I couldn't keep living in the past, clinging to the ghost of Sophie.

"Sorry. It doesn't matter. I'm here with you," I said.

Delilah smiled and twirled a lock of hair with her index finger. I blinked, and Sophie stared back at me, twirling her hair. I blinked again. No. I was with Delilah. I took a deep breath and looked around to clear my head. We'd been strolling around the campus grounds and were outside the old chapel, sharing a thermos of hot chocolate Delilah had brought with her. Stone flowerpots lined the path leading up to the chapel entrance. It was a quiet, peaceful spot, one of the oldest buildings at Draycott. Moss half covered everything. Sophie used to love this place. She'd come here and sit by the gravestones to think, running her fingers over the carvings, reading the names out—

Stop thinking of her!

It was this place, I realized. It was Draycott. Sophie was everywhere here. If I went to the Eastern Gardens, she was there, bending over to stroke the petals of a flower. If I went to the pool, she was there, tucking her hair into her swimming cap, swinging her arms 'round and 'round to warm up her muscles. She was in the library, the gymnasium, the corridors. Draycott was saturated with her. The only way I could be rid of her ghost was to leave this place.

If things went as planned, Delilah and I would be in NUS by this time next year. A whole new place just for Delilah and me. Our futures gleamed in front of me, perfect and golden.

"So I told my mom we sent in our applications on Tuesday," I said, my voice coming out louder than I'd expected in the silence. "She said she'll make sure the dean gets it."

Delilah's mouth twitched. "I'm still not used to the idea that you could just hand your application over to the dean instead of mailing it to the admissions office like everybody does."

"Hey, that's life. You have to use whatever advantage you have."

Delilah sat down on a bench and tucked her feet under her. I got a flash of Sophie once more. My head felt fuzzy. Damn that Mendez. The conversation with her had really thrown me off balance.

"Any other schools your mom is affiliated with that she can get you into?" Delilah asked. At least she didn't seem to notice I was hanging on to reality by the tips of my fingers.

"Maybe. Does it matter? NUS is a given for you and me," I said.

Delilah gave a nervous smile. "Hah. I'm not going to count on it until I have the acceptance letter in my hands." She took a sip of hot chocolate.

"Suit yourself, but get used to the idea," I said, gesturing for her to pass me the thermos. I sat down next to her and leaned my head back, gazing at the sky while I took a big mouthful of the rich, molten chocolate. The side of my left leg touched Delilah's, but she didn't move hers away. I closed my eyes, trying to preserve this moment, this perfect moment with the girl of my dreams.

"Logan," she sighed, and I realized I'd put my arm around her shoulders. I hadn't meant to, but now that I had, it felt absolutely perfect. She fit into the space like she'd been made just for me. When she tried to move away, I held tight. "Logan," she said again, and now there was a touch of panic in her voice.

"Isn't this perfect?" I almost couldn't recognize my own voice, it came out all high and chirpy and weird, almost like a screech. I cleared my throat. "This is great."

"I don't feel comfortable."

I hated that note of fear in Dee's voice. Why was she still so fearful of me? After all this time, couldn't she tell how pure my intentions were? Had I not been patient enough? I hadn't even tried kissing her again. Speaking of kisses, she was the one who first kissed me, after that magical first date. It wasn't like she asked for my consent, so why couldn't I put my arm around her? It was just one arm. And she was always baking for me, surely that meant she loved me. Nobody bakes for people they're not in love with.

Only when silence fell, sudden and heavy, did I realize I'd spoken this out loud. Jesus. Delilah was staring at me wide-eyed, like a trapped deer.

"Sorry, Dee. I didn't mean, I—"

She swallowed thickly. "No, it's fine." A forced smile.

"You're right, I did kiss you after our first date, and I wanted to at the time, but…"

"Not now? Why? Why not?"

"Because of the video, Logan!" she cried. She stopped herself and took a deep breath. "Look, I didn't want to tell you this before, because I guess I've been fighting it for so long, and I keep telling myself this is wrong, but—" Another deep breath, this one lasting a whole eternity. Her eyes sparkled with tears when she looked at me. "I like you."

The words were hushed, and yet I felt them searing through my entire being, blasting through my skin, my flesh, and drilling straight to the marrow of my bones. She liked me. Delilah liked me.

"What?"

"You're right," she continued, "no one would ever love me the way that you do. The way that I want to be loved. You know everything about me, and you accept me for who I am. How can I not like you, Logan?"

There were no words. I kept opening and closing my mouth, but nothing came out. I was a bubble. Floating, flying, zipping through the clouds. I wanted to shout it from the rooftops. Delilah liked me! I grabbed her arms and pulled her to me. Her mouth was so close, so kissable, just a single inch separated us, but she pulled away. What the fuck?

She put a hand against my chest. "Logan, you don't get it, do you?"

I shook my head. No, I sure as hell did not.

"I—I'm falling in love with you," she whispered, "and it scares me to death. I've never loved a guy before, not like this. And I want it to be perfect, do you understand?"

"It is. It's totally perfect."

"No, it's not. How can it be perfect when you have that video over my head? When I fall in love, I want it to be pure. Nothing between us but pure, innocent love. When I kiss you again—and I will, I've been dreaming about it—but when we do kiss again, I want it to be like our first kiss, where all I wanted was you and there was nothing hanging over me."

I gaped at her as her words swam through my head like a school of fish, whirling this way and that one second and dispersing the next. I could hardly fathom what she was saying. My mind was still singing with the joy of having her tell me she liked me. No, not just liked. She said she was falling in love with me. It was finally happening!

But no. It wasn't. Something was stopping her, she said. Clarity plodded in on painfully slow legs. The video. I struggled to understand. But why? The video was safe with me, surely she saw that. But maybe she was right. The video made our relationship different. We weren't on the same level as each other.

I nodded slowly, and Delilah visibly relaxed. Anger shot through me, sudden and surprising. Why was she so fucking worried about that video all the time? She squeaked, and that was when I realized I'd tightened my hold on her arms. I loosened my grip, but she still looked scared, and I hated that, I had to explain to her that she was safe. There was nowhere safe for Delilah except with me.

"You need to trust me, Dee, do you trust me?"

"Yes."

But she didn't. She looked like she wanted to run away from me. I knew then that I had no choice. I *had* to kill her, to stop her from running away from me. To save her. The video didn't matter. I could delete that, no problem. It wouldn't make a difference. All that mattered was making sure she was mine. Mine for eternity.

CHAPTER TWENTY
delilah

Aisha and I walked toward the boys' dorm, taking the long route to avoid the streetlights. It was way after curfew. Mom would have a shit fit if she knew I'd stolen out of the house and gone to school, but Mom was fast asleep; I'd made sure of that before I left.

"Okay, you remember what you're going to say to him?" I asked.

"I heard something about someone saying something that might be related to Sophie," she recited.

I swear, I could kill her. She didn't understand just how precarious everything was. How dangerous Logan was. After our last date, when he'd grabbed me with surprising strength, I hadn't been able to sleep. Each time I dozed off, I'd startle awake, convinced I'd find Logan standing at the foot of my bed, watching me with that intense gaze of his.

I glared at Aisha, and she rolled her eyes. "Obviously I will be a lot more specific than that," she said. "Dude, you're being a bit of a control freak right now, just so you know. Have more faith in me, okay? I'm in your corner."

Guilt sank its teeth, sharp and quick. I'd been so fixated on finding the video I hadn't stopped to think what a huge favor Aisha was doing for me. If we got caught, that would be the end of her future too. Aiding and abetting. I didn't want to think of how many years she'd get for it. No, I wouldn't let that happen. I'd tell them she knew nothing, that I'd been manipulating her all along. "Thank you," I said.

"You owe me. Okay, go hide. I'm gonna call him."

I slipped around the corner and watched as Aisha dialed his number. Her phone screen flashed bright in the dark. I breathed into my hands to keep them warm. I'd worn layers and gloves, but winter was nudging in; the air was crisp and my fingers were numb. Draycott at midnight was different, witchy and wild, like creatures could come out from the woods at any moment and take over the campus. Snatches of Aisha's voice floated to where I stood.

"—meet—now—outside—"

She hung up and flashed me a quick thumbs-up. Holy crap, we were really doing this. Now that it was about to happen, it felt unreal, a game, some sort of bad joke. A shrill bout of laughter threatened to overcome me. I pinched myself to keep silent.

The door swung open, and my breath caught in my throat. Logan walked out. I crept forward, willing every muscle to move as silently as humanly possible.

"What is it?" Logan asked, so close, his voice so clear. God, if he turned to his left just a couple of degrees right now—

"Not here," Aisha said sharply.

Wow, go Aisha.

"Come on," she said, and strode off to the other side of the building, leaving Logan with no choice but to follow.

I had a moment of panic once the front door slipped shut behind me. The world went silent, save for flutters of noise from within the rooms: a sudden loud snore, the creak of a bed, the tap-tapping of a keyboard, probably some kid finishing up a last-minute paper.

I'd done my research, I knew where Logan's room was, but for one second, I was rooted to my spot, frozen. Surely they could sense me here, an intruder, my breath so loud in the enclosed space. And what the hell was I doing anyway? I couldn't go through with this. It was completely hopeless. I couldn't—

Then, as suddenly as it captured me, panic's grip released, and I crept forward. One step, two, silent as a cat. I glided up the stairs to Logan's room. I'd been given a key, but his door was unlocked anyway. I slipped inside and let my breath out.

Unlocking my phone, I propped it up on the floor, facing away from the window. It gave me enough visibility to avoid crashing into things but was dim enough so no one outside would be able to see the light through the window.

I opened my bag, took out a few baggies filled with assorted pills, and rummaged about the room, looking for good hiding places. The other steps in my plan had finally become clear: I had to frame Logan as the school's drug dealer. Everyone could see he was on something; it wouldn't take too big of a leap to conclude that he was selling the stuff. I didn't allow myself to pause. I had to keep moving, otherwise, guilt would catch up and paralyze me. The place was a dump. I'd expected Logan to be a bit neater, but maybe he hadn't been in a cleaning mood lately. Quite honestly, it stank. Piles of dirty laundry were strewn everywhere. I checked his wardrobe, rifled under his mattress, searched all of his drawers, and every place I searched, I left a little plastic baggie behind. I hated the fact that this place reminded me that Logan was a person, a human being with a whole life. I felt sick at the thought. I should stop. But still I moved around, stuffing the little bags in every hiding place I could think of, feeling shittier by the minute. Aisha didn't know about this part of the plan. And I hoped to god she never would. She'd never look at me the same way again. She'd never forgive me.

At last, I was done. And still no flash drive or anything that looked like it could contain the video. If it wasn't on his computer or in his room, where else could it be? I guess he could've uploaded it onto the cloud somewhere, but I couldn't imagine Logan being that brash when it came to the video. It was way too precious to him. The last possibility was that he had it on him at all times. Maybe in one of his pockets, maybe—oh.

That cheap pendant he always wore. I'd dismissed it as a silly trinket, but now I recalled how he was always handling it, how his fingers curled around it from time to time, as though it was some touchstone he had to keep coming back to. It was big enough to harbor a secret USB drive.

Why had I never thought of that?

I peered out the window. Aisha and Logan were silhouettes in the distance, their heads bent low. *Good job, Aish.* But even as I thought that, Logan suddenly grabbed Aisha. I heard her squeak, the sound a small, furry animal might make right when a clawed predator snatches it. My chest tightened. I couldn't breathe, couldn't move. Logan shook Aisha, hard, and she cried out as her head flopped back and forth. His hand shot out, covering her mouth. No, no, no. *Oh god, what have I gotten Aish into?* I had to move, I had to get to them, I had to—

But just as suddenly as he'd grabbed her, Logan shoved Aisha away and started walking back toward the building. My breath released in a rush, my blood pounding. No time to waste. Spying his sport coat on the floor, I grabbed it and stuffed it into my bag. My phone buzzed.

"He—he's going back," Aisha gasped. "Holy shit, he's awful, he—get out of there!"

I packed my stuff and slipped out of the room. I was about to head down the stairs when I heard the front door open. Crap. If he found me here...

Luckily, the bathroom was only two doors away. I slunk inside just as Logan thudded up the stairs. Every muscle in my body tensed at the sound of his approach. Only after his door clicked shut did I release my breath. Oh my god, I did it.

I snuck outside and went to the back of the building, where Aisha was pacing with her arms wrapped around herself. She looked so tiny and scared that my breath caught in my chest. Guilt sat in my throat, hard and heavy. I did this to her. I'd known how dangerous Logan was, and still I roped her into my mess and put her straight in the middle of his path. I whispered her name, hating myself even more when she literally jumped.

"Holy shit, Dee!" She caught me in a fierce hug.

"Aish, I'm so sorry, I—"

"What?" Aisha looked at me with a frown. "Why are you sorry?"

"I saw him grab you. I—god, Aisha, I'm so sorry I pushed you into doing this—"

"Dee, you didn't push me into doing anything. Logan..." Aisha shook her head. "I had no idea—I guess it never really hit me what he was doing to you, but...fuck. He's danger-ous, Dee."

I nodded. "Come on, I don't wanna hang around." We started walking back to the girls' dorm, keeping our voices low.

"I didn't know he was like that," Aisha whispered.

I was about to comfort her when the seeds of another idea sprouted. "Yeah, I didn't want to tell you because I didn't want you to worry, but—" I let my voice tremble a little. It wasn't hard to do; I was actually pretty shaky after everything. "I'm scared of him, Aish."

"Oh god. I'm so sorry, Dee."

"I think he's on drugs. I found some stuff in his room, like bags and bags of pills. He's so unstable. I just don't know what he might do."

"Tell me you found the video," Aisha said.

I shook my head, and she visibly deflated.

"Are you sure you didn't—"

"Yes, I'm sure I didn't find what I was looking for," I sighed. Guilt snaked through my veins at having to lie to the only friend I had, but I couldn't risk telling her I'd found the video of me supposedly cheating on a test. What if she asked to see it?

"Ugh. This was supposed to work! In the movies, you know, at the last second you'd walk over like, a loose floor-board and you'd pry it open and the thing would be there." She swung to face me, her eyes shining. "Did you search the floor?"

"It's carpeted."

"Oh, right. Yeah, of course. Dammit! So the whole thing was a bust?"

"I guess I'm not much of a spy. Wait, are you sure you're okay? It looked like he hurt you—"

Aisha sighed. "I'm okay. But I don't like the thought of Logan having something over you. Something is seriously wrong with him." She took my hand and looked into my eyes. "Dee, I'm scared for you. I think he might do something. I think he might hurt you."

I tried to laugh off the fear that was clutching my throat, but my voice came out cracked. "I'll be okay. I'll think of something."

"You sure we shouldn't just go to the cops?"

"Yes!" I cried. "Please, Aish, no cops, okay? I'd be expelled. Please? You have to trust me. I'll be okay." *Will I?* Now that I was actually carrying out my plan, it felt even more dangerous than I'd expected. Even if I were to get away with it, it would change me for good. Turn me even more monstrous.

There were moments that I'd look in the mirror and see a complete stranger. Someone capable of carrying out true evil. Someone who was no longer a passive victim. If Brandon were still around, would he notice this stain spreading through my very being? Would it scare him, make him think twice about raising his fist at me?

Aisha shoved her hands in her pockets, her mouth pinched. "Did you check behind the posters or picture frames on the wall? There could be like a hole or something—"

"No posters or pictures up on the wall."

"Damn."

"Yeah."

We were quiet as we shuffled inside the girls' dorm and crept down the hallway to Aisha's room. Inside, I shrugged off my stuffy jacket and slumped onto the bed. I was glad we'd agreed earlier on that I'd stay over for the night instead of going all the way back to my house.

Aisha climbed in next to me and propped her head up on one hand. "I'm sorry it didn't work out. We'll find another way."

"Yeah," I said, staring at the ceiling. I couldn't bear to look her in the face and continue lying to her. I kept expecting Aisha to notice the corruption in my soul and figure out what my actual plan was. Surely she'd know. Surely she'd see it, this shadow lurking underneath my skin.

"Hey, you okay?" Aisha asked.

I shrugged. My stomach writhed in guilty knots. There were so many things I wished I could tell her. I was being the worst friend in the world, and here she was, trying her best to help me out. "Thanks for helping me tonight, Aish."

"Shut up, you'd do the same for me." She narrowed her eyes. "You would, right?"

"Duh."

Aisha bounded off the bed. "I'm way too keyed up to go to sleep right away. I'm gonna have a smoke. Do you mind?"

I shook my head and sat up in bed, watching as Aisha rummaged through her bottom drawer and took out a small vaping tube. She grunted as she pushed up the heavy, old window, and then sat on her desk and lit up.

"Can't believe that by this time next year, we'll be off in college, doing whatever the fuck," she said, blowing out a stream of white vapor. "I'll be in New York, fingers crossed, and you'll be in Singapore." She glanced at me, and her face turned sad. "You're gonna be so far away from here."

I slumped onto the pillow and gazed at Aisha, leaning against the windowsill and watching the sky, and I tried to memorize this moment. After tonight, there was no going back. My plan had to be carried out to the very end. I blinked away my tears, biting down hard on my lip to keep myself from sobbing out loud. I had to go through with it. And this quiet moment with my best friend could be the last peaceful one I had. Who knew how long this would last?

CHAPTER TWENTY-ONE
logan

I shivered myself awake. My bones had turned to chunks of ice. Everything inside me was frozen. Slowly, my surroundings came into focus. I was in the glade. How the hell—

Lolo.

I startled. "So—Sophie?" My words came out in broken bits, my teeth were chattering so hard. I looked around for her, but she was nowhere to be found. A whimper escaped me. How did I end up here?

Her voice came again, a whisper at the edge of my hearing. *Lolo, I've missed you. I'm so glad you're here.*

I nodded, but for the first time, being in the glade didn't bring me the sense of peace I used to associate with it. Uneasiness lurked in my gut, and my head was a mess, thoughts flying everywhere, half-baked, shattering before I could catch hold of them. "How did I end up here?" I whispered. I got to my feet and jogged in place, trying to generate some body heat. Fear lurked nearby, waiting to pounce and overcome everything. I could no longer pretend that I was in control of anything. Maybe I should make an appointment to see Ms. Taylor. Maybe I should take some time off school. Maybe—

Oh, Lolo. You sweet, confused little thing. Did you sleepwalk?

I shook my head. "I—I don't do that. And where are you? You're dead. You're not here. I'm just imagining things. Maybe this is a dream." I was babbling and I couldn't stop it.

That's not very nice. Her voice was all wrong, warped and devoid of emotion. Something inside me twisted to get away from her. But where would I go? Her voice came from everywhere and nowhere, all at once.

"Why're you here?" I squeaked. And yeah, it really did come out as a squeak. Shit, I was so scared. "You're not—you're—" *You're dead.* But I couldn't say it. Even now, here in our glade, I just couldn't.

I'm dead? Yeah, I am. But that's not a big deal, is it? You know what is?

"Wh—what?"

The fact that you failed to save me. Her voice came out in an angry hiss that made me jump.

"I tried, I really did, I—"

And now you're going to let the same thing happen with Delilah. After I sent her to you as a gift.

"You sent her to me as a gift?" I repeated, stupidly. Then I realized, of course. I'd known it all along. Delilah was my gift. I just hadn't known she was from Sophie.

Are you going to make the same mistake, Lolo? Are you going to let her slip through your fingers like I did?

"No. NO. I won't. I'm going to save her. I'll do it. I'll even destroy the video, I'll tell her, so she won't die hating me. We'll be like Romeo and Juliet, our love will be preserved forever."

Forever...

The last word echoed in a mix of my voice and Sophie's before melting away into the night. I clenched my hands into fists, digging my nails into my palms until some semblance of clarity returned. Sophie wasn't really here. That was just a dream. But Delilah was real, and after tonight, Delilah would be mine forever.

Once I showed Delilah that I fully, 100 percent trusted her, I would be unshackled. I could fly, I really could. If I had a running start, if I launched myself at the sky, I'd stay there.

I wanted to run all the way to Delilah's house and tell her what I was going to do, but I still had enough sense to realize this was probably not the best way to tell her. Might freak her out to find me outside her room at four in the morning, screaming about how much I loved her. And I did love her. So fucking much. Delilah! We were finally going to be together as a true couple, without anything between us.

I was too keyed up to sleep. I ran back and paced around my room for a while, but then Adam, who was next door to me, pounded at the wall and yelled at me to be quiet, goddammit. I tried, I really did, to calm myself down enough to go to sleep, but I couldn't keep still, not when my blood had been replaced with champagne, so bubbly, so much fucking joy! I took out a foil-wrapped package from my bag. Dee had baked red velvet cookies for me. God, I loved her. I ate half of the entire batch, they were so good. Then I put on my hoodie and went outside. I hurried to the gym, but it turned out to be locked. Finally, I went down to the track and ran laps until the sun rose and chased the darkness away. I raised my hands at the sun in greeting, then I took out my phone. My chest expanded as I scrolled down the screen and found her number. The thought of speaking with Delilah sent darts of excitement shooting down my limbs.

"Hello?" Her voice was slurred with sleep, which was when I realized that just because the sun had risen didn't mean it was a decent time to call. Oh, no, had I fucked this up already?

"I'm sorry, I didn't mean to wake you," I babbled.

"No, it's okay," she mumbled. "What's up?" Hardly the

affectionate greeting I wanted, but at least it was no longer her saying, "What do you want?" or worse, "Ugh, what?"

"I—um, I have something to tell you. I want to do it in person," I said. Surely she could hear the joy in my voice. The world could hear the joy in my voice!

She was quiet for a while.

"It's—it's good, Dee. Really good. Huge. You're going to love it," I said.

"Okay," she said, her voice cautious. "How about telling me tonight? Meet by the river at eight?"

Well. This was new. I didn't bother fighting the dopey grin that stretched across my face. Delilah wanted to go out with me. For once, I didn't have to fight to spend time with her. She was taking the initiative to suggest going out, and the river was the perfect spot. Delilah had been waiting all this time to open up to me, to truly connect. I'd been the one holding us back.

Since it was a Saturday, there wasn't much going on. I spent the rest of the day working out, trying to get rid of some of the excess jittery energy. I had to be on my best game tonight. I loaded on weight after weight onto the bar until the other guys at the gym came over to take a look. After some time, Josh came forward and said, "Let's go, Logan."

Confused, I let him lead me out of the gym. "What's up?"

"Dude, you look bad," he said, his voice low. "Stop using. Everyone can see it, okay?"

I shrugged him off. "I'm not using."

Josh shook his head. "Come on, I know when someone's using."

This fucking guy, I swear. He thought he knew what was best for me. The old concern was back on his face. I pushed him away lightly, but he stumbled back and crashed into the weights.

"Whoa, hey! The fuck, man?" he said, clambering to his feet. Heads turned to face us.

"Everything okay?" A couple of guys came over, both of them looking at me warily. What was going on? Couldn't they see I was perfectly fine? I took a step forward to assure them I was okay, and suddenly, the two guys were in front of me, their hands on my shoulders, their grip soft for now, but with a promise that it could get a lot harder if I continued coming forward.

"Logan, chill out, please," Josh said. He looked so worried. Frightened, even.

"I'm okay, hey, I'm totally fine!" I said.

"C'mon, Logan—" Josh's hand wrapped around my arm, and I—

I blinked.

And suddenly, my knuckles felt like they'd just gotten crushed, and an alarm was shrieking through my head, and Josh was on the floor, and *what the hell just happened*—

People were shouting, someone else came at me, but I

turned and ran away, every muscle in my body screaming tight. I needed a drink. I could down an entire gallon of water right now. When I got back to the dorms, I stood in the shower for a long time, trying to get my heartbeat to come back down, the room to stop seesawing. Was Josh okay? I should really go check on him. I remembered blood—

Shit. Did I hit him? I couldn't remember. No, he must've fallen. Once I was dressed, I'd go check on him, make sure he was okay.

Back in my room, my phone was ringing.

"Hello?" I said.

"Logan? This is Ms. Taylor."

The school counselor. I took a silent breath and made my voice come out pleasant, deferential. The way she liked me to sound. "Hi, Ms. Taylor, what's up?"

There was no kindness in her voice now. She was all business. "We were just informed that you attacked another student. Please report to Mrs. Henderson's office right away."

I attacked another student? Me? There must have been some mistake. "Yeah, I'll go to her office," I said and then hung up.

I stood there for a while, unmoving, trying to piece together the last few days of my life. Hell, the last few hours. They were all broken up and mixed together, and Josh, there was something about Josh and *oh*.

I'd hit Josh. I remembered now, the white-hot moment

where my fist met his face. That sickening thud underneath my knuckles.

Draycott had a zero-tolerance policy on physical violence. The realization hit me like a storm. I was going to get expelled. I would never be able to get into NUS. Hell, I wouldn't get into any college. How the fuck would I protect Delilah then? I couldn't just let her leave. Look what had happened to her with Brandon.

I had to go see Delilah. I had to save her. I had to make her mine forever. And before that, I'd destroy the USB drive in front of her, see the look of gratitude in her face before I did it, so I'd know that she died loving me. Yes! Joy rushed through my veins, breathing new life into my chest. Yes, this was perfect. This was how it had always been meant to be. I could fly, I really could.

I wasn't sure how long I remained in my room, pacing, but when I next looked out the window, the sun had dipped low in the horizon. What had happened to the day? I quickly styled my hair and got dressed. Ten minutes of heavy searching and rooting around in the depths of my closet, I still couldn't locate my favorite sport coat. What the hell? I stood surrounded by mounds of clothes, scratching the side of my cheek, trying to recall when was the last time I'd worn it. Was it two weeks ago? Three? Maybe yesterday?

Whatever. I picked a sweater out of the pile and pulled it on then checked my reflection in the mirror. I looked terrible.

I was sickly pale. My lips were cracked, my eyes bloodshot and empty. It was all that time I spent obsessing about how to win Delilah over. But I was going to be okay now. Tonight was going to be special for both of us.

At seven o'clock, I started walking toward the river. I was going to be early, but I couldn't help it.

I was literally skipping by the time I reached the river, a huge, shit-eating grin on my face. And lo and behold, she was there already. The sight of her stopped me in my tracks. She was so luminescent even in the dark, standing there, gazing at the flowing river, surrounded by late blooms and greenery. What a vision. And she was mine, mine, mine.

She turned when she heard my footsteps and gave me a small smile. Shy, sweet, and utterly lovely.

"You're early," she said.

"So are you. Come," I said to Delilah. When she hesitated, I said, "I have what you want." She swallowed, and I knew I had her. I held out my hand, and after a moment's reluctance, she took it.

Hand in hand, we headed off the path, into the cozy dark. Delilah had brought a bottle of hot chocolate, and we passed it back and forth as we walked. I wasn't sure how long we walked, I only knew we had to go far enough from the school, deep in the forest where no one would stumble across us while I did what I had to do. Once we'd traveled a good distance, I stopped close to the river and turned to her.

We smiled at each other, and I knew then, this was it. This was the moment.

"Dee—" I took a deep breath. "These past weeks, I could feel you'd been opening up to me. And you said you're starting to fall in love with me, which—god, I can't even tell you how much that means to me. I decided we couldn't have this thing between us anymore, I have to let you trust me, and I—I'm going to do it."

Her gaze burned into mine. I could almost see her pupils dilate. "What are you going to do?"

I caught my pendant in one hand and unscrewed it, showing her the USB drive hidden inside. "This is the only copy of the video."

A short gasp escaped her lips before she caught herself and swallowed. She nodded ever so slightly. "Do it, Logan. Do it and I'll be yours forever. All of me."

"I know." I took the drive in both hands and, in one swift move, broke it in two.

The breath rushed out of me. Delilah sagged with relief. Both of us stared at the broken pieces in my hand, and one of us laughed, I wasn't sure which, but soon both of us were laughing, and it felt so good, so right.

And her reaction was so much better, so much purer than what I'd dared imagine. I'd thought Delilah looked beautiful before, but now she became transcendent. Little worry lines I hadn't even noticed were there disappeared.

Her eyes brightened. She was radiant, completely, wholly. She shone so brilliantly.

"Oh, Logan." She flung herself at me and grabbed me in a huge hug. "I can't believe it."

I laughed, buried my nose in her hair, and inhaled the wholesome scent of her. My god, if I'd only done this sooner...

"Thank you for destroying the video, Logan," she said. "I'm just—I'm so grateful. I don't even know what to say."

I wrapped my arms around her waist and pulled her close. "You don't have to say anything."

Through my happy haze, I heard Delilah say, "You left this at my house the other day." She pulled something out of her bag. My sport coat. I grinned stupidly and reached for it, frowning when I missed and the coat dropped onto the ground.

Delilah watched as I bent over to pick it up.

"Here, I'll help you put it on," she said.

"Naw, I can do it myself," I said. I shook my head, trying to clear it, and almost fell over. Somehow putting the coat on had become a huge ordeal. Finally, I gave up and raised my hands like a little kid to let Delilah pull the coat on.

An annoying ringtone pealed loud and sharp, shattering the silence. We both froze. Belatedly, I realized it was my phone. I fumbled for it, dropped it on the ground. Mom's name was blazing across the screen.

"Hey, Mom, can I call you back, I can't really—" I mumbled, my tongue thick and useless as a slab of meat.

"Logan, why would you do that?" she said. "Your dad and I are mortified."

"Wha?"

"The school called us. You hit Josh? What's going on, Logan? They said you were supposed to be at the principal's office two hours ago and you never showed!"

"But—" I tried to say something more, but none of my muscles worked properly. Josh was right, I shouldn't have exerted myself at the gym like that—

"I can't believe—why would you do that, Logan? And the dean at NUS called. I'm so disappointed in you. I can't believe my own son would plagiarize his college essay! I've told him to reject you. Did you think they weren't going to find out? Did you think because I know the dean, nobody's going to look at your essay? How could you be so—I just—I have no words."

But I didn't, I wanted to say. All that came out was an idiotic, babbly snort.

"Logan? Are you drunk?" Mom asked. "You are in so much trouble right now. Your dad is going to—"

The phone slipped out of my hand. My chest burned freezing hot, because I'd just recalled my study session with Delilah, when she'd asked to read my essay to NUS, I'd left her alone with my computer. I'd thought she was snooping to try and find the video, but now I realized what had happened.

I looked at her, and I couldn't help the way my upper lip

curled up with rage. "Did you do something to my essay?" I asked, tripping over the words. My tongue wasn't moving properly.

"Why would you do that?" I shouted. Or rather, tried to shout. My words came out all garbled, my tongue a thick, dead thing I couldn't control. Tears pricked my eyes. Why would she do such a horrible thing? Why would she ruin us like this? How much more shit did I have to take from her before she realized I was right about us? "Stupid bitch," I growled, reaching out for her.

She dodged to one side as I moved closer, and I lurched forward. My balance was off. My knees buckled under me, and suddenly, Delilah was behind me. How the hell did she move so fast? I tried to turn, and the world spun around me, wild and fast. From the corner of my eye, I caught sight of Delilah, and I lunged for her. But she was gone again, and suddenly the river was speeding up to meet me.

Water crashed into my face, so cold, stabbing me like knives. I screamed, and water rushed into my mouth. The freezing onslaught of it woke me up, gave me renewed energy, and I thrashed around. I broke the surface at some point, sucked in a mouthful of air. Delilah ran toward me, panic written all over her face, but as I reached for the bank, something in her features changed. In that split second, she hardened, turned to stone. Gone was the fear on her face. Now she wore the same expression she had when she'd turned into a vengeful Valkyrie and crushed Brandon under his own car.

"Dee, please—"

She lifted her foot and stomped on my injured hand. I screamed, an animalistic sound. Then she reached out, grabbed me by the hair, and in a split second I was back underwater, and it was cold, cold, cold, and the river was sucking everything out of me, relentless, pounding. This was not how it was meant to go. I was going to save her, I was going to—

CHAPTER TWENTY-TWO
delilah

Time lost all meaning, warping, going both fast and slow, trapping me in that moment where I caught hold of the back of Logan's hair, shoved his head into the water, and held him there. The generous mix of downers I'd put into the hot chocolate—Ambien, mostly, plus a bit of MDMA to really fuck him up—made sure he wouldn't fight hard enough to actually overpower me. It was too easy, actually, which made it harder. He should have been given a fair chance. Murder shouldn't be easy. Not like this. It shouldn't feel natural.

Logan's arms were floating, the sleeves of his coat ballooning with trapped air. *It's done.* No, not yet. I wasn't stupid enough to let go right away. God help me, I was a natural. I held fast for one more minute, just to be sure. No room for errors, not down this dangerous path. A minute passed. I pried my frozen fingers loose. Logan veered downriver, but his legs were still on the bank, and he stuck fast. I gave him one last push and watched as he floated downriver.

I blinked away my tears and took a deep breath. No time to mourn the loss of what little innocence I had left.

Breathing hard, I stepped away from the river and gathered the broken pieces of the USB drive. I picked up my bag from the ground then made my way back toward campus. I stripped off my jacket as I walked, stuffed it into a plastic bag I had prepared, and put the bundle into my bag. The last thing I needed was to be seen by other students walking around in wet clothes the night Logan drowned. I put on a clean sweater without breaking stride.

The sadness caught me unaware, punching me in the gut hard enough to take my breath away. That same strange, calm rage had taken over me. The exact one that had pushed me into kicking out the car jack. I'd gone to that same place, where time stopped and I could practically see the air molecules around me freezing and all that existed in the world were me and my prey. I'd struck again, and this time it was even worse, because this time, it wasn't just a matter of a brash kick. I'd grabbed Logan and held him down while he drowned under my hands.

I could no longer stop the tears. By some stroke of luck, very few people were about, and none close enough to notice me crying. I pulled my hood down over as much of my face as I could as tears burned down my cheeks. Oh my god, I killed him.

I hadn't planned on killing him. Truly, I hadn't.

The thought of killing another human being made every fiber in my being recoil. My plan had been to frame Logan as Draycott's drug kingpin. It would be so easy to do. Even Mendez thought Logan had something to do with the drug business. But then he'd attacked me, and I couldn't not react. It was self-defense.

Except it wasn't. Not really. I could've let him go once he fell into the river. I could've just turned and run away. But no, I wanted to do it. The chance for freedom practically fell into my lap. Yeah. This was fate. This was meant to be. He deserved to die. I was just defending myself—

My phone rang then, startling me so badly that I actually gasped out loud. Oh god, who was it? Did somebody see? Did they report me to the cops?

It was Lisa. She didn't even give me a chance to say hello before she said in a clipped voice, "Come to the stacks. Now."

My breath caught in my throat, and I very nearly started hyperventilating. I forced myself to slow down and take a deep breath. And another. I was okay. I knew what this was going to be about. She didn't know what I'd just done.

Then it hit me. So what if she knew what I did? She of all people wouldn't be in a hurry to go to the cops.

I paced for a bit, trying to smooth out my frantic thoughts, reminding myself to breathe deep, to gather myself before walking back to campus. This was okay. This was good. In fact, yeah, this was how things should have gone. Because even if I pinned the drugs on Logan, he was never going to let me go. He'd spend a few years in prison, or maybe in juvie, and once he was out, he'd hunt me down. This had to happen for me to have a future. I took in a shaky breath and calmed myself. I was okay. And even if I wasn't right this very moment, I was going to be okay.

I hurried across the quad toward the library and went through the side door, which I knew would remain unlocked. Inside, it was so quiet that I could hear my own heartbeat. My footsteps sounded thunderous in the large, silent space.

Lisa practically pounced on me when I unlocked the door to the office. Her eyes were wild, her face red with barely repressed anger. "I know you've been sampling the product. I've got thousands of dollars of merchandise missing here!" This was the first time I'd ever seen the timid librarian act crack, and it caught me off guard. I stumbled back a bit before catching myself. "Dee, I told you, if you ever steal from me—"

"There would be grave consequences, emphasis on the *grave*," I said. "Yes, I remember." I had to work hard to keep my voice from trembling. *Be strong. You've got this.*

"So where's the stuff? There are six packs of MDMA

missing, two bottles of Ambien, not to mention the coke. My profits—"

"They'll take a hit, yes, but it's better than getting arrested for being a drug dealer." I was speaking sense, I knew. She wouldn't be able to refute this.

Lisa froze and gaped at me. "What?"

My voice solidified. I'd planned for this, hadn't I? Everything, down to the last meticulous detail. I'd tied up all the loose ends. There was no reason why my plan couldn't go on, just because Logan was dead. "Haven't you noticed that Detective Mendez is closing in? She came down here, for god's sake. It was only a matter of time before she realized we're the ones dealing."

"No." Lisa shook her head and pushed up her glasses. "She didn't—she didn't think I was a threat."

"Oh, right, and she came all the way down here and asked us about the Post Ur Secret board just for fun. Face it, Lisa, we were gonna get caught. I chose to take the initiative to save us."

"What? How?"

I shrugged casually, even though I was sweating like mad. If this didn't work, if I couldn't convince Lisa, it would be the end of me. "I pinned it on someone else."

Lisa's mouth dropped open. With her glasses and her ridiculous outfit, she looked so much like a caricature, I almost broke into hysterical laughter. I must be reeling from all that adrenaline that killing Logan had pumped through me. "You what?" she breathed. "Who?"

"It doesn't matter. Consider the missing product payment for taking the cops off our backs. You can afford to take a cut from the profits this month. I mean, it's not like you're living large or anything."

Lisa shook her head with disbelief. "I can't—" She sighed. Took another deep breath. Sighed again. "So you're confident about this?"

"Yep."

"And the person you framed, they won't be able to prove it was you?"

An image of Logan's lifeless body floating downstream flashed through my head. "No."

Lisa studied me for a long while, and maybe she saw something, maybe she caught a glimpse of the red beast that lived inside me. She took a step back. Lisa was scared of me. Lisa. I wasn't sure how I felt about that.

"Okay," she said, after a beat. She broke eye contact first. "Fine. But you're no longer welcome here, Delilah. You don't work for me anymore."

I felt a sudden zap of anger, but as quickly as it came, it fizzled away. I didn't need the job anymore. I'd saved up enough to at least get me to Singapore. Mom would help me out the rest of the way.

"Okay," I said. Lisa looked visibly relieved. "But I

need you to do one last thing for me." She stiffened. "I need an alibi."

Now the fear was clear as words on a page. "An alibi? Jesus, Dee, what the hell did you do?"

"Don't worry about that. I fixed everything. Log me in so it looks like I was here working the whole evening." I nodded at her computer. Lisa hesitated, but I held my ground, gazing at her until she moved to the computer. She typed in her access code and did as I asked, logging me on the roster from 6 p.m. to 9 p.m. "Thank you."

She swallowed and refused to look at me. "Get out."

It stung a little. We'd worked so closely for so long, and she wasn't even the least bit grateful that I'd saved her ass. I shook my head and sighed as I left the library for the last time.

The night air was cool and refreshing on my skin. I breathed deep and my eyes fluttered closed. The air tasted of freedom. Despite everything that had happened tonight, a laugh escaped me. I was free. Of Brandon. Of Logan.

And I realized then why Lisa had been so eager to get rid of me. Why I shouldn't take her rejection personally. Because one thing I had learned about predators is that there can only be one around. Lisa, Brandon, and Logan were all predators, in their own ways. And, as it turned out, so was I. Maybe Lisa sensed that I was a bit of a natural when it came to killing predators. That I was the snake after all. And maybe, just maybe, I liked it a little.

acknowledgments

First and foremost, thank you to my husband, Mike, who supported me in every way that a spouse could. Thank you for working so I didn't have to, for watching the baby at dawn so I could write, and for brainstorming with me on my wild ideas.

I will be forever grateful to Uwe Stender for selling my debut book and setting me on the incredible path I now travel. He not only made this book stronger, he also picked the best possible editor for it. I am so happy that *The Obsession* found its home with Annie Berger and the team at Sourcebooks. Annie's input made the story sharper, more exciting, and about a million times better than it previously was.

The Obsession was my fifth book, and it didn't sell until

after I finished writing my eighth. This journey has been a horribly long and twisty one, and I would have quit writing a long time ago if not for the love and support from my online family. A special thanks to S. L. Huang, who was there from the very beginning and continues to be my guide in everything from writing to how to be a less crappy person. Toria Hegedus, who is always patient and loving. Maddox Hahn, whose wit makes me jealous. Lani Frank, who I can count on to spot all the plot holes (and fix them). Tilly Latimer, whose superpower is always getting us out of tricky spots. Elaine Aliment, for her unflinching and brilliant observations. Rob Livermore, the best cheerleader and also our generation's Dahl. Emma Maree, who is the purest soul in the world. Mel Melcer, for being a source of wisdom and calm. Taylor, my mind-mate (Delilah!)—we drive each other up the wall, but if I ever crush someone with a Camaro, you'd be the one I'd call because you know everything about everything and I have no idea how you're that smart? Nicole Lesperance, who is incredibly talented and just about the sweetest person I know. Shannon Morgan, whose tenacity and productivity humbles me.

I wouldn't have found any of these amazing writers without the Absolute Write forum, which is the best resource there is for writers. Thank you to the wonderful, hardworking mods—Lisa, MacAllister, Calla, and so many others, for making AW a safe place for writers to learn and grow.

To my family—my Mama and Papa, for giving me

everything you never had growing up. You sacrificed everything for my sake and gave me the best education possible. I wouldn't have been able to do any of this without your help. And to my babies, Emmie and Rosie, my little warrior princesses. Thank you for pushing me to want to be better.

And of course, to you, dear reader. Thank you so much for picking up a copy of my debut book. I am so grateful for your support, and I hope that you have enjoyed reading *The Obsession* as much as I enjoyed writing it.

about the author

Photo © Michael Hart

Jesse Q. Sutanto grew up shuttling back and forth between Indonesia, Singapore, and Oxford, and considers all three places her home. She has a master's from Oxford University but has yet to figure out how to say that without sounding obnoxious. She has forty-two first cousins and thirty aunties and uncles, many of whom live just down the road. When she's not writing, she's gaming with her husband (mostly FPS) or making a mess in the kitchen with her two daughters.

FIREreads

#getbooklit

Your hub for the hottest young adult books!

Visit us online and sign up for our
newsletter at FIREreads.com

 @sourcebooksfire

sourcebooksfire

firereads.tumblr.com